PRAISE FOR THE WITCH'S CURSE

A thrilling followup to *The King's Curse*: after Colleen has freed the people of her father's kingdom from the terrible curse that gripped them, she and her friends are on the run. The people blame her for what's happened and they are furious. Colleen's only recourse is to go to Queen Rhiannon, but getting there will not be easy, for she must cross the dreaded Divide, which is controlled by a powerful and evil witch.

Part Wizard of Oz and part Promised Land Odyssey, *The Witch's Curse* is a captivating adventure story that highlights the importance of faith in God during difficult times and the strength of friendship in supporting that faith. Plus, there's an adorable dragon! Fans of the Ariboslia series and Young Adult Christian Fantasy will love this one.

Gina Detwiler, author of The *Forlorn* Series

THE WITCH'S CURSE

THE CURSED LANDS BOOK 2

J. F. ROGERS

NOBLEBRIGHT
PUBLISHING

www.noblebrightpublishing.com

The Witch's Curse - The Cursed Lands Book 2

Edited by Brilliant Cut Editing
Cover design by 100 Covers

Library of Congress Control Number: 2023944332

Paperback ISBN: 978-1-955169-19-6
Hardcover ISBN: 978-1-955169-20-2

Published by Noblebright Publishing
Sanford, Maine
www.noblebrightpublishing.com

"The fear of man brings a snare, but whoever trusts in
the Lord shall be safe."

— Proverbs 29:25

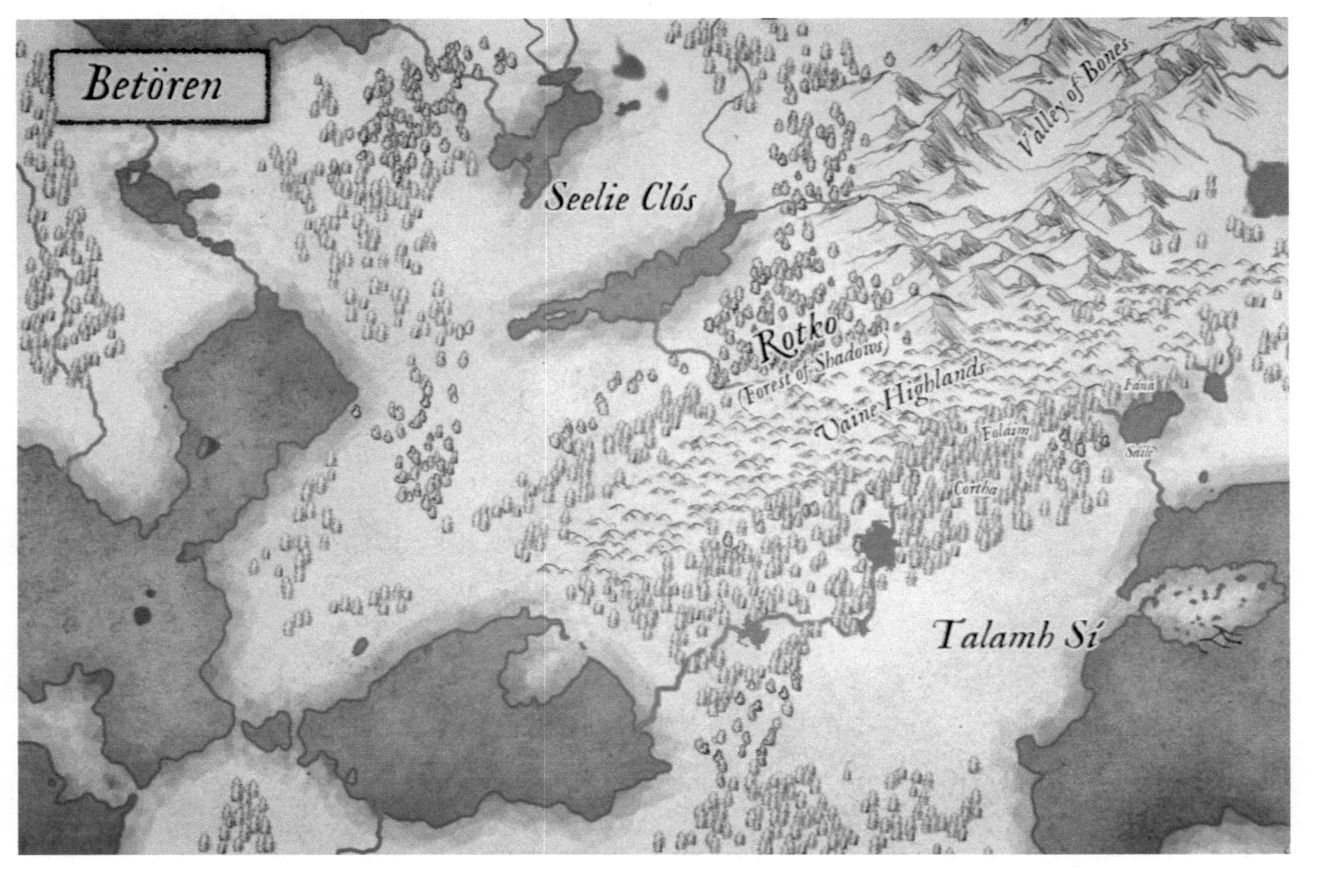

Betören
Seelie Clós
Valley of Bones
Rotko
(Forest of Shadows)
Väine Highlands
Fann
Folaim
Sáile
Cortha
Talamh Sí

PRONUNCIATION GUIDE

PEOPLE

Auberon \ O-bər-ahn \ the king of Talamh Sí

Aune \ OW-nah \ a villager from Sáile

Eerika \ EH-ri-ka \ the princess

Eerikki \ EH-ri-ki \ King Auberon's father

Fallon \ FA-lən \ Colleen's adopted mother

Balder \ BAHL-dər \ a strange man

Beagan \ BEE-gun \ Colleen's youngest adopted brother

Carr \ kahr \ a villager from Sáile

Corwin \ KAWR-win \ Colleen's adopted brother

Delyth \ DEL-ith \ Colleen's mother

Eliina \ eh-LEEN-ah \ the witch's captive

Fergus \ FUR-gəs \ a shepherd

Fiske \ fish \ a villager from Sáile

Hadwin \ HAD-win \ a human

Jaakko \ YAH-ko \ a pooka

Liam \ LEE-əm \ a defender

Nialla \ NEE-al-ah \ Colleen's adopted sister

Noita \ Noy-tah \ the witch

Pirkko \ PIR-ko \ a member of the Saoirse Trodaí

Rhiannon \ ree-AN-ən \ the queen of Seelie Clós

Ruuta \ ROO-tah \ Colleen's lady-in-waiting

Rhys \ REES \ a boy who joins Colleen in her quest

Sakki \ sah-ki \ the dragon, formally known as Iisakki

Silja \ SIL-yah \ the ogre's daughter

Simo \ see-moh \ an ogre

Taneli \ TA-ne-li \ a member of the Saoirse Trodaí

Valtteri \ VAHL-te-ri \ the leader of the Saoirse Trodaí

Zorac \ zohr-ack \ a fallen angel (demon)

GROUPS

Fasgadair \ fahs-geh-deer \ Ariboslian vampires
Gachen \ gah-chen \ an Ariboslian race of shape-shifters
Saors \ SEE-ores \ those who have been freed
Saoirse Trodaí \ SEE-er-shay TRAH-day \ freedom fighters
Seelie fae \ members of Seelie Clós
Unseelie fae \ exiles from Seelie Clós
Vapaus \ vah-pows \ a rebel group

PLACES

Ariboslia \ air-eh-BOWS-lia \ Colleen's realm
Betören \ beh-TUHR-ən \ the new realm
Folaím \ FALL-eem \ the veiled forest city
Hiekka \ yay-gah \ a desert
Kylä \ GOO-lah \ a village in Rotko
Pohjola \ POH-hya-lah \ a territory in Rotko
Sáile \ SOH-leh \ a fishing village
Seelie Clós \ SEE-lee clohs \ the seelie court across the Divide
Rotko* \ ROHT-goh \ the Divide, aka the Forest of Shadows
Synkkä \ SIN-kah \ the swamp of sadness
Talamh Sí \ tall-um she \ King Auberon's kingdom

THINGS

Aivopestä \ I-voh-pest-ah \ the king's curse
Ankerias \ AHN-keh-dee-ahs \ a lake monster
Croí \ kree \ a spelled tree in Folaím
Éin bís \ AY-uhn BEE-sh \ waterfowl
Jumala \ YU-mah-lah \ the fae word for God
Jyrsijä \ YER-see-ya \ a large rodent-like creature
Kani \ GAH-nee \ a rabbit-like creature
Käärme \ KAH-are-may \ a large serpent/worm-like creature
Keino \ GAY-no \ a synthetic version of aether
Krokotiili \ krock-oh-TEE-lee \ winged crocodile-like creature
Makea purukumi \ mah-kay-ah pur-ooh-guee \ seed containers
Matka \ MAHT-kah \ a seelie ward

Olikissa \ Oh-lee-kee-sah \ a werecat
Outo \ OW-ooh-tah \ a strange fruit
Pakana \ pah-kah-nah \ slang for heathen
Socrú \ suh-CRU \ a bond mark
Värikäs \ VAH-ree-kahs \ the color of aether smoke
Vastalääke \ VAHS-tah-lah-geh \ antidote to the king's curse

*Trill the R

ONE

Ashrieking horn pierced the night, spooking Clover. She bolted through the underbrush. The blast continued, drowning out my heartbeat thrumming in my ears. Branches reached for me, whipping my face, scratching my arms, threatening to tear me from the saddle as I clung to Clover's reins in her mad dash to escape the alarm.

That sound! It rammed into my unprotected ears. Where was it coming from?

Were the others still with me? I couldn't hear anything over the shriek. It was too dark to see. What if I lost them? I'd be trapped in this realm, hunted, alone....

Sweeping beams of light penetrated the treetops, illuminating the shrubs.

A ship.

Creeping crabs! The siren had masked the airship's approach. They were sure to spot us. I pulled the surrounding air to form a veil. Where were the others? I needed to hide them too.

But the veil was no use if we crashed through the woods, rustling the trees. I had to make Clover stop. The only way was to calm her. But first, I had to calm myself.

I lay on Clover's back to protect myself from the branches, found her rhythm, and rode in tune with it as I worked to steady my heart, my breath.

Light in. Dark out.

Light in. Dark out.

I gathered the reins in one hand and held fast, then touched her neck with the other. My arm tingled as I pushed my life force through my arm to my hand, setting it aglow. Then I pushed it out through my fingers. Tendrils reached for the breath of life within the horse and made contact. Clover shook her mane and staggered as I fueled her with my calm.

She stopped. I dismounted and led her into thick brush under a leafy canopy. The sweeping lights had moved on, yet the siren continued.

As I worked to keep her calm, I scanned the woods for the others. *Sakki! Where are you?*

Sakki is hiding from the ship with Ruuta. The horses bolted like Colleen's.

The spotlight continued past me. *Are you near the ship?*

No. Airship passed Sakki.

Okay. Stay where you are until the siren quiets.

I stroked Clover's neck. If only I could speak into the other's minds too. Where were they?

Please, God, don't let the ship spot them.

How had things gotten to this point? I'd done what needed to be done—freed the people from my father's curse. They were no longer under a spell to believe he was God. They had their minds back—their free will.

So why did they want me dead? I wasn't my father. I barely knew him. And he'd manipulated me too. I was as much a victim as his subjects.

They were confused. The curse had kept them united. Now they had differing opinions and no leader to guide them. Not everyone wanted me dead. But most people did. The Vapaus certainly did. How could the Saoirse Trodaí not have noticed the rebel group in their midst? Now Valtteri, a man who might've been a good leader, was dead.

I'd barely had a moment to grieve his loss. Or Pirkko's. Or Taneli's.

I squelched the anger coursing through me before it affected the calm I needed to keep feeding Clover. Taneli... part of the Vapaus. I still couldn't believe it. I thought he was a friend. An image of his gun barrel filled my view with his face behind it, twisted in anger, bent on causing me harm. Nay, Taneli was no friend. And yet, I felt the pain of his loss. And worse, his lost soul.

What a mess that turned out to be.

What was I supposed to do now? Go to Seelie Clós to my aunt, Queen Rhiannon, as Ruuta insisted? She was certain I needed to be queen of Talamh Sí to break the divide between the kingdoms. But wouldn't that cause *more* mayhem? Should I go home to Ariboslia? My family must be off their heads with worry.

But my dragon, Sakki, wanted me to see Queen Rhiannon too. God had told him so.

Where was the resolve I'd had moments ago? Before the siren. Before the ship.

God, help me.

The light from the airship was gone. The siren was quieting. I should search for the others. Something nudged my side, and I pitched forward onto my knees. My right knee collided with a rock, sending a jolt up my thigh.

Sakki didn't mean to startle Colleen. He prodded me with his doggy muzzle again.

My riding pants now had a tear in the knee, but I didn't feel any blood. Just a scratch. *How is it I didn't hear you coming?* My hearing was better than most, probably because of my elfin ears. One of the many things I'd forgotten to ask my father. The only other elf in existence. Now there was none. Only me.

Same reason Sakki's ears aren't working so well. The ship's roar makes Sakki's ears ring. He splayed his legs and gave his ears a good shake, making a flapping sound, then stopped to scratch his left ear. *The better the hearing, the worse that roar.*

Ruuta's outline appeared in the moonlight behind him, straightening her white gloves. "There is no time to dawdle. We must find the others."

Sakki will find them. He lifted his doggy nose and sniffed the air in several directions.

The night seemed quiet now, but for the ghostly echo of the ship's siren. There would be more. We needed to put as much distance between us and the Atonement Center as possible.

This way. He dashed through the dense greenery.

We mounted our steeds and followed him to Rhys squatting in the thicket. His unearthly blue eyes gave off a surreal glow in the moonlight. The trees rustled behind him. Liam held a branch aside to allow Iida and their horses to pass through.

Relief filled me at the sight of them, like a puffy chair refilling once relieved of the weight sitting upon it. "Thank God. You found us."

Rhys crept from his hiding place, his gaze scanning the skies. "More ships will come. To be sure, to be sure."

"Like I said"—Ruuta smoothed a stray strand, apparently unaware of all the other untidy hairs crowning her head—"let's not dawdle, shall we?"

As much as I wanted to stop running, they were right. "Then let's go. And try to stick close. I'll cover us with a veil. But if another ship comes, we need to stop, or they'll notice our movement, even if they can't see us."

Liam riffled through his satchel. "I need to keep Nessa from bolting if she hears that sound again."

"How are you going to do that?" I asked.

"With this." He retrieved a cloth, tore it into shreds, and gave two to each of us. "Roll them up and put them in your horse's ears."

Clover flicked her ears and jerked her head away. But with my calming energy, she relented. Too bad there wasn't extra to shove into *my* ears. Everything still sounded tinny.

"I'm not going with you." Iida swooped back into her saddle. "You'll need friends on this side of the Divide. I'll return to the hideout with Reko and see what I can do here and in the castle."

I looked at her, my maid, companion, friend. Darkness obscured her face and her aura, so I couldn't read her. But she was one of the strongest people I knew. "Thank you for all you've done, Iida. You are loved."

"And you as well." She turned her horse south and galloped away.

The rest of us followed Rhys in the opposite direction.

God, this is Your plan. Please hide us. Help us get through these woods. And get Iida safely to the hideout.

The blaring alarm returned, strengthening as it neared, masking the telltale chug of the ship's engine.

Two

"Quick, under these trees!" I had to yell to be heard over the siren, hoping no one on the ship could hear me.

We scrambled to huddle under the canopy. I gathered the air around us and wrapped us in my veil.

The horses nickered and bounced, threatening to bolt despite their stuffed ears. Liam tied his horse to a branch, then tugged Clover from me to tie her as well while Ruuta and Rhys did the same for theirs. The earplugs only helped so much. If we didn't calm these horses, they'd give us away.

Light in. Dark out.

Light in. Dark out.

An idea sparked. *God, please let this help.*

I breathed deeply, then reached for God's breath from within, and pushed it out. Rather than feeling through soil or a living being, I felt through the air. Tendrils of my life force weaved through the air within the veil, reaching out like foggy fingers. The horses breathed it in. Their stomping hooves stilled, and their nickers softened.

I continued infusing the veil with my energy. The sound intensified, and lights swept over us. Though it was difficult to see auras at night, theirs were lightening. Everyone's. My energy was calming everyone within my veil. Despite growing weary, I persisted until the sound lessened once more. My life force recoiled back to where it belonged, and I slumped.

"Colleen!" Liam caught my limp body. "Are you all right?"

"Aye." With his help, I righted myself, gripping his arm as I teetered.

"What was that?" His aura was darkening, but still lighter than usual, and he wore a strange smile. "I've never felt so... calm."

"We can discuss fae magic later." Ruuta's gaze darted in every direction. "We need to keep moving, or do I need to use my fae magic to compel you?"

Fae magic? That's not what I did, was it? The veil was. But the calming energy was from my elf side. Or so I thought. But Ruuta's certainty made me uncertain. If only I had an elf to ask. Another pang for my father's inevitable death struck me in the gut.

"No need to get snippy." Liam guided me to Clover. "Are you able to ride?"

My legs were holding me up better now. I was tired, but even calming multiple horses at a time didn't spend nearly as much energy as I'd expected. And riding would be better than walking. "Aye."

"Let's hope you don't need to do that again." He helped me into my saddle, then returned to his horse, and we continued our mad dash through the seemingly endless forest.

Eventually, dawn's early light brightened the sky to a dusty gray. Hours ago, while it was still dark, I knew my father was dead. God had said he'd die by midnight. Now, with the morning sun greeting us, there was no question. He was dead.

If only we hadn't wasted our time together. What might've happened if he'd trusted me instead of trying to control me? To erase my memories every time I questioned his methods? My heart sobbed for the missed opportunity.

Colleen should stop blaming herself for Auberon's choices.

I know. I forced a smile back at Sakki's cat body sitting on

Clover's rump. I took a deep breath. He was right. I did what I could. At least his soul was saved now. His body may die, but his soul would live on.

But what if he was the last elf in existence? I'd missed my opportunity to get to know my father... and myself. I didn't understand either side of me. But I had Ruuta, and we were on our way to a land full of fae. But the elves were... gone.

Colleen needs to stop worrying about things Colleen can't control.

He was right. But what else could I do as my body plodded onward, leaving my mind free to roam?

We hadn't seen a ship nor heard an alarm for hours, yet my ears continued to buzz. Clover clomped along. Our poor horses traversed the wooded area as if slogging through mud. We dismounted to give their backs a break and trudged on, hunched over, our minds perhaps more willing to continue than our bodies, refusing to drop.

"Do you think we're far enough away?" I searched the sky—again.

"I hope so." Ruuta blew a stray hair from her face.

"I doubt anyone is pursuing us." Liam slowed his labored steps even further. "Their hands are full occupying the city and subduing it."

"We should rest." Rhys made no move to stop. Like the rest of us, his body seemed stuck in a slow gear with no brakes.

I desperately wanted to sleep. But more than that, I wanted to get as far, far away from those who sought to kill me as possible. Was anywhere in Betören safe for me now? Once we escaped Talamh Sí, what was next? Rotko, the Forest of Shadows? That sounded worse than ducking lights from passing ships. Much worse.

Sakki leaped from Clover's rump as a cat and landed on the ground as a dog. He made his way into my path and stopped. *Colleen must sleep.*

I nearly fell over him. "We can't sleep. What if someone finds us?"

He stretched and grew, limbs and neck elongating, morphing from gray-and-white fur to green-and-yellow scales.

Wide awake, I searched the skies as if each star were a ship waiting for us to make the wrong move. "What are you doing in your dragon form? They'll find us."

Iisakki spread out a wing. *Sleep here. Sakki will cover Colleen.*

"But they'll see you."

Liam turned back to us. "What's going on?"

"Iisakki wants me to sleep under his wing, but if a ship flies overhead, they'll spot him. He's too big."

Sakki is green.

I eyed him against the greenery surrounding us. The greens were similar. Enough that, from above, he might look like a patch of shrubs. But the yellow streak starting from his forehead, running between his eyes. What would that look like from the sky?

Sakki will tuck Sakki's head under Sakki's wing.

Could he read my mind all the time, not just when I sent him messages?

"And what of the horses?" Ruuta asked.

Liam rubbed the back of his neck. "If we took turns keeping watch, we could wake Colleen to hide us."

"If time allows." Ruuta's lips formed a doubtful pout.

I surveyed our surroundings once more. Iisakki was right. We were unlikely to be spotted by a ship, and we needed rest.

"We have no choice. We must sleep if we're to get out of Talamh Sí alive." Liam planted himself on a patch of grass. "I'll take first watch."

THREE

I woke sandwiched between Rhys and Sakki, nestled under Sakki's wing beside his warm belly. His chest rumbled with each breath, lulling me back to sleep. But I shook it off. Snippets of the prior day assaulted me in reverse order. Running from the airships to our escape from the Atonement Center to finding my father in his cell.

My father.

He was dead by now. Assassinated.

Something stabbed me deep, to the very core of my being. A low wail began as almost a growl within, but I stifled it before it grew. Never had I felt such heartache. I pulled the ring from beneath my neckline. His gift to me. My mother's ring. I clutched it tight.

We didn't have time for this. I swiped at the escaping tears and blinked the rest away. I'd grieve later. Right now, we had to keep going. I pressed the velvety underside of Sakki's wing.

He rumbled and rolled, lifting his pinion.

Chill air rushed in. It carried the fresh after-rain smell, but there was no visible dampness. Bright light reached under the canopy, blinding me. Liam and Rhys groaned. Liam's aura darkened while

Rhys's remained unchanged as they winced and shielded their eyes. Liam scrubbed a hand down his face. He looked adorable with tousled hair and sleepy eyes.

What happened to us? Was there still something there? The beginnings of something more than a friendship? I remembered the way he'd looked at me when we were about to go into the boutique, when he'd begged me not to go to my father. There'd been something in his eyes then. And I'd seen traces of it here and there once our memories were restored. But we'd been too busy plotting, traveling, and escaping to develop anything further. Would we ever?

I shook the thought away. There wasn't time for such frivolity.

When did I start sounding so... old?

A breeze swept through the new holes in my pants and the thin tunic. I hugged myself. If only I'd packed a cloak. Traveling with Sakki would be convenient, though. A warm shelter that slept three. Possibly four if we packed ourselves in.

Rhys sat in the fetal position and rubbed his arms, surrounded by his infuriatingly never-changing aura. "I miss my fur."

"No one said you couldn't be a rabbit." Liam bowed and raised his palms to offer this idea on an invisible platter.

"Pooka." Rhys grumbled and scratched behind his ear.

"You look like a rabbit. A big, black, walking, talking freakish rabbit." Liam winked at Sakki. "Food for dragons."

Sakki chuffed.

Rhys threw Liam a half-lidded, unimpressed look. "The princess prefers this form."

"Colleen." Why did it irk me to be referred to as the princess? I pressed the darkening light surrounding me as if I could push it into my skin. "Rhys can take whatever form he likes... except Balder." I squirmed at the thought of the angular man with the top hat who'd accosted me in the woods back home. "If you want to be in your true pooka form, feel free."

Ruuta's shadow crossed before us, easing the strain on our eyes. "Or shift into your pooka form at night, like sleepwear."

"Sleephare." Liam barked a laugh at his own joke.

We groaned at his painful pun, but his rising laughter infected us all. Then, one by one, our gazes landed on Rhys's frown, and our laughs died but for stray chuckles.

Sakki staggered to the clearing and collapsed.

I rushed to his side. *Are you okay?*

Yes. Sakki worried about rolling over and crushing Colleen and friends, so Sakki didn't sleep well. Sakki just needs a moment in the sun to get warm.

Why don't you shift into your cat form? I'll warm you.

He seemed to think that was a good idea. His limbs retracted like a recoiling measuring tape. Gray-and-white fur sprouted where his green-and-yellow scales had been as he shrank to a gazillionth of his size.

I gathered his cat form into my arms and snuggled him to my chest, then sat beside Ruuta, facing the rising sun. "Did you get any sleep?"

"I got enough." Her dim aura told me otherwise, but I wouldn't argue. She stood and brushed off her pants. "I eagerly await reaching civilized society and wearing proper attire. If Mother could see me now. She raised me to attend a queen, not gallivant through the forest and sleep under a dragon's wing in the dirt."

"It's grass, actually." I scratched Sakki's chin.

His squinty face seemed to smile as he stretched to give me better access.

"And dirt." She smacked at something on her hip, then rubbed her gloved fingers together. They were still white. Mostly.

Liam came up beside us, contorting himself, stretching every which way. "We don't have time for a proper meal. Even in daylight, we can't risk a fire. We're still too close to the city."

"To be sure. To be sure." Rhys tended the horses. He pulled a blanket out of the satchel and tossed it to me.

"We had these the whole time?" I bundled myself up.

"We didn't need them under Sakki's wing." Liam turned to Rhys. "How many blankets are there?"

"Enough."

"We should make a quick meal of the leftover fish and food Iida packed for us." Ruuta riffled through her horse's satchel.

"Not too much. We'll have to ration it." Liam accepted a wheel of cheese Ruuta slapped into his hands.

"No, we should eat it now. Travel lighter."

Liam's expression morphed into his ready-to-fight face. Then he read the twinkle in Ruuta's eyes that contrasted with her serious expression. He heaved a sigh and set to work on the cheese while the rest of us made fun of him for being gullible.

After we ate just enough of our rations of bread, cheese, and crunchy fish, we took one last drink from the stream, filled our water-skins, and returned to the horses. On my way, something snagged my foot, and I tripped. Arms windmilling, I caught my fall, but something ripped. I peeled a prickly bramble from my boot and another from my pants. It had torn another small hole by my shin below the one at my knee from colliding with a rock last night. "Creeping crabs, these are the only clothes I have."

Iisakki bounded over to me in dog form. *Is Little One okay?*

"I'm fine." I brushed off my pants and straightened. "Since when am I 'Little One'?"

Sakki morphed into his dragon form, his head towering over me. He bent his long neck so he could come down to my level and peer into my eyes. *Since Sakki is bigger than Colleen.*

I pushed his gargantuan head away, hoisted myself into Clover's saddle, and sat tall. "Well, I'm still older."

He snorted a laugh, sending smoke tendrils from his nostrils, then slipped back into dog form, and sauntered up the hill.

"And much more mature!" I called after him.

"Shhh!" Ruuta admonished, her gaze darting in every direction as the horse beneath her spun.

I cringed. Her aura didn't change much. She seemed to have good control of her emotions, but it flared with black. We were only a day's journey from the Atonement Center. Auberon's defenders roamed these woods. As much as I didn't like being shushed, she wasn't wrong.

I lowered my voice. "What if we run into a defender out here? Would they still be under the curse?"

Liam mounted his horse. "Depends on if we're anywhere near an outpost. I'm not familiar with this area."

Ruuta gathered her horse's reins. "If they followed us from the city, no, they're not cursed. But if they were out here when we administered the antidote, they wouldn't have been close enough to inhale the cure."

"Unless there was a strong wind." Liam bathed us in his dancing shadow as Nessie flitted underneath him.

"Even with my father..." I couldn't bring myself to say the word.

"Dead?" Leave it to Ruuta to say what others preferred not to. "Highly unlikely. Noita's twisted fae magic is unpredictable and powerful, but it's unlikely Auberon's death was enough to free them. For one, it wasn't his curse. He didn't craft it. For another, it was administered individually."

She guided her horse to fall into step beside Clover. "Many outside the city may continue their loyalty, believing Auberon to be immortal, until they receive the antidote."

I padded my pocket to ensure my sprayable vial was still there.

Liam pulled Nessie as close up behind us as possible. The trail only allowed for two to travel side by side. "If we come across anyone under your father's curse, I wouldn't recommend freeing them, if that's what you're thinking."

"What? Why?"

He scoffed. "Did you not just see what happened after freeing people? They want to kill you."

"So did you," I said in a low voice, sorry for making him wince, but not sorry enough to stop talking. "Aren't you glad to be free? How could you, of all people, let anyone continue to believe the lie when we have the means to free them?"

His emotions were typically stronger and darker than most. My comment sent oranges and reds blazing. "And how could you not care that your life is in danger?"

Ruuta sighed in her regal way. "Let's agree not to free anyone until we've discussed it and come to a consensus."

"To be sure. To be sure." Rhys's voice floated from behind.

For now, I'd hope the situation never arose. But I couldn't imagine I'd be capable of leaving someone in such a sorry state. Not if I had any say in the matter. If I had to risk my life to free someone, I would.

God, I hope it doesn't come to that.

FOUR

Sakki came charging through the woods and leaped at me. His dog form sprouted dragon wings long enough to get liftoff. Then he shifted into cat form midair, fell onto my lap, and settled in.

As we rode north, my gaze kept gravitating toward the blotches of sky peeking through the trees. How I yearned for the ease of floating above the terrain and arriving in the Seelie court within a few days, as opposed to however many weeks this would take. We'd flown on his back with two before. But now we had four. As big as Sakki was, he wouldn't likely get far with that many. Would we even fit? Plus, we had the horses.

It hadn't been long since we'd slept, but that had been little more than a nap after a long night. My body felt night growing near. A breeze swept through the trees and into the holes in my pants. Too bad we couldn't have flown back to the castle for more supplies. All we had was what we'd packed in the saddlebags when we left the hideout. And blankets, apparently. But we couldn't risk returning to the castle or the cabin, even hidden under my veil. People who opposed me infiltrated the ranks in the castle and the Saors' lair.

There was no going back now.

If only I could go home to Ariboslia. But even if I could find the megalith, I had no way through. No amulet. And Sakki wouldn't let me go while God had other plans.

But we were headed to Rotko—the Divide—the Forest of Shadows. Why did one place have so many names? I still wasn't sure which to call it. "Has anyone been inside Rotko?"

Noes came from everyone except Rhys.

"Have you been there, Rhys?" I twisted in my saddle to see him.

He grimaced and seemed to shrink. "No?"

I narrowed my eyes at him again. His steadfast aura may refuse to give up the truth, but I was beginning to be able to read him without it. And when his answer sounded like a question, that was a telltale sign. "You're lying."

He flinched as if I'd hit him. "Noita the Witch created me. I escaped her once. I don't care to do it again."

I couldn't conceive of such power as to create a living, breathing creature such as him. Other than God. And except for his aether-smoke-like aura—värikäs, Ruuta called it, a color only fae could see— Rhys seemed so... so... human. I kept forgetting he was a pooka. A shape-shifter. He was right. I much preferred his twelve-year-old boy form and appreciated him choosing it despite missing his fur. But, even after all he'd done for us, suspicions tangled through me. "So you've never been in the Divide?"

He squirmed under my stare. "I may have been once, to assist Auberon."

"Assist him in what?" Liam closed in on Rhys.

Rhys shifted in his saddle and pointed at Sakki on my lap. "Him! To get his egg!"

Liam, Ruuta, and I exchanged glances. His excessive response to a simple question rang warning bells. Yet, we all seemed to agree his claim made sense.

"Look." Gathering the reins in one hand, Liam placed his other one on his thigh. "If you've been in there, you need to help us. What should we expect? What's in there?"

"Nothing natural, to be sure." Rhys shrugged. "Well, not anymore. Noita twisted everything."

"Twisted?" That word piqued Ruuta's interest. "As in... with fae magic?"

"As in, whatever Noita uses to manipulate things, directly or indirectly."

"How do you indirectly manipulate something?" Liam screwed up his face.

"By twisting minds into seeing it differently." The flash in Rhys's eyes seemed to ask why we weren't understanding such a simple concept.

"Noita is the witch who gave Auberon the curse?" Ruuta sat in the saddle with perfect posture.

"Yes." Rhys guided his horse around a tree. "She controls the Divide."

"We need to know what we're facing," Liam said. "What kind of danger are we walking into?"

"I would tell you, to be sure. But Noita has a way of scrambling one's mind. The Divide was one way when I entered and another when I left. What is memory, and what is nightmare? My mind is a jumble of images—a witch with horns growing like a dead tree from her skull, a swamp of gators with glowing red eyes, dead earth unfit for growing anything green, unseelie fae ready to steal or trick you out of your possessions. Sand. Blackness. Char. Death."

Was that all he remembered? Rhys had rarely been forthcoming in the short time I'd known him. He tricked me into coming to Betören. He lied about being a pooka in the king's employ and now again about having been in the Divide. He'd given me the wine that altered my memory... several times. And he was conspiring with the Saoirse Trodaí. He'd planned to bring me to them from the beginning.

Whose side was he on?

The Saoirse Trodaí.

Then again, hadn't I been on their side too? I did everything they asked of me.

Were they to blame for all that had happened? They manipulated me into freeing the people of my father's curse. Granted, it needed to be done. It was not okay for my father to make anyone believe him to be God. To take away their choice... and their chances of getting into heaven. Definitely not okay. But where were the Saoirse Trodaí now? They lied to me. They lit a ship on fire to trick everyone in the city to gather outside at midnight when they released the antidote into the air.

Or were the Vapaus, the rebel group within the Saoirse Trodaí, to blame? Would the Saoirse Trodaí have accepted me, made me their queen, if not for the Vapaus?

Probably not.

Even so, this was all my father's fault. He started the whole thing when he cursed the people into believing he was God. But he'd repented before he died. He was in heaven. I would see him again without all the distrust and memory wiping.

Thank You for saving my father in the end.

Iisakki nuzzled his cat face on my leg. *Sakki isn't God.*

I huffed a heavy sigh. *I know you're not God, but if you're going to be in my head, you're going to need to learn the difference between my prayers and communication with you.*

He snorted and rubbed his whiskers on me again.

And thank you for Iisakki.

He looked up at me with a kitty grin.

I could trust Sakki. Though he was young, he was the only one I could say for sure I trusted fully, aside from God. Maybe Liam as long as I could keep him at arm's length and never... ever... give in to whatever strange feelings a mere look from him invoked. I still wasn't sure about Ruuta. She claimed to be here for me, but Queen Rhiannon and the fae still held her allegiance. I knew nothing about the queen to know if I could trust her or not. And Rhys? Well, he'd proven himself untrustworthy again and again. He didn't seem to understand that lying was even a problem. Why I continued to forgive him, I wasn't sure. Yet something told me not to give up on him.

You brought me this unusual group, God. Please see us through the Forest of Shadows with our lives.

FIVE

Though we tried to use our water sparingly, between us and our horses, we were out. So the telltale babbling of running water pushed new life into us as we hurried to find the source. Water peeked through the greenery, and I smacked my lips together, eager for a drink. The moment I reached the dirt bank, I dropped to my knees and dunked a hand beneath the cool surface. As I relished the relief to my dry throat, I glanced across the way to the other bank. It was quite far. "Where are we?"

Rivulets leaked through Rhys's fingers as he swallowed his handful. "I believe this is the Bealach River which leads to Sáile, a fishing village. There are many villages along the river."

"Shouldn't we avoid people?" Or was it God's plan to free people along the way?

He took another drink, stood, and wiped his hands on his pants. "Perhaps yes, perhaps no."

Ruuta clicked her tongue as she filled her waterskin, not willing to look uncivilized for even a moment to quench her thirst. "It's not worth the risk. Let us keep to the woods."

"Won't it be patrolled by defenders?" I unscrewed my canteen to refill.

Liam scoffed, his aura flaring red. "Unlikely. Auberon didn't like to waste resources. One defender typically patrolled a large area and didn't stay long in populated areas. Not that he needed many defenders when all the villages were cursed." He mumbled that last part under his breath, then splashed himself with the water, and scrubbed his face.

"But will the Saoirse Trodaí send people in search of us?" I tried not to look at Liam as he washed his exposed areas, longing to clean up as well, but it would have to wait.

"I was never one of them and can't know their plans, but between your veil and Ruuta's compulsion, they shouldn't know you were at the Atonement Center. By going to the hideout, then the Atonement Center, we haven't taken a direct route. All they know is when you escaped the castle. You could've gone anywhere with a dragon."

"But they know something unusual happened at the Atonement Center." My voice bordered on whiny. "Wouldn't they suspect us?"

"The whole city was in a state of chaos." Liam huffed.

"The perfect time to escape unnoticed." Ruuta took delicate sips, then dabbed at the corners of her mouth. How did she have such restraint? And what did she look like under the glamor enhancing her face? Did the blue markings emphasize her beauty, or were her perfect features also an illusion?

"And no one has reason to suspect you'd venture into Rotko." Rhys hopped to a stone to bypass us for better access to the water.

Ruuta raised a perfectly shaped eyebrow. "Unless they suspect she'd seek Queen Rhiannon's assistance."

"Perhaps." Liam waggled his head as if tossing the thought about. "But it's more likely they'd think you've returned to your realm. You disappeared once. You could do it again. Searching is a wasted effort right now. They need all their resources to gain control."

He was right. Still, I hated feeling like a fugitive on the run, especially when I'd done nothing wrong. "But what of the ships?"

"The ships we haven't seen since last night?" He stared for a second to let that comment sink in. "My guess is they sent them out to search the perimeter and we're outside of it. I doubt we'll see another."

I hoped he was right on that too.

Once the horses had had their fill, we gathered their reins and led them to a grassy spot.

Liam wrapped Nessa's reins around a low branch. "Come. We'll sleep here. Let's see if we can find something to eat. I'm famished."

None of us had a net. Nor were we swift enough to catch a fish with our bare hands. After bringing Clover to rest with the other horses, I searched for what I knew best—plants. Night was nearly upon us, and my stomach rebelled for want of food. But the vegetation wasn't the same here as in Ariboslia. What was edible? There were no recognizable berries, nuts, mushrooms, or roots. I was about to give up when I spotted a patch of green leaves with silver serrated edges. My breath caught. "Is that silverweed?"

Rhys inspected the plant and shrugged. "I haven't studied botany."

I didn't know what botany was, but I didn't feel like listening to him regurgitate a lesson from one of the many books he'd read. I loved books. But I was more of a fiction reader. "I think..." I broke off a leaf and licked the torn piece. The familiar nuttiness of the leafy greens only I seemed to enjoy back home begged to be eaten, and I crammed a leaf in my mouth. "Definitely silverweed."

I laughed as I chewed, not caring about my manners. Just what we needed. *Thank You, God!*

After plucking a leaf, Rhys took a bite. His face screwed up as he chewed, and his tongue expelled the moist clump onto the ground. "I'll find something else."

Something passed overhead, bathing me in its temporary shadow. I ducked and looked up. *Sakki!* I released my held breath. *Don't do that! I thought you were a ship.*

He dropped beside me, shaking the ground as I dug up the plants.

His mouth opened, and a waterfall of fish splashed onto the ground. I jumped away from the deluge.

"Fish!" Rhys clapped his hands together. "Thanks, Sakki. Are you going to cook it for us like you did the rodents?"

Step aside. Iisakki used his bulk to push me, then took a deep breath, and huffed out fire. When the blazing stream ended, scorched grass and fish remained.

Rhys picked one up and flipped it over. It was raw on the other side. "How about cooking the other side, friend?"

A rumble rose from Sakki's throat. He pawed at them, tossing them over. Rhys helped flip those he'd missed. Then Sakki cooked the other side.

Rhys crunched on a fish. "They're a little crisp."

Sakki shot a small stream of fire toward Rhys, who got the message. Rhys sat and chewed his cremated fish carcass in silence.

Liam tossed sticks onto the scorched grass. "Care to light a fire for us?"

"Is it safe to have a fire here?" I picked up a fish and gagged at the head.

"I hope so." Liam's aura flickered, demonstrating his uncertainty.

I hated to be a princess, but... "Can someone remove this for me?"

His aura dancing with light colors now, Liam laughed a silent laugh. He yanked the fish from me, retrieved the knife from his waist, and lopped the head clean off.

I gagged again and accepted the headless carcass.

Sakki blew onto the sticks, and they turned to ash. He grimaced.

Liam's shoulders slumped. "I'll get more."

"No hurry." Ruuta dropped an armful, then wiped the residue from her formerly pristine sleeves.

We tossed more sticks onto the ashes. Iisakki threw us a wary glance, pursed his lips together, and released a puff. The sticks ignited.

"Well done, Sakki." I rubbed the soft scales on his shoulder.

He loosed a rumbly dragon purr, shifted into cat form, and

circled a tuft of grass several times before settling down to sleep. He must've already eaten his fill of fish. Would he wake to shelter us again tonight? Sleeping under his wing beside his warm belly was comforting.

But we had silverweed, fish, and water. It made me more optimistic about this journey. God would provide along the way. If only I would remember and continue to trust Him, even when I didn't have food or water.

Once my stomach was full, my eyes grew heavy. I didn't have the heart to wake Sakki to sleep beside him. We hadn't seen a ship all day, by air or by river. It should be safe. Rhys distributed blankets while I made a more comfortable spot to sleep. My hands brightened as I summoned energy, and I pushed it out over the grass, teasing it to thicken. The grass I'd manipulated was noticeably different, even in the dim firelight. It felt like fur.

Ruuta sucked in a breath. "Might you do that for me too?"

By the time everyone had a bed of plush grass, I was exhausted. I wrapped myself up in my blanket, snuggled beside Sakki's kitty body, drifted off to sleep, and dreamed my father was still alive, but he wanted me dead. Though it felt as if I'd been running for days, I'd only gotten as far as the beach. The castle was still in view. My father had sent Rhys after me. And Rhys kept prodding me in the side with Balder's cane.

I swiped at whatever was poking me. "Stop."

But my protests just made Rhys more angry. He prodded me again with more force.

"Ow!" I smacked the thing and opened my eyes.

A man with pasty white cream slathered on leathery skin and clumps of damp red hair sending rivulets of water down his shoulders crouched over me with a spear. My heart seized as I gasped. I pressed into the ground, wishing it had more give as my gaze darted back and forth from the man's face to the tip of his spear.

He had no aura.

Six

Another armed man with the same white smeared across his face and longer clumps of twisted red hair aimed his spear at Rhys who looked equally terrified.

Clickkk.

"Get away from them." Liam emerged from behind a tree, his pistol trained on the man holding the spear at me, then flicked it to the man by Rhys, then back as he took careful steps closer. His red aura had never been more steady.

Liam's presence distracted the man threatening me. I rolled away from the weapon and into a crouch, jostling Sakki in my haste. He stretched and yawned before noticing what was happening. His eyes widened. His aura blazed red.

Don't change! Stay in cat form. I gathered him up in my arms.

What's happening?

I don't know, but you're a lousy watchdog.

Because... Sakki's a cat right now.

This was not the time for... whatever this was. *Just stay as you are.*

But wait. Both men's weapons... "Don't shoot! Their spears are backward. They don't mean to kill us."

Ruuta came running from the woods. She clutched the stone about her neck as she strode toward the one closest to me.

"Don't." I held a hand, staying her. We didn't need her going around compelling everyone and scrambling their brains unnecessarily.

These men could deal damage with a stick, but if they meant to kill us, they wouldn't have turned their spears around. But what *was* their intent? To prod us from our slumber? And they had no aura. Either they were something new I hadn't encountered in this realm yet, or they were cursed.

"Who are you?" I hoped they spoke English.

"You're on my land, lass. I'll be doin' the askin' if you don' mind." The man's accent sounded much like those in Talamh Sí. But thicker and more difficult to understand. "Who are you? And what are you doin' on my land?"

I wanted to know what land we were on, but I didn't want to anger him further. I took a deep breath. Time to tell the truth, come what may. "I'm Colleen. Er. Eerika."

"No!" Rhys reached out as if he could remove my words from the air.

I braced myself for whatever response my next words might elicit. "King Auberon's daughter."

Rhys slumped to the ground, deflated, like he'd given up on life.

"Princess Eerika?" The man yanked the spear away and sank to one knee. "My most sincere apologies."

That settled it. He was under the curse. The tension ebbed from my muscles, and I breathed easier. And hated being so relieved.

"Is he with you?" The other man held his ground, keeping Rhys pinned.

"Yes, we're traveling together." I motioned toward Liam and Ruuta. "These two as well. Please, put your weapons away."

The young man retreated and gripped his spear like a walking stick. He looked a lot like the older man, but smoother and thicker.

Liam didn't move to holster his pistol, so I nodded to confirm I meant him too. His face twitched. Then he huffed and holstered his gun, though the red penetrating his aura didn't let up. He didn't trust these men, and I didn't blame him.

The older man's gaze roamed over me, lingering on the tears in my pants. "You're in need of new clothes, ma'am."

Ma'am? I was only twenty. But I still felt like the seventeen-year-old I thought I was before my father told me my true age. My elfin age. I assessed his attire. He thought *I* needed new clothes? He was right, but judging from his threadbare trousers and lack of anything else covering his tanned skin, he needed them more.

He caught my eye, then looked down at himself, and laughed. "This is my fishin' attire. No need wearin' nice clothes for such a task."

I glanced at the river. Why would he need to wear nothing but tattered pants to fish?

The man laughed again. "We were headin' out to dive for mussels. Some of the village children found you and came a runnin'. Forgive us, for we're not fit to be in the company o' royalty. And the children were afright when they happened upon people in the woods. Visitors come by road or by port. None visit these here woods but the children."

"They were right to notify you," I said.

"Forgive my terrible manners." He placed a hand over his heart. "The name's Carr. This here's my son, Fiske." He motioned to the younger man. I would've guessed they were brothers, not father and son. The younger man didn't look young enough, nor did the older man look old enough. But they had to be human, not elves or fae, to be under Auberon's curse. "Come with us. We'll get you some food and clothes."

"That's not a good idea." Liam splayed a hand out, blocking me.

"For once, we agree," Ruuta muttered.

Liam rolled his eyes at her.

Rhys smacked the wrinkles from his clothes, shot Fiske an

insulted look, then addressed Carr. "From which village do you hail?"

"Sáile." Carr pointed through the trees. "It's not far from here."

"Highness?" Rhys sidled up to me. "Perhaps we should take a moment to confer amongst ourselves."

Since when did he speak so formally? "Would you please give us a moment?" I asked the men.

"O' course." Carr bowed and motioned to his son. Both walked out of earshot toward the river.

Liam glanced over his shoulder to ensure the men were a safe distance away. His head snapped back to me. "What happened to not telling strangers who you are?"

Ruuta shook her head and judged me harshly without words.

"I felt I needed to be honest."

"You could have said, Colleen. That's honest!" Liam dragged a hand down his face with a groan.

"We can fix this." Ruuta slid the stone from beneath her neckline. "I'll compel them before they return to their village and not tell anyone." She swiveled back to the men.

"Nay." I grasped her arm and pulled her back.

Liam blew out a sharp, scoffing breath.

Sakki nuzzled my leg. *Colleen must free the people, then go to Sáile.*

Which people? All the people?

The dragon held his tongue.

I patted my mother's ring, then reached beneath the neckline to fiddle with it as if it might give me answers. *What if they turn on me? Liam did. The men on the ship did.*

Not all the crewmen turned on Colleen. The captain didn't.

I growled. The furry-brained beast wasn't getting the point. *What will happen to me if I free them?*

How should Sakki know? Does Sakki know the future?

What are you, Rhys now? Stop being evasive. I tried to hurry this along. By their auras and expressions, Ruuta and Liam were growing impatient. *Did God say to go?*

Of course! Sakki wouldn't tell Colleen to do something risky without God's say-so.

That should have settled it. Yet my heart still waffled. But I had to trust God. The only way to do that was to practice. Take leaps of faith. I relayed the message. Rhys nodded, looking doubtful yet satisfied. But Ruuta and Liam weren't believers. Liam might be teetering on the edge, but he wasn't there yet.

He massaged the back of his neck and squinted. With how pained his face looked, his thoughts might be physically hurting him. "I don't like it."

That meant he'd go along with it.

Ruuta puckered her pert mouth. "I'll follow you anywhere." She pointed a gloved finger in my face. "But if anything goes wrong, I'm compelling them."

I plucked the vial from my pocket. Purple swirling vastalääke filled the bottle. "Does everyone still have their antidote?"

The others retrieved theirs and checked the contents. All full. None of us had used any, except Liam.

"Mine's still mostly full." He shook it, sending the purple swirls mixing with the pink liquid. "I only sprayed one defender."

I studied his vial. You wouldn't be able to tell he'd used any. "Good. We should be able to free a lot of people with this."

We found Carr and Fiske.

"We will accompany you, but you must agree to receive an antidote." I held my vial out for them to see.

"An antidote?" Father and son exchanged identical confused expressions.

"Aye. You're under a curse."

"I know of no curse, but far be it from me to second-guess the princess." Carr planted his spear in the ground to punctuate his decision.

"If the princess insists," Fiske agreed.

With a firm nod, I gestured to our camp. "Please lay down on our bedding."

Wait. I did a double take at the spot where I'd slept. Twin dark spots in the grass. *Dead* grass where my hands would have been when I woke to find a spear in my face.

A memory sprang to mind—sitting in the garden with Iida and Liam as they told me, yet again, that my father was manipulating my memories. The flower in my hand. I'd siphoned the energy from it. I *killed* it. Had I—? Had I done it again?

Could elves remove a living thing's life force as well as give it? Or was that the fae side of me?

I hoped no one noticed the spots as the men exchanged more doubtful looks. Finally, they agreed. Once they were lying down, I sprayed Carr's face whilst Ruuta doused his son. Their eyes rolled up, and they were out.

Not-so-hushed voices came from a shaking bush. Liam sneaked to the offending shrubbery, reached in, and hauled out a boy by the arm. "All of you, come out."

The boy dangling from Liam's grip gaped at him, horrified.

"You're scaring the poor boy." I raced over and tugged him from Liam's grip and smiled. "It's okay. You're safe." I beckoned to the bush. "You're all safe."

Three more children emerged from their hiding place with sheepish expressions. Ratty clothes hung on skinny frames. Leaves and twigs clung to knotted hair.

"Are you really Princess Eerika?" asked a girl with twists of matted hair bound together in a ponytail.

All four children huddled together, reminding me of my siblings. I smoothed back some unruly locks from the girl's forehead. "Yes, I am."

A boy with similar twists of hair like a mop stepped forward. His skinny chest puffed out. "What have you done to my uncle?"

The others wouldn't approve of what I was about to say, but I said it anyway. "Your uncle is under a curse. We're freeing him."

The four gave a collective gasp. The girl's aura had begun to lighten. Now, it went black, like the others, and she scooted out of reach.

"Why don't you sit with us while we wait for them to waken?" I sat and patted the grass beside me.

They held a silent meeting with their eyes alone, then Sakki wove his cat body through their legs, taking swipes as he went. The kids laughed and reached for him, passing him along as they scratched under his chin to get him to smile. I breathed a relieved breath, grateful for the distraction. If only we'd packed our bedding rather than giving it to the men. I'd hate to have to flee without it.

SEVEN

Carr bolted upright on my bedding, and Fiske groaned. Our gazes darted toward them, and we stopped chewing on our charred fish.

Liam's hand crept toward his holster as Ruuta clutched her amulet. They waited, watching what the men might do. We all did.

"What happened?" Fiske asked.

Carr peeled himself from the ground. He took a wide stance and gripped his back as he straightened, his sinewy arms and torso flexing.

I rushed to his side. "You should sit a moment." I waited for him to comply, then asked, "How do you feel?"

"My head feels like it's bein' crushed in the maw of an éin bís." Fiske remained seated, clutching his head.

I had no idea what that was, but he clearly had a headache. Plus, it was a common side effect of the antidote. "Do we have any soothing tablets?"

"There might be something in the tin in my saddlebag." Liam made no move to get it, his hand still ready to reach for his weapon.

"Rhys, can you please find it?" I asked.

With the way Rhys sprang for Nessa, he might think he was being timed.

"Your father, King Auberon." Carr gripped his brow, wincing. "What did he do?"

I steeled myself for the anger I'd received from Liam and others I'd saved. These people were as likely to be angry... and unreasonable. But I had to tell the truth. "He cursed you into believing he was God." I prayed my father hadn't manipulated their memories as he had mine. "Do you remember everything?"

"Huh?" Carr squinted at me like I were the sun. "Remember what, specifically?"

"You're not remembering anything you might've forgotten?"

"Not that I'm aware. I'm a simple man with a simple life. There's not much to remember or forget."

That was a relief. "Have you always lived in this village? Have you always been a fisherman?"

He nodded, then winced, and rubbed his temple. "Not many folks come or go from this tiny village."

Good. Maybe my father hadn't taken anyone away or caused any other damage. Maybe I could free these people and get out cleanly. "What about you?" I asked Fiske.

"Don't feel much of anythin' but a throbbin' head."

Their dull auras flickered in and out, trying to start up again. It would take them time to return to their full range of emotions. Liam's had flashed red fairly quickly. But then, he'd had reason to hate my father beyond being cursed. Perhaps, if nothing happened to these men, their emotions would return with them no worse for the wear.

We packed our things while Carr and Fiske waited for the soothing tablets to take effect. Then we followed them down a well-worn path along the riverbank. The river widened, and brilliant blue waters appeared. I longed to jump in for a bath.

The children waved to people floating by in boats. Rather than wave back, the occupants stared at us. Everywhere we went, people stopped what they were doing and stared. Oars stilled and boats drifted. Women washing clothes dropped their garments in the water. People carrying baskets across wooden paths to huts hovering over the waters tripped over each other, nearly toppling into the river. Eyes watched us from everywhere.

"We rarely get visitors 'round here." Carr gave small waves to the onlookers with a sheepish smile.

"We get defenders." Fiske's upper lip twitched, and his aura flared red. He shared a look with Carr that sent all the alarms within me pinging. "They take our catch."

Carr's aura blipped red, then morphed to a blue that deepened with his sigh. "And deliver supplies."

Fiske's anger, I understood. But Carr's sadness? Was he trying to reconcile what my father had done to him and consider the good? Or was he concerned about what would happen to his people now that the king was gone? The people who'd taken over the castle weren't likely to consider the needs of villages on the outskirts.

Nay, he didn't know of my father's death yet. I wasn't looking forward to that conversation.

Carr's home was one of many thatched-roof huts on stilts all strung together by a rickety walkway overhanging an inlet. The planks complained and threatened to dump us into the waters below. Villagers stepped out of their huts, stilled their boats, and stopped their chores to watch us until we disappeared inside the unfurnished shack. A slender woman with dark hair tied in a loose bun sat on the floor stirring something in a pan over an open fire. Her inquisitive eyes glistened like polished charcoal as she looked at her husband with unspoken questions. Like the rest of the adult villagers, she had no aura.

"This is my lovely bride, Aune." Pride warmed Carr's voice. "Aune, this is, uh... Princess Eerika and her friends."

Aune jumped to her feet and scrambled to curtsy, sending the hut rocking. I tried to steady myself, but finding nothing solid to hold on to, I opted for Liam's shoulder and regretted it. The energy within him jolted at my touch. But, if he felt it, he gave no indication.

Sakki crossed the dubious floor with his lithe cat form. With ease, he leaped over the gaps revealing a cerulean glow lapping beneath and wound himself around Aune's legs. She startled, then extended a tentative hand to pet him. When his head met her and he rubbed himself against her, she gushed.

"Princess, would you allow me a word with my wife?"

"Of course." I gave a curt nod and backed toward the doorless entrance. There was nowhere for them to go for privacy in the modest room. But they retreated to a corner and spoke in low tones while Fiske motioned for us to sit on the floor.

Once Aune seemed to understand what was happening, she agreed to take the vastalääke. As she lay on a mat, we crowded together, waiting for her to recover. Carr's gaze continued to drift toward her, his face and aura illustrating his worry. But every time Fiske's gaze snapped toward his mother, his aura flared red as he sat wringing his hands.

Water lapped below the floorboard gaps, and I shivered, expecting the floor to give way.

Laughing called my attention to the glassless window. Children stood on a long log-like boat. With their feet planted on the rails, arms splayed for balance, they rocked. A boy fell over the side with a splash while others pitched back and forth, fighting to regain balance. One more fell overboard while those still standing laughed. Once they recovered, they rocked the boat again. They needed decent clothes, a brush through their long hair, and regular meals for their sunken bellies, but despite all that, they looked happy. Genuinely happy. Happier than the children in the city.

All but one child capsized. The last one standing thrust his hands in the air and shouted something. Then he sat as the children scrambled to get back in the boat and start their game again.

How did these people have so little? My father may have been misguided, but he had cared about his people. Even his jail cells were cozy. Was it possible he didn't know what was happening outside his city?

If I became queen, I'd improve their living conditions... somehow. Until then, I had to find my way to Queen Rhiannon, assuming we survived the witch in the Divide. A sense of urgency rose within me, pushing me to my feet. "We should be on our way."

Carr grasped my hand and pulled me back down. "Please stay. I have so many questions. How did we come to be under such a curse? How did you know about it? How did you free us? Will we fall under the curse again?"

I held up my hands to hold back his rapid-fire questioning. "My father cursed everyone in his kingdom." I decided not to confuse the issue by mentioning their lack of auras had confirmed my suspicions. "They receive the curse at the age of—"

"Atonement." Fiske sneered.

Carr's gaze pinged back and forth as if he was searching his memories, piecing them together. "Yes, I see it now." Once he finished processing, he skewered me with a determined stare. "You can't leave. Not until all of Sáile receives the cure."

Liam leaped to his feet, making the hut sway. I grabbed his pant leg, silently imploring him to sit back down. With pursed lips and a subtle headshake, he complied.

Ruuta clutched her compulsion stone. "Remaining that long is unwise. Princess Eerika plotted against her father and risked her life to free the people. Many of them are so angry with Auberon—they're calling for her blood. Then there's a rebel group scheming to overthrow the monarchy. She isn't safe. We must get her as far from the city as possible, and once Sáile is freed, we'll need to keep her away from here too."

"How many atoned live here?" Rhys's voice squeaked.

"Forty-two. We're a small village." Carr scratched his chin.

"That's because we don't live long." Fiske's right eye twitched as his aura raged. "We have one widow in her sixties. Most folk pass on in their fifties."

I gasped. "Why so young?"

Fiske scoffed. "Lack of food, medicine, accidents... Diving is dangerous. Defenders confiscate most of our catch. Little remains for us."

"What else do you have to eat?" My voice came out thin as I barely breathed.

Carr twisted his hands in his lap, his aura a myriad of colors blinking in and out. "We eat what others have little interest in—mollusks, taro root, lotus root, water chestnuts, algae... But defenders deliver milk, eggs, vegetables, supplies—"

"Not enough." Fiske smacked the floor, and I feared his hand going right through the boards. "We don't have enough to feed us, nor do we get the medicines we need."

Or clothes. But I wouldn't mention that.

"You see?" Liam jabbed a finger at Fiske. "That's what I'm talking about. Once your sleepy community wakes up, they'll want to take it out on Colleen. We can't let that happen."

"He's right." Ruuta pulled her vial of vastalääke from her pocket and handed it to Carr. "This is the cure. There's enough to free everyone. Take it. And we'll be on our way."

I was surprised she'd give up her vial rather than attempt to compel them. But listening to these arguments made me nauseous. They were right. I was a fool. I'd put us all in danger.

We all stood to leave.

Fiske blocked the doorway. "You're not going anywhere."

"Fiske!" Carr's confused aura and expression made it clear he wasn't conspiring with whatever nefarious plot brewed in his son's mind.

"Oh?" Ruuta straightened her spine. She grasped her stone.

"Nay!" I yanked the amulet from her grip.

"What would you have me do, Colleen?" She cut a gloved hand through the air. "These people intend to hold us prisoner."

"Just till the defenders arrive." He bit his lip and looked up without lifting his head, probably sorting out the plan and convincing himself all at once. "If they find out the princess was here and we let her go, they might not look kindly on us. What if the new government decides they don't need our fish? We won't survive on our own."

Ruuta gripped my hand holding her stone and stared me down. I held my ground, unwilling to let her impress upon me the direness of the situation and that compelling them was our only option. She had a point, but fleeing now would set us up for more difficulty later. It might look as though I'd abandoned them, which was not something I wanted to do.

But I also wouldn't hand myself over to those who wanted to kill me.

Yet my friends were all awaiting my decision. How could anyone expect me to be queen when such a situation as this left me at a loss?

God, please tell us what to do.

Sakki, do you know what to do?

Sakki knows nothing new. Colleen and friends are to go through Rotko to Queen Rhiannon.

Then we had to escape. But how?

EIGHT

Groaning came from the corner of the hut. Carr jumbled the table to sit at Aune's side. He smoothed his wife's hair while Fiske stood his ground, blocking the exit.

"Do you have more of those..." I rubbed my fingers together, imagining them in my hands as my brain searched for the word.

"Soothing tablets?" Liam fetched the tin from his pocket and shook out two, then handed them to Carr.

He pressed them into his wife's hand. "Take these, my love. They'll help your achin' head."

Wincing, Aune dragged herself up to sit on the mat. Her nose wrinkled as she chewed the medicine, then chased it down with water. A wall of people stood around her. I motioned to my friends to sit back down. Liam and Ruuta complied, but their expressions and orange auras rebelled.

Aune massaged her furrowed brow. "What's happening?"

"Your son wants to keep us prisoner." Liam scoffed.

Her aura chugged like an engine attempting to start, spitting out strands of dark-purple light to illustrate her confusion. "They freed us. Why would you repay them like that?"

"Mum." Fiske grasped his mother's hand, leaving the doorway unblocked, and I gave the others a stern look to stay put. "What if the defenders find out she was here? What if they decide they don't want our fish? There are other fishing villages." His shoulders inched up by his ears. He probably already felt guilty for what he planned to do. "We may need leverage."

"How could you think like that, my son?" With her free hand, she waved to her husband. "Do you agree with this?"

"No. They've given us enough cure for everyone. We should repay their generosity in kind. The defenders needn't know they were ever here."

"Kids saw them, Pa! The entire village knows by now. Can you guarantee the defenders won't find out? Auberon will have our heads! You heard what they said. She conspired against him. That's *treason*. If we help her, we become conspirators. Traitors. They'll hang us!"

"My father is dead."

The small family gasped as one.

Fiske's aura waned. "But the defenders—"

"Aren't coming." Liam huffed.

Their gazes snapped to him, then back to me, seeking answers.

"He's right. Talamh Sí is in mayhem. They need to get the city under control." I didn't want to tell them that, if defenders appeared, it was because they were hunting me.

Ruuta smoothed away a loose golden curl with a gloved finger. "The Saors who freed the kingdom had another rebel group in their ranks, the Vapaus, who wish to overthrow the monarchy. They are likely fighting for control. The victor, whoever that may be, will have their hands full restoring order."

The blood drained from our captors' faces as their auras blackened. "They've abandoned us?"

"It will take time to consider communities on the outskirts." I spoke with certainty though it was an assumption.

Fiske's Adam's apple dipped.

"If Talamh Sí remains a monarchy and I'm placed on the throne" —I took a deep breath—"I will protect and provide for Sáile."

What was I saying? Had I lost my mind? I don't know if I'd survive the journey to Queen Rhiannon, never mind become queen. And besides, I knew nothing about ruling a kingdom.

All these thoughts plagued my mind, and yet I wouldn't take back what I said. Sakki rubbed his kitty face on my knee, confirming I'd done the right thing. That made me feel better... and terrified.

Fiske stared like he might see the future and determine the truth of my words if he looked hard enough.

"What do you think will happen if the Vapaus overthrow the monarchy?" I asked.

"They'll form a new government?" He raised an eyebrow.

"Aye. They want to form a democracy. But it won't be a true democracy. The Vapaus will be in control. The people will have no say. They have manipulated, schemed, and killed—"

"Like your father?" Fiske scowled.

That comment could go two ways. Either he meant my father had done those things or he was one of their victims. Perhaps, rather than sort out his meaning, I should tell him what he needed to hear. "My father deserved to die for his crimes."

The family straightened, holding a silent conversation with their eyes as their auras sparked purple. Confusion was better than fear. It meant they were thinking.

"Valtteri, the leader of the Saoirse Trodaí. And my friends, Pirkko and Taneli..." My voice caught and my vision blurred. "All died because of the Vapaus."

Taneli had been part of them and the reason for Pirkko's death, but I blamed the Vapaus for his death too. If they hadn't sunk their claws into him... twisted his mind...

A tear escaped, and I wiped it away. "Any government formed by such people will be to the detriment of all."

Their auras were blue now. Sad was even better than confused. They cared.

Ruuta laced her gloved fingers. "If we can get to Queen Rhiannon, she will help us restore order, place Princess Eerika on the throne, and ensure everyone has enough keino and supplies to run their communities. And, from what Princess Eerika just said"—a dimple appeared as her blue eyes sparked with gloating—"she will ensure you are provided for as well."

Fiske gave his father a sheepish look. "We should let them go."

His parents nodded.

"What if defenders... or someone from Talamh Sí does come?" Carr asked. "What should we say? Will they know we're free from the curse? Will it matter?"

"I won't ask anyone to lie on my behalf. Tell them we were here and we've gone."

"Tell them we've gone through the Divide." Glee blazed in Ruuta's eyes now. "They're welcome to attempt the journey as well."

Rhys paled, and Liam pressed his lips into a thin line, probably to keep his thoughts from escaping. But the family nodded again.

"Then you should leave under cover of night so none see the direction you take," Carr said.

"In the meantime..." I stood and eyed Sakki. "Maybe we can help gather more food for you and your people."

WE TRAVELED UPSTREAM, away from the villagers, for Sakki to shift into dragon form to fish. The poor things fighting to travel upstream leaped straight into his mouth. Ruuta and I gathered silverweed and berries. On our way back with bulging pouches and a wagon filled with Sakki's flopping catch, we spotted a wild pig. While Sakki chased it down, Liam and Rhys met us with rabbits dangling from each hand. The villagers didn't know what to do with the animals, so for those willing to learn, Liam demonstrated how to skin the rabbits. The children cleared an area on the riverbank where I instructed on how to make a spit.

Night waned on as the pig spun above the fire, sending a wonderful aroma into the air. Villagers took turns spinning the beast while others played tiny drums like nothing I'd ever seen. They were attached to sticks, like big lollipops, with mallets dangling on strings. One child taught me to beat the drum by spinning it in my hand. Many of us drummed together. Or *they* drummed together, and I tried and failed to spin the thing in time to the beat. Some clapped along. Others danced in the water.

I felt guilty. What would these people think of me if their eyes were opened as they would be tomorrow? Carr, Fiske, and Aune all drummed and laughed. Perhaps, like these three, they'd just take time to adjust. At least we'd left them with food. And now they knew to look outside the waters for more should they be abandoned for any length of time. Only God knew when—or *if*—we would return to help.

How I hated making a promise I couldn't keep.

The fire died down, and the villagers dispersed. Once they were asleep, Carr led us across the rickety walkway. Soft snores escaped the huts as we passed. Nothing sounded outside but lapping water, creaking boards, and bumping boats jostling against the docks. Moonlight reflected on the river's surface, seeming to move with the water, sparkling as it went.

We reached the bank. An owl hooted, then flew away. The branch on which it perched swayed.

"Thank you, Carr." I tipped my head to him when he brought us to our horses. "I pray we return to assist your village."

"I'm holdin' you to it." He smiled and grasped my hands. "Thank you for the food and the cure. We'll free the others in the morn."

"I pray it goes well." I quirked my lips. "And that the villagers aren't angry with you for letting us go."

"Bah." He waved it off. "Don't you worry about that a'tall. There are so few of us. Most will be like Fiske. If you could talk sense into that stubborn boy, we can with the rest. Especially after that feast." He patted his stomach. "Never have we eaten so well."

We mounted our horses, waved goodbye, and set off through the woods to the north.

God, I don't know what possessed me to make such a bold promise. Please help me keep it.

NINE

Riding through the dark woods again was slow going. We were tired. There hadn't been enough room to lie down in Carr's hut. But the horses had rested. We'd eaten well and left the villagers with more food than they had when we arrived.

"Are we too far east?" Ruuta stopped her horse and spun, studying the sky. "Seelie Clós is northwest of Talamh Sí."

Liam tugged his sleeve, revealing the timepiece on his wrist. Looked like it had a compass too. He consulted it and shifted his body. "Sáile is northeast of Talamh Sí." He checked his compass again. "Yeah, we're too far east."

"We need to cut back toward the west." Ruuta's horse side-stepped beneath her.

He cupped the back of his neck. "That will bring us close to Folaím."

"The veiled village? Where we stayed with Valtteri?" The mysterious tree village filled me with warmth despite the unfortunate circumstances of my last visit.

"Yes. We'll have to be careful. The Saoirse Trodaí may still be there." He leaned forward to scratch his steed's neck. Black hair spilled into his eyes. "We don't know whose side they're on."

"Or if there are Vapaus among them." Ruuta inspected her gloves.

"Should we continue north, then? And cut back west in Seelie Clós?" I didn't want to take any longer than necessary in the Divide.

"It's better to spend longer traveling here." Still scowling at the smears on her gloves, Ruuta adjusted her grip on the reins.

"With the Vapaus trying to kill me? Seelie Clós must be safer."

"Not for royalty outside of Queen Rhiannon's protection." She clicked her tongue and spurred her horse west.

"But—"

"We need to move, then." Liam cut me off. "We'll travel by night and sleep by day while someone keeps watch." He took off after Ruuta.

Rhys gave me a lopsided smile, then followed the others.

"But—" I wrinkled my nose. How could Ruuta say something like that, then leave without another word? If more dangers awaited me once we made it through the Divide, I should know. And traveling all night after we'd been up all day? I slumped in defeat and sighed, then nudged Clover to catch up. We had enough to contend with now and soon in the Divide. Whatever awaited me in Seelie Clós could wait. For now.

LIAM FOUND a place he recognized and led us to a cave that wasn't out of our way. The news would have thrilled me if I'd had the energy to be excited. I kept nodding off and jerking awake. One of these times, I would slip from Clover's back. I never thought I'd miss the noisy autos in my father's city. At least I could sleep in those if I was too tired.

My father's city.

It wasn't his anymore. It never was. But would I ever think of it as anything else?

Dawn's gray light filtered through the canopy, leaving me more tired than ever. "Where is this cave already?"

If anyone heard me, they gave no sign.

An hour or ten later, when we arrived, Liam insisted on taking the first watch.

"If the Saoirse Trodaí and defenders aren't following me, is it necessary to keep watch?" I searched the terrain for anything menacing.

"I assume they're not searching for us. Not very hard, anyway. We still need to be prepared. And there are animals—"

As if waiting for their cue, cries erupted in the distance. Eerie, like a cross between a wolf's howl and a woman screaming for her life. Every hair on my body woke and would have fled if not attached. "Creeping crabs, what was that?"

"Olikissa." He sat on a rock and draped his rifle across his lap.

"What in God's world is that?" I accepted the blanket Rhys offered and wrapped it around me.

"A large cat. Most cats are solitary creatures. Not the olikissa. They travel in packs." Liam scrubbed his sleeve along the rifle, wiping something away. "Another reason to keep watch. You do *not* want to come upon them or have them wander into your camp."

I hated to think it was better for him to keep watch, then. What would *I* do against a horde of such creatures? I doubted I'd stay awake, anyway.

After offering everyone blankets, Rhys placed the lantern on the ground and spread his blanket beside it. "They're nocturnal, so they should be going to bed soon."

Behind the cave's depths loomed utter darkness. I swallowed. "I hope this isn't home."

"They sleep in trees, mostly." Rhys lay down and pulled his blanket around him.

That didn't make me feel better. Had we passed trees laden with olikissa hidden in their branches? I'd never travel through the woods the same way again.

After I settled down and Liam took his post with Ruuta, we snuffed out the light. I tried to sleep, but the morning light was brightening the cave. We should have gone deeper into the darkness.

But what might be lurking back there... in the dark?

Perhaps it was best to stay closer to the light.

I must've finally slept, but barely. I seemed half aware of sleeping on the stiff ground and half in dreams, like a shark, with only one side of my brain sleeping. I watched everyone who'd died die again—my father, Pirkko, Valtteri, and Taneli. Over and over again. In different ways. I rose not because I was no longer tired but because I couldn't lie like that for one more minute.

Rhys and Sakki were gone. They'd already risen?

Liam and Ruuta headed toward the cave as I emerged. He gave an eye rise and smile that made my stomach flutter. He walked like all his limbs were in splints. A clump of hair stuck up on one side, looking like he'd slept with it in his fist. I fought the urge to rub his shoulder as I passed. Was that even appropriate?

Rhys's eyes widened at my approach, and the corner of his upper lip rose. "You look terrible."

Great. I tried smoothing my curls. What kind of rat's nest had they converged into with all that tossing and turning and after days without proper care? Is that why Liam had smiled at me? Because I looked ridiculous? "What time is it?"

Rhys tipped his head back to squint at the sky. "Nearly midday."

It'd been what... five, six hours? And he looked refreshed. That must be enough if you actually slept... or if you were a pooka. I sighed and stepped into the sun to the rocky slope near the fire.

I moved to sit beside Sakki gnawing on a bone. *There you are.*

His tongue lolled out one side of his mouth in a smile-like pant. Then he resumed chewing his bone.

Nothing to say to me, huh? Not good morning? Nothing?

He watched me but continued chewing. *Nom. Nom, nom, nom.*

Rhys handed me a skewer of leftover pork. Not a favorite meal. I preferred vegetables. And what would happen to my body over time without them? I'd have to keep an eye out for anything edible in our travels. At least the pig meat helped wake me up.

I spent the afternoon sunbathing on the rock and perusing the land for vegetation, firewood, and skewer sticks. But I didn't know these lands, and I didn't dare venture too far with the threat of olikissa in the limbs hanging over me. So, when the time for the evening meal drew near, I helped Rhys reheat more leftover pork.

The porky scent must've awakened Liam and Ruuta. They emerged from the cave looking hungry and well rested. "We should reach the highlands by morning. How much further east do we need to go?"

Ruuta consulted the sky, shielded her eyes from the sun, then reached for a meat stick. "Another day's travel, I should think."

"The highlands." Hope stirred in me, and I smacked Rhys's arm. "Isn't that where we arrived in Betören—where the megalith is?"

He shrugged. "The highlands are vast. They stretch the entire length of Rotko."

Ruuta narrowed her eyes. "Does it matter?"

All watched me, probably trying to weigh my desire to escape through the megalith and go home. What must my family be going through? No doubt they'd scoured the woods and waters in search of me. Had they found the megalith? Would they assume that's where I'd gone? But I'd told Fallon about the stranger in the woods. They'd think I'd been kidnapped. If only I could go back and assure them I was okay. Well, as okay as I could be in a land where people wanted me dead. My friends continued to stare, midchew, waiting for me to say something.

I swallowed my mostly chewed mouthful. "No worries. I can't get through the megalith without Sakki's help anyway, remember? And I'm sure he's not willing to bring me home."

Sakki lifted his doggy head from resting on his paws. *Colleen is correct.*

I needed them to stop gawking like they expected me to take off running on my own in search of the megalith. "Once we reach the highlands, how much longer until we reach the Forest of Shadows? It didn't take long to go from there back to the valley."

"That valley was part of the highlands," Rhys said. "It will take another night's walk or so."

"Are we going to make camp during the day and travel through the Forest of Shadows at night?" We'd seemed to be unintentionally forming that pattern, but the Forest of Shadows at night sounded like a bad plan.

Rhys raised a hand like a student in class. "I suggest we enter Rotko in the morning. We'll want to travel by day and hide at night."

"Hide?" I clattered my bowl to the ground, every bit of me twitching to fulfill their expectations and run away.

"There are troubling things in Rotko, to be sure. But the worst things come out at night."

Well, that was terrifying. "Speaking of the worst things coming out at night, do we plan to travel at night with olikissa out there?"

Liam poked the fire, toppling what remained of the pile of sticks. "They're unlikely to attack a large group."

"Unless they view us as a herd and try to separate the weakest from among us." Rhys tossed his fish bones on the dying fire, then shrank from Liam's deadly stare.

Liam shifted to face me, and his gaze softened. "We're rested and need to keep moving. It will be all right."

I plucked a blade of grass and rolled it in my fingers. Now I really wanted to go back through the megalith and home, rather than subject myself to whatever nightmares awaited me. Something crumbled in my fingers. The piece of grass was dead.

TEN

While I welcomed a break from the trees and scratches from invisible branches—and I no longer feared olikissa hovering over me, ready to pounce—traveling through the highlands presented new struggles. The bright moon played tricks on us in the mountains' shadows, making it more difficult to judge our steps. The ground grew steeper and rockier. Icy winds swept through my torn clothing. Then the rains came, starting with a gentle mist, then thickening to a steady sprinkle. My curly hair frizzed and swelled nearly to double its original size. Everything was damp, making the winds feel colder. I wanted to hug myself to conserve warmth, but I had to guide Clover. Sakki left his usual spot on Clover's rump to sit in my lap. Though he had to deal with my movements and occasionally getting squished, he opted for more covering and warmth.

Why, God? Don't You want us to go to Rotko? You could give us decent traveling weather. Are we going the wrong way? Are we doing something wrong?

Jagged mountain peaks loomed like giants with spears warning trespassers to keep a respectable distance. We couldn't be anywhere near the megalith. The highlands I'd seen when I'd arrived were rolling hills lush with green. Cozy. Inviting. Nothing like this treacherous path.

Clover skidded on pebbles, and I pitched forward, squishing Sakki—again. "How will the horses endure this?"

Liam held up a fist, alerting us to stop, then leaped from his saddle. He ran his hands down his horse's right hind leg and lifted her foot to inspect it, focusing on the heel. After doing the same with her other hind leg, he combed his fingers through his black hair, making it stick up in droopy spikes. "We need to free the horses. They won't scale the highlands with riders."

"We can't leave them!" I didn't want to hurt Clover, but I didn't want to abandon her either. Sakki leaped out of my lap, landing on the ground as a dog, and I dismounted. "What if we walk them?"

"This terrain is too hard on them, even with their shoes." He unpacked his saddlebag, his decision apparently made.

Ruuta made no move to dismount. "But what of the trek through the Divide?"

"Are your legs broken? We'll have to make do without them." His irritated glare at Ruuta softened when his attention returned to me. "Horses have a good sense of direction. They'll find their way home."

"Back to the city?" I hugged Clover and stroked her neck, seeking forgiveness for what I was about to do.

"Her home is Folaím." Rhys was already unpacking. "Less than a day's walk."

"How will they find it behind the veil?" I looked into Clover's big brown eyes.

"It's not hidden anymore, now that Auberon is dead." Ruuta was going along with this? And why didn't she look like a partly drowned, partly electrified swamp rat, like me? No frizz marred her golden updo. Was she using her illusion to mask how she looked? No way fae were impervious to the elements, or I didn't inherit those features.

I'd forgotten she was aware of the Saoirse Trodaí. Queen Rhiannon had helped them rise up against my father. The fae had created the spell that hid the village. Had Queen Rhiannon been in on that too?

"How can you be sure they won't die out here... alone?" I buried my face in Clover's damp mane. She smelled... ripe.

Sakki will tell them. His limbs, face, and neck elongated as he transformed from dog to horse. He teetered on unsteady hooves. Once he righted himself, he shook his mane at the other horses. They perked up, ears erect. He flicked his ears and shook his mane again. Then his limbs retracted as he shrunk into his dog form. *Horses will return to Folaim once Colleen and friends are ready.*

How did you do that?

He sat to scratch behind his ear. His stretch made him appear to smile. *Animals are simple creatures—easy to communicate with.*

Was there no end to the things I'd learn about him? I relayed the message, and we collected whatever we could carry. Once we had all we needed and said goodbye, the horses plodded back the way we'd come. Though I was grateful Sakki had somehow told them where to go and they'd be safer there, leaving them stabbed at me, poking holes in my heart where I'd held back the tears I'd yet to shed for those I'd lost. Their faces flashed in my mind. Valtteri. Taneli. Pirkko...

My father.

My heart twisted, wanting nothing more than to release the wail pent up within. I blew out a breath to keep my face from crumpling.

Light in. Dark out.

Light in. Dark out.

I steadied my breath and squared my shoulders.

God, please keep them safe.

We returned to the steep incline that grew steeper still until we were nearly scaling a wall. The horses never would have survived this, even during the day. Night made it all the more challenging. The full moon cast shadows that tricked my mind into seeing hand-holds where there were none. The only way was to feel my way along. I stayed behind the others and to their left in case they slipped.

Let Sakki bring Colleen to the top.

You know we can't. What if someone sees you? I couldn't look at Sakki, and he didn't say another word. But I sensed his annoyance.

Colleen won't make it without help.

Yes, I will.

Nay, I wouldn't. My fingers burned as I clung to the ridge. They tingled with fright, knowing they couldn't hold much longer. How far we'd come at an almost vertical climb, I didn't want to know. But if I fell, it was sure to hurt. A lot. Assuming I survived. I didn't dare look down. Nor could I look up other than to find the next handhold.

A bead of sweat dripped into my eye. I tried to blink it away.

"Keep climbing, Colleen. You can do it." Liam's voice fluttered down from above. He'd made it to the top? "Reach for that rock to your right."

I searched for the rock in question, then found what he must be talking about. Hoping it wasn't a trick of the moonlight, I took a deep breath, then scrambled for it. My fingers got a decent hold. I searched for a new foothold. As my foot shifted about, my fingers lost their grip, and I slid.

ELEVEN

I screamed. My stomach remained where I was as the rest of me plummeted, scraping against the rough surface, scrambling to catch hold. I landed on something, and my wail cut short as I bounced away from the wall onto the scaly surface. Sakki's back. I clambered to get a better hold as he lifted me higher. *What are you doing? You're not supposed to fly. What if someone sees us?*

Sakki will not let Colleen fall. He huffed a puff of steam. *Unwanted attention is more likely to come from Colleen's scream.*

I couldn't help it.

Neither could Sakki.

He flew us past the others, through a patch of fog, to the crest. Crosswinds blasted us as we landed and I collapsed into him. The air was chillier here. I rubbed my arms and snuggled closer. "Thanks, Sakki."

Hopefully, no one had spotted him. "Why aren't there any ships? When I arrived, the sky was teeming with balloons and ships."

"Do you see the weather?" Liam grabbed my wrist and twisted it to inspect my gritty wounds. As the energy within me danced at his touch, I fought the urge to yank my hand away. He checked the new tears in my clothes, now in my knee and elbow, then dropped his pack, and rummaged through it, probably in search of his healing balm.

With a rag, a vial, and his balm in hand, he ordered me to sit.

"My clothes will be nothing more than rags by the time we arrive before the queen." I croaked a laugh and sat on the cold stone.

He kneeled before me, his eyes looking unimpressed. He was so close. I tried not to squirm under his gaze. His focus returned to his task. He poured something on a rag, then dabbed at my forearm.

"Ow!" Now, I yanked my arm away. "That burns."

"And it will keep your wounds from getting infected." He held the rag ready, waiting for me to toughen up and return my arm.

I grumbled, but complied, wincing at each dab. When he finished, he switched to a clean part of the rag and applied the balm. That felt much better.

Patched up, I moved to the ledge to search for the others and grew dizzy despite the dark sky and fog. Where were they? I stepped back to ease the sick feeling I might fall at any moment. Something pinged to my right. Rhys clung to the edge several feet down. I was about to offer Sakki's services when Sakki broke through the cloud cover with Ruuta on his back. They landed behind me.

While Liam attended Ruuta, I crouched closer to Rhys.

His form twisted. I wiped my eyes. Was I seeing things? No, where Rhys had just stood clinging to the rocks as a boy, was now a goat. His clothes disappeared. He wore nothing but a goat fur coat and no clothing fell.

The goat skimmed along the slim ridges as if there were more of a floor than there was. My heart clenched as the animal defied gravity. His feet slipped. All four stick legs slid, scrambling to catch hold. Rocks pinged and bounced along the wall as I held my breath. Then he caught himself and made his way up and over the edge.

At the top, he morphed back into Rhys, clothes and all.

"How do your clothes come and go as you transition? Gachen's clothes can't do that."

He shrugged. "I was created by fae magic."

That still made no sense. But what was this fae magic, exactly? Was it bad? Was that why lies sprang so easily to his lips? He wasn't just a liar. He was a traitor too. He served the king and the Saoirse Trodaí, playing both sides.

But then, didn't I do the same? I swished the spoonful of guilt in my mind, then spat it out. Nay. It wasn't the same. Lies spray easily to his lips. He was a magical being created by a witch. For all I knew, he was her spy.

But he was trying. And he'd proven his loyalty time and again. Or was that part of his programming?

"Why didn't you transform into something that could fly?" I asked. "Why a goat?"

"I would have if I'd fallen, to be sure." He brushed himself off.

After Liam applied his balms, the cuts on Ruuta's hands vanished. Had she reenacted her glamor? That unnerved me. I wouldn't want to see things differently from how they were. She tried to put her gloves back on, but they were all torn. Sighing, she stuffed them into her pack. Apparently, she couldn't glamor their way into working despite the tears. "At least we're far from the iron-infested city. I shouldn't come across much, if any, out here." She wiggled her fingers at us all staring. "Shall we continue?"

Ruuta's hands seemed naked. She always wore gloves. But if iron was such a problem for the fae, there mustn't be any in Seelie Clós.

Liam handed out blankets. "It's going to get colder the higher we climb."

I wrapped mine around my shoulders, covering my pack. We still had more of an incline left to ascend. But the rolling hills were much tamer here. The rocks strewn about the greenery would be easier to navigate. The continual wind blew my hair into my face. The light rain had puffed into snow.

As we trudged on, the snow and winds picked up, coating me in a chilling white sheet. The moonlight reflected off the snow, so all I saw were white flecks coming at me. I hugged the blanket tighter as we walked, head down, fighting the unrelenting onslaught. My teeth chattered and my skin burned. If we didn't do something soon, we'd freeze out here.

"We'll have to stop soon!" I had to shout to hear myself, never mind for anyone else to hear me.

"What?" Liam probably hollered, but I barely heard him.

The others closed in to hear me. "We can huddle under Sakki's wing!"

"What about Sakki?" Rhys shouted, pointing to the dog who seemed unfazed by the weather.

"With the snow covering him and our heat beneath him, he should be okay." Liam dropped his pack, the plan settled.

A faint sound came from up ahead. We gawked at one another, then went to investigate with Liam in the lead. Was that... bleating? Aye. Sheep. A pen full of them. Perhaps we could find warmth with the sheep. Seeming to have the same thought, we walked along the circular wall, searching for the gate.

Rhys smacked Liam's shoulder, then pointed in the distance to pinpricks of light. Had those been there a moment ago? One of the lights swayed and grew brighter. We stopped, frozen, staring at the light like deer, then gave a collective gasp as the lantern came into view. It dangled on the end of a rifle pointed at us.

Twelve

"Don't shoot!" Liam raised his hands and motioned for us to do the same.

Our blankets fell from our backs.

"Get away from my sheep!" The rifle's aim swept over us all.

"We don't mean you any harm." Liam stepped in front of me. "Or your sheep."

The earflaps on the man's hat flapped along with his open coat, revealing striped pajamas. He didn't lower his weapon. "If yer not here to steal, why are ye?"

"We seek shelter from this storm." Ruuta fought the snow whipping at her face to tip her head as if speaking to royalty. Her snow-laden lashes fluttered.

Should I mention who I am? Or would that make things worse?

"Why"—the man repositioned his weapon, readying his fingers to use it—"are ya here?"

I stepped forward.

The barrel snapped to me. The swaying lantern made it difficult for him to hold his aim.

"Don't," Liam growled and snatched me, pulling me back.

"I'm Princess Eerika."

The man's furry eyebrows raised the rim of his fuzzy cap. He aimed his rifle up, so the lantern came close to my face.

"Well, I'll be..." He coughed. "Spittin' image of the king and queen if I do say so." He lowered the lantern, bowed, then spun, and waved an arm for us to follow.

We pushed one another in our hurry to get inside the cabin. Warmth greeted us like a long-lost loved one. We hung our soaked blankets, freed ourselves from our packs, and shook off the snow in the entryway as our host closed the door on the raging winds threatening his warm home. I made for the potbelly stove, sat before it on the threadbare carpet, and held my hands to receive its heat. Melting snow dripped from my hair.

The man stomped his feet in the entryway, peeled the hat from his bald head, and shook the snow from his bushy beard. He shrugged out of his coat and kicked off his unlaced boots. "What are ye doin' out here, never ye mind a night such as this?"

The poor man's entryway was a snowy mess.

Rather than wait for an answer, he started mumbling. "Lights. And coal. Mustn't forget the coal. And food. What have I got? Nothin' befittin' royalty. That's fer certain." His gaze drifted from the cooking area to us. "Plaids. That's first. Definitely plaids." He darted across the humble cabin to an armoire and pulled out a bunch of blankets.

I gratefully accepted a green-and-white checkered one.

He noticed me eyeing a big hole in the side. "Ain't never seen a shepherd's plaid? Ye can wear it like a cloak or use it as a blanket. Comes in mighty handy out in the fields. Keeps ye dry in the rains and just fold it and throw it over yer shoulder when it's too warm to wear."

Rather than put my arms through, I bundled myself up. He reached for my hand. "Are ye warm enough? Come. Sit in ol' Fergus's chair. Can't have the princess sittin' on the floor. No, no."

When he led me to a well-worn padded chair, I spread the clean blanket down first to protect me, for the chair was clearly well loved.

"Sit. Sit."

As I lowered myself, snug in the cozy blanket, the chair engulfed me in a hug. Sakki leaped onto my lap and kneaded the blanket to his liking.

After giving us each a plaid, the shepherd bustled about in holey socks, lighting lanterns and adding more coal to the stove, all the while verbally ticking off and adding to the checklist in his head. Once the chores seemed complete, other than food, he bent beside me, hands on his knees, to look into my face. Deep lines waved across his forehead and crinkled his kind brown eyes.

"Princess Eerika. Well, I never..." He jolted, and his face turned stricken. But he had no aura to match his expression. "Forgive me for—"

I waved his request away. "There's nothing to forgive. You were protecting your sheep. Thank you for giving us a warm place to stay..."

"Fergus." He pressed a hand on his heart.

"Thank you, Fergus."

Words of agreement came from the couch.

Fergus waved us off with a bah. Then he frowned at Sakki on my lap. "Is that a cat?" He surveyed the cabin. "Thought I saw a dog with ye."

"Uh, this is Sakki. He's the only animal with us." It wasn't a lie unless Rhys counted as an animal. But he knew I was the princess and, therefore, part elf. Would it be a problem to know a dragon existed still? Something told me to keep that part quiet.

"Drinks. How could ol' Fergus forget drinks?" He hurried to the counter at the other end of the cabin. "Let me get ye somethin' to warm yer insides."

"Thank you." I bit the inside of my cheeks. How could I sit here, accepting his help while he was under my father's curse? Should I give him the cure and hope he didn't kick us out? Or wait until we'd rested and the storm passed? That felt wrong.

Fergus pumped water into a tall kettle. Iron. So much iron here. The stove. Wall hooks. Lanterns. Much of the furniture.

Ruuta cocooned herself in her blanket and sat in the center of the cloth sofa between Liam and Rhys. At least she was protected.

Fergus dumped something inside the kettle, stirred it, then clattered it onto the stove. The aroma of coffee warmed the cozy cabin. Then he turned from his brew and smiled, revealing crooked yellow teeth. "Cozy, innit?"

I sighed. "I could fall asleep."

"Sleep. Sleep! A princess needs her rest. Seems the others beat ye to it."

On the couch, they looked like they'd all tipped over. Rhys leaned on Ruuta. Ruuta rested on Liam. Liam slumped into a pillow propped against the wall.

Fergus peeked inside the kettle. "Ah, it's rollin' nicely. Shan't be long now. If ya stay awake, that is."

I didn't want to continue taking advantage of him while his mind wasn't his own. And with the others asleep? Well... they wouldn't know. I grasped the vastalääke vial in my pocket. *Should I cure him?*

Are you asking Sakki or God?

You. I didn't hide the huffiness in my mind's voice.

Sakki doesn't know when Colleen doesn't use an address. Besides, Colleen should ask God first.

I know. I know. More guilt welled up for not doing that. But He so rarely answered. It was easier to ask someone I could see. Someone who would always answer.

God, should I cure him?

As expected, I got nothing. But I knew I had to free him. How could I not? Sometimes it seems that gut instinct is actually God. But I couldn't be sure. So infuriating. But allowing this man to help me while under my father's curse was taking advantage of him. It was wrong. "Fergus?"

"Hmm?" He placed the last mug from his cupboard onto the counter and turned to me.

"I have something difficult to tell you."

He crossed the room. "Are ya here to take my sheep? I've been wonderin' what yer doin' all this way from the castle. But why send a princess? Why not a defender?"

I shook my head. "Nay, nothing like that."

He picked up a wooden chair and sat in it backward, leaning on the backrest, facing me. "What is it, Yer Highness? There's nothing ya can't say to ol' Fergus."

"I'm afraid it's rather unpleasant. My father. King Auberon..."

Fergus nodded emphatically, his head leaning closer and his eyebrows rising higher with each nod.

"He put his people under a curse."

Fergus shot back so far, his neck formed multiple chins despite his thinness. His graying red eyebrows obscured his eyes. "How could ye speak about the king that way? Yer own father?"

I reached out from the blanket to stay him. The last thing I needed was a cursed man defending my father. I readied the cure in my grip under the blanket, just in case. "Please, hear me out."

Tiring of this conversation, I aimed the vial at him. It would be better to spray him and get it over with. But, by God's grace, I held back. "I don't want to do this without your permission, but you can't fully understand until you receive this cure. Will you trust me? Will you let me help you?"

His face twitched through an array of expressions, never landing on one. Then he scrubbed his face. "Oh, why not. If I can't trust my king's heir, who can I trust? And what does ol' Fergus have to lose but his sheep?"

I freed myself from his stinky chair and instructed him to sit. His neck fell to an awkward angle. If only I'd had the foresight to place a pillow there to spare his neck. As I debated lifting his head and stuffing a pillow there, he came to. Wincing, he gripped his head.

"Sorry! I should have had the soothing tablets ready. The cure causes quite a headache."

"And a headache only, so it would seem. I told ya. Nothin's changed. I feel no different."

Was it possible the vastalääke wasn't working? Did it expire? I looked at the vial almost expecting an expiration date like medicines from America. Or some evidence of going bad. But it looked the same as always. An orange glow sparked around Fergus. His aura was returning. It *had* worked.

"Are you sure you don't feel any different?"

The orange flared brighter. "Well, maybe a little?"

And now the part I feared most. "Do you remember anything? Anything you may have forgotten?"

"Well no... I..." His aura flashed again, blinking in and out like a faulty bulb. "My... family? I had a family?" Purple flashes intermingled with the orange. Then blue. Then red. "I had a family."

Oh no.

His face twisted. "Your father took them from me!"

The others stirred in their sleep. Their cloudy eyes sharpened as they jumped to their feet.

Red blazed like a raging inferno around Fergus. Sinews protruded from his neck. He closed in. "Where's my family?"

"I—I don't know." I slid from the chair and away from him.

Fergus rounded on me. Hands poised to catch my throat.

THIRTEEN

“You cured him?” Liam lunged between us, ready to protect me. “How could you—”

“I had to! I couldn't let him serve us while he was blinded by the curse.” I looked past Liam's incredulous eyes, stolen from sleep to Fergus's fiery gaze and sizzling aura.

Ruuta clicked her tongue and clutched her amulet to compel Fergus into submission.

“Where's yer father?” He rammed into Liam. “I'll kill him fer what he's done!”

Liam seized Fergus, legs splayed, holding him back.

“He–he's dead.” I said over Liam's shoulder.

The blaze surrounding Fergus died as it would if I'd doused him with water. He dropped his hands, and his face went slack. Then his aura sparked again, flickering purple. “The king is dead?” He clutched his forehead and returned to his seat. “Are ya queen now?”

I kept a wary eye on him... and my distance. “Nay.”

“Is that why yer out here? Others want to kill ya?”

I nodded. “We need to get through the Divide to Queen Rhiannon. She'll know what to do.”

"Will she, now?" His question sounded like a statement.

Ruuta lowered herself to the edge of her seat, still clutching her stone. "Queen Rhiannon *always* knows what to do."

"But what of my family?" Blue flashed around him, and a pleading burned in his eyes. "How do I get my family back?"

"You can search for them in the city." Liam's aura calmed, but he stood his ground.

Rhys flopped onto the couch, disturbing Ruuta.

"Do you remember where you lived? You can start there. But be aware, my father likely told your family you were dead. It might come as a shock to see you." I waited to make sure he wouldn't erupt again. When he groaned and massaged his temples, I slinked back into the well-loved chair, and Sakki jumped onto my lap like nothing had happened. I petted his furry shoulders, starting his purr motor. "Do you remember your hearing? Why my father took away your memories?"

Fergus squeezed his eyes shut and deepened his massage. "I worked in the aether power plant. King Auberon suspected me of workin' with some group... Saors?"

"They're the group who freed the people from my father's curse." No need to tell him that I helped.

"That's why I thought he was God?"

The way he sneered at God's name disturbed me on levels I couldn't comprehend. Creeping crabs! How many people would never accept the real God because of what my father had done? Even now that their ability to choose had returned, would they refuse Him because my father had poisoned them to the very idea of God?

Fergus's aura mellowed, returning to oranges and purples. "Ye cured me with that spray?"

"Aye."

"Knowin' I might wanna kill ye?"

Words eluded me. I shrugged.

"Well, that says somethin', donit?" Still bent over, he squinted at me like I was as bright as the sun. "Yer not like yer father, are ya?"

"Nay." I would never do what he did, even if it did keep peace.

THE SMELL of cooking meat and something else roused me from my sleep. My stomach growled. Fergus stirred a pot over his stove while the others slept.

"What time is it?" I didn't realize how much my body hurt until I tried to rise. Every muscle and bone in my body cursed me.

"About midday." He frowned. "Stay where ya are. The stew's almost ready. I'll bring it to ya."

I placed Sakki on the armrest and peeled myself from the depression in the chair that didn't want to let me go. My spine had conformed to the chair's contour and refused to straighten as I stood. "Nay, I need to move."

"Suit yerself. Ye can take a seat at the table if ye prefer."

"Thank you." I neared the pot and sniffed. The meaty aroma incited my stomach to rumble, but I couldn't identify something. "What's that smell?"

"Mutton and potatoes. But ya probably smell bog myrtle. Makes fer a good stew, it does."

"Bog myrtle? I never heard of it."

"I don't have much out here. Defenders bring a meager supply when they rob me of my lamb. Gotta take what the land offers."

"Does bog myrtle come from a bog? Are there bogs in the highlands?"

"Yep. Blanket bogs. On account of it bein' so wet." He fetched bowls from the cupboard and mugs from the counter. "Don' have enough bowls fer everyone. Mugs will hafta do."

Rhys snorted a loud snore and woke himself up. The others stirred while he pressed his fingers to glazed eyes, his nose twitching. He must've caught a whiff of food cooking. Liam stretched and yawned, disturbing Ruuta who backed away from him with a glare. She rubbed her stone as if considering putting him back to sleep.

Fergus served his stew, and I slopped it down so fast I hadn't noticed it burned the roof of my mouth until it was too late. He laughed as he doled out more for the others. "It's nice ta have company fer once."

Ruuta clutched the surrounding blanket in one hand. With the other, she reached for the bowl Fergus offered, then jerked it away, pointing a questioning finger. "Is that iron?"

"The spoon?" Fergus eyed the utensil like he'd never seen it before. "Think so."

She shrank away as if iron spores might leap at her. "Might you have something less... ferric?"

Judging from his glow and expression, he didn't know what that meant. I didn't either. "Got a wooden spoon in the drawer just there. Will that do?"

From the drawer, I retrieved a wooden spoon and passed it to him. "She's allergic to iron."

"Iron? Why I never... Except..." He studied her, the light surrounding him darkening to a deep purple. "Yer fae, aren't ya? Ain't never seen a fae. But yer about what I'd expect."

She flinched, then recovered her proper composure as she took the food with the acceptable spoon. "I'm the princess's lady-in-waiting assigned by Queen Rhiannon herself."

Fergus screwed up his face, then gave me a conspiratorial look. "I don' trust the fae. Shifty lot, if ye ask me."

"I'm part fae." I didn't know any fae other than Ruuta, but a wave of protectiveness washed over me. She'd been nothing but loyal. And she freed me from my father's control, restoring my memories, helping me see his wrongdoing.

"Do *you* work for Rhiannon too?" Keeping a sharp eye trained on me, Fergus scooped his food backward, away from himself, then slurped his spoonful.

"Nay." At least, I didn't think so.

Sakki hopped onto the table and stuck his head in my cup. I relocated him to the floor and gave him the rest of my meal.

"Good. I don' trust Rhiannon or anyone in her employ." Fergus glowered at Ruuta.

Her simmering purple aura blazed red, yet she kept her composure. "You mightn't be so bold, sir, if you were capable of comprehending all that Queen Rhiannon has done for this kingdom. She supplies you with keino—"

Fergus dropped his spoon into his bowl and waved his arms. "Does it look like I got all kinds of fancy contraptions around here, flameless lights and whatnot? I got no use of keino."

She pressed her lips together as red engulfed her in flames. She worked to steady her breath, tame her aura, and keep her voice low. "You've benefited from her cure for Auberon's curse."

"Princess Eerika here's what cured me."

"With Queen Rhiannon's cure!" Ruuta bolted from her seat, spilling some stew.

Liam gripped Ruuta's arm. She looked into his eyes. The lights around her pulsed in time to her measured breathing. With each breath, the red dissipated, lightening, but never leaving. He pulled her down to sit. I never thought I'd see them on the same side.

"Now I'm not sayin' I know all. But workin' at the aether plant, I saw some things." Fergus twisted his mouth as his aura sputtered through a wide range of colors. "Now that I think on it, I believe I was framed."

"For what?" The interest on Liam's face contrasted with the disdain on Ruuta's. Rhys appeared only mildly interested.

"The aether plant is misnamed. We process keino, the fake stuff."

"Your intellect astounds me." Sarcasm laced Ruuta's voice.

"But is it really?" He cocked his head at me, awaiting my answer. "I don' think keino exists."

Purple lights flared around us. Well, other than Rhys's. His never changed. But he sat up, looking equally confused, and awaited Fergus's explanation.

"I studied keino. There was no structural difference between the so-called keino Rhiannon shipped to us and true aether."

"No difference you could find." Ruuta yawned.

"How can you know that?" Liam's aura flared.

"Aether collection is forbidden," Rhys said. "To be sure, to be sure."

"We didna kill anyone." Fergus punctuated the air with a skinny finger. "We collected aether from dyin' animals. Ya know... fer research."

"But to take their aether *is* to kill them!" Luminescent static obscured Ruuta's features.

I glimpsed her face. Plain. No paintings to enhance her beauty. Was that her real face without the glamor? Her anger must be depleting the energy needed to keep the illusion.

He held his hands to hold back her arguments. "We only took aether from animals who wouldn't survive. Put them out of their misery, we did. And we had aether to study. I'm telling ya. What Rhiannon supplied us with wasn't keino. It was aether. I'd stake my life on it."

"I refuse to waste any more breath or even share the same air with a nitwit bent on slandering my queen." Still clutching Fergus's blanket, Ruuta turned to me. "It's time we took our leave."

FOURTEEN

As the sun lowered in the sky, we trekked up and down the lolling hills over grass, boulders, and dirt. The snow had melted, and it was warmer than yesterday. But the gray sky prevented the sun from doing its work. Though the cool air kept me from breaking out in a sweat, I was damp all the same.

I longed to dry myself beside Fergus's fire.

But Ruuta had ruined that. And why did her comments bother me so much? My queen. *My* queen. She'd said such things before, and they hadn't stuck in my mind like this. But now I couldn't help but wonder whom Ruuta served. She claimed loyalty to me. But what if I decided not to follow Rhiannon? She may be my aunt and ruler of the fae, but I didn't know her. Would Ruuta abandon me for her *true* queen, Rhiannon, even if I became queen too?

Hopefully, it wouldn't come to that. And I needed to stop dwelling on it. So, we had to leave Fergus's earlier than I would've liked. At least I had his wool plaid to wrap around me to cover my tattered clothes. And there were places for my arms so I didn't have to cover my pack. Glad for it, I hugged it tighter as the wind picked up.

Ruuta clutched hers. Fergus had been good to let her keep it.

One day, God willing, I'd do something to help him. To help all the people my father misplaced. All the people my father manipulated.

No matter how far we walked, the highlands here didn't look like the place where I'd arrived in Betören. Wherever that was had been beautiful. Warm. With flowers I'd never seen before and a sweet smell. But then, it had been summer. What was it now, fall? Winter? With my father messing with my memories, I'd gotten turned around. Whatever the season, I couldn't recognize anything. Fog dusted the earth, obscuring my feet. A persistent wind battered my woolen protection, chilling my face and hands. Haze dulled the rising sun, smelling like rotting heather.

This was paradise compared to what awaited me.

An image of the Forest of Shadows invaded my mind. The glimpse I'd gotten from the outside when I'd arrived in this realm with Rhys. Everything had looked and smelled dead.

Was I going in there? Willingly?

We reached a summit just as the sun was setting. My throat tied up in knots, stopping up my breath. Rotko sprawled before us like a never-ending nightmare. Diseased trees waved twisty arms, ready to catch innocent victims in spindly fingers. The lowering sun refused to waste dying light on such darkness.

I pivoted toward the hills we'd climbed. It would be so much easier to go back.

"There's no going back." Ruuta tugged my arm, urging me forward.

"There's a cave!" Liam rounded a corner on the hills below. I hadn't even seen him descend. "Let's make camp. We'll rest for the night, then enter the Divide tomorrow."

Tomorrow. Aye, tomorrow was much better than today. And yet, tomorrow was much too soon.

We sat around the campfire, eating a deer Sakki killed. Why was it so much easier to find meat than vegetables? I wasn't likely to find any vegetables *there* either. But the venison wasn't bad. Rhys hung strips to dry so we'd have food later if we found none in Rotko. For that reason, I forced myself to eat, but it sat like lead in my stomach.

The Divide loomed before us. Tomorrow we'd go inside. I had to get Rhys talking. He had to know something about the place. He'd been there. "What else can you tell us about Rotko? Or the witch, Noita? There must be something."

Rhys rushed to chew and swallow his bite. "As I said, Rotko has a way of scrambling one's mind. But I'll say one thing—Noita thrives on fear. To be sure, to be sure."

"Then we'll have to be on guard." With a raised eyebrow, Liam caught our gazes one by one, forcing his words into our minds. "The best way to instill fear is to divide people. Isolate them. We all stick together. No matter what."

"To be sure, to be sure." Rhys stamped his foot twice.

Ruuta gave a firm nod.

Sakki blasted smoke through his puppy nose.

I felt the color drain from my face. If Noita wanted to separate us, could we stop her? With them, I might survive that place, but alone? Even when I was trapped in Bandia, I wasn't alone. My brothers and sister were with me, though they were just babies... and burdens. "What can we do to keep from being separated?"

"Be alert. Don't let your guard down." He spoke too nonchalantly.

I grasped Ruuta's ungloved hand, desperate for something to grab onto to keep me from falling into a pit of despair. Something to help me sleep before entering a living nightmare. "None of your protection spells will help?"

Her lips formed a grim line. "There are no wards against whatever unseelie magic Noita employs. They tap into demonic forces. And there's something beyond our comprehension about how such evil magic infiltrated the power that existed here before. Our magic is powerless against it, excepting matka. We cover ships in it so all on board can safely travel through the Divide by air where the unseelic magic is thin."

I wanted to say the power she referred to was God's. "Do you have any... matka? Can we take turns flying through the Divide on Sakki's back?"

"My potions are laying to waste in the castle—assuming they've not been pilfered. Nevertheless, there is no matka among them. Nor would it help us had we any at our disposal. Matka covers the ship, thereby protecting everyone inside. But the magic is too powerful for use on any living thing. It burns flesh. Even Sakki's scales wouldn't stand up to it."

Sakki snorted, rejecting the idea through his nose.

I rubbed my arms to brush away the phantom lethal magic burn. "So we've no choice but to walk into that unholy place and pray we don't lose each other."

"Or ourselves," Rhys said. "As I said, Rotko scrambles the mind. You can't trust your own eyes. We must stay together. That's our only hope of getting through alive."

This couldn't be all there was. "You must have something more... helpful. What happened to you in there? You got out." My voice was growing shrill. "How did you escape?"

"I can't recall." He wrinkled his nose, and I shrank back, expecting a sneeze. "The Divide was darkening when I entered with King Aub—"

I gasped. "You were there with my father?"

"To be sure, to be sure. But we got separated. I'm sure Noita allowed King Auberon to leave. He was doing her bidding. But me?" Rhys scratched behind his ear. "I've already told you everything. Why don't you believe me?"

"Because since I've known you, you've been less than forthcoming. You're holding something back. You must be."

"Argh!" Rhys danced in a circle, shaking his arms like he was fighting off a swarm of bees. Then he stopped and sliced the air with one arm. "What can I say? We went to stop the witch. The Divide was dying, but not dead. The greenery... browning. From there, my memory is nothing more than snippets and flashes."

He poked at his temples. Maybe he thought he'd jab his memories into alignment. "Noita... her horns looked like dead trees growing from her skull. Auberon and Toini fighting—"

"Toini?" The question escaped before I could stop it. I didn't want to interrupt his train of thought.

"His dragon. I don't know what happened to her other than they had an argument I couldn't hear. She blasted warning flames at him and flew away. Never seen a dragon and their bonded elf like that. Ever. Auberon... he—"

Rhys's thick eyebrows shot up. His eyes went wide as his jaw hung open.

"Auberon what?" Liam asked.

"What happened?" I barely breathed.

"He gave me something to drink. I'd... I'd forgotten that. It must've been the same elixir he gave you each time he erased your memory. The next thing I can recall was being back at the castle in my bed. Auberon acted like nothing out of the ordinary had happened. But something had. Toini never returned. Your mother never returned with you. The Divide had gone dark. And the people treated Auberon like a god."

Rhys shrugged, holding his arms up in his attempt to convince us. "That is all I remember, to be sure."

What choice did I have but to take him at his word? How many times had my father erased my memories? It was something he'd do. But Rhys knew that. He'd administered it every time my father commanded it. Was he making this up to avoid speaking the truth? Nay. His story matched what Father said when he spoke of getting the curse from the witch.

I gripped my aching head and sighed deeply, all this thinking hurting my brain. "We'll just have to face whatever is in there blind."

"My most sincere apologies, Princess." Rhys's face fell. Perhaps he meant it. Who could tell since his aura never changed?

"I was thinking." Liam broke the silence. "The Divide was created to protect the elves from the fae, right? So, can she even get inside?" He waved the remains of his venison steak at Ruuta.

"It did at one time." Rhys gnawed at his steak with his front teeth.

Ruuta wiped her mouth. "Fae can get in."

"They can?" I discarded the inedible remains of my meal. "How do you know?"

She tugged at her wrists as if to straighten the gloves she was so accustomed to wearing. Finding them gone, she pulled at her sleeves instead. "When fae are banished from Seelie Clós, they're sent into the Divide."

Liam leaned closer to her, propping his elbows on his knees. "How long has that been happening? Since before it went dark?"

"Since as long as there have been fae to banish, to my knowledge." Her mouth flattened to a grim line. "There were some who believe it to be a death sentence, that the light killed them. Now the fae believe the banished survived, though that may be wishful thinking. But if going in there kills them, it wasn't the light that did the killing."

"If they survive..." I swallowed. Hard. "Can they get back out again?"

"No one has." She rose and smoothed her riding pants. "I suppose we'll find out tomorrow."

I stood to prevent her from leaving. "Why would you risk it?"

"What choice do we have? We must find our way to Queen Rhiannon." She pushed past me. "Now, if you'll excuse me."

As she retreated to the cave, I returned to my seat by the fire. "How can she do this?"

"You can't talk her out of it." Liam rubbed the back of his neck. "She's the most stubborn fae I've ever met."

"She's the only fae you ever met."

He winked at me, and my insides went gooey, despite the horrors facing me.

"To be fair, there's a chance none of us will be able to get out once we enter." He scraped the flesh from bone with his front teeth like he was eating corn on the cob in neat rows, seeming oblivious to the fact that he might get trapped there too. "The Divide changed when it went dark. Who knows what will happen?"

"But God said to go through to get to Rhiannon." I pivoted to my dragon. "Right, Sakki?"

He picked his head up from resting on his front paws and huffed. *God said go through the Divide.*

"But there has to be another way. Another protection spell? A potion? Anything?"

No one answered... because there was no other way. "Then we'll have to do as God said and trust He'll see us through." But, despite all that...

Were we walking into a trap?

FIFTEEN

Tomorrow took forever in arriving. And yet, it came sooner than I'd have liked, and after a long night of tossing and turning on the hard cave floor, I found myself at the border of the Forest of Shadows. I stood there staring. Shaking for what I was about to do. What would happen when I crossed the border? Would it hurt? Would I get out alive? Would I get separated from my friends? Would they make it out alive? What would the witch do to us if she—

Stop. Colleen will drive Colleen and Sakki mad with such questions. God said go, so Colleen and Sakki must go.

How are you reading my mind?

Sakki isn't reading Colleen's mind. Colleen's anxious thoughts are leaking into Sakki's mind.

His distraction helped, but I couldn't stop trembling. The smell of rotting eggs burned my eyes like a dozen chopped onions. We all stood in a row an arm's length from the shimmering border.

Was everyone else contemplating the sanity of this mission? "Are we going to do this?"

Ruuta clicked her tongue. "I see no other way to get to Seelie Clós."

"Does anyone have a teleview?" Liam pressed around, feigning searching through his pockets.

Ruuta was having none of his antics today. She threw him her most disdainful look. "We require Queen Rhiannon's help. This is the only way."

God told Sakki this is what Colleen is to do, travel through the Forest of Shadows to Queen Rhiannon. Has Colleen forgotten?

"Nay." I drew out the word like a bored child.

"No, what?" Liam asked.

It would be so much easier if they could all hear my dragon. "Sakki reminded me this is God's plan. If it's God's plan, we'll succeed."

"We might succeed, but will we survive?" Liam eyed us askance with a lifted eyebrow.

I gave his shoulder a light smack. "That's a terrible thing to say!"

Good question, but terrible.

"This is what God instructed me to do, so this is what I'll do." I took a deep breath like one readying to travel underwater and stepped into the stench.

The others stepped forward too.

A cloud swept over us, changing our appearance.

Ruuta's hair turned gray. The butterfly-like glamor painting her face fell, leaving black streaks like she'd been wearing too much face paint and had cried rivers. Her skin wrinkled and took on a leathery appearance. Horns sprouted from her head and curled like a goat's.

Liam also grew horns. But they rose up, angled, then shot back at pointy tips. His face elongated, giving him more of a snout. The shadows of dark hair covering his jaw spread out, masking his beauty.

Rhys remained unchanged—other than his missing, unchanging aura.

Wait. *All* our auras were gone. What did that mean? Were they just not visible here? We still had emotions. Aye. There was no misinterpreting my rising fear. It began in my heart, making it thump erratically, then sank into my stomach, leaving me sick with it and turning me cold. My arms shook, and I clutched the shepherd's plaid in hopes it might protect me from whatever unholy wraiths chilled the air.

Had we fallen under another curse by entering this place?

I held out my arms. Nothing seemed different.

I prodded my face. Everything felt like it remained in its proper place.

"What's happening? Why is everyone except for Rhys and me mutating?"

Ruuta and Liam gawped at me, both looking as sick as I felt.

"You're covered in green scales." Ruuta's fingers poked around her face and hair. "What of me?"

Liam smiled, revealing sharp canines. "You look like a cross between an old hag and a goat."

Rhys swirled his fingers above his ears. "You have horns like a goat."

Her eyes widened to impossible lengths as her fingers rooted around. "I don't feel any horns." She peeled back her sleeves and inspected what she could of herself. She jerked in several directions.

"Are you looking for a mirror?" I asked.

"I don't think you'll find one," Liam added unhelpfully.

She pressed her lips together, breathed a heavy breath through giant nostrils, and spoke in slow tones perhaps to calm herself. "It's just an illusion, nothing more."

Liam seemed like he was already growing accustomed to our new looks. He flung a loose arm in my direction. "You almost match Sakki with your scales."

"Scales?" I rubbed my arms again. My skin looked and felt normal. "I don't see any scales."

"Your eyes are yellow, and"—she nodded to my head, then averted her eyes—"you have no hair."

Oh no! Were my pointed ears exposed? My hands met thick

curls. I could see my blonde hair. Why couldn't they? "You can't see my hair?"

Ruuta and Liam shook their heads.

"I can," Rhys said.

"You can?"

"I can see you both ways. As Noita's magic wants you to appear." He tilted his head to get a new viewpoint. "And as you are."

"Are you unaffected by this magic?" Ruuta jammed her hands on her hips, perhaps equally surprised and annoyed, then jerked her chin at Liam. "You look like a wolf man with horns."

"Nice." He grinned, revealing sharp canines.

Was he seriously not bothered by this?

"We must move." Rhys thumped a foot. "This place is already affecting your minds."

I waved at my hideous friends. "This isn't permanent, is it?"

Ruuta quirked her lips. "It's an effect of the magic ruling this place. I'm sure it will wear off the moment we step through the other side."

"What about him?" I pointed to Rhys who didn't appear any different. "Does he look normal to you?"

"Depends on how you define normal." Liam laughed.

"I'm glad you don't find any of this disturbing." I sneered, hoping my scaly façade gave it more impact.

Ruuta shrugged. "He looks the same to me."

"I'm an aetherian creature, to be sure. A shape-shifter no less." He met our blank stares in turn. "That means I have control over how I appear, even in here."

I looked back the way we'd come and sucked in my breath. "Why do the highlands look as dead as this place now?"

"I'm sure it's another illusion," Ruuta said.

"Or everything is dead." Again with the unhelpful comments from Liam.

"Won't that make it difficult to know when we've reached the boundary? Where's Sakki?" I searched in every direction. My heart sped up, trying to keep time with my thoughts as I stepped back the way we'd come, but I hit a wall. "Nay. Nay, nay, nay, nay..." My heart squeezed, feeling the confinement in my chest that I felt now as I smashed my fists against the invisible wall.

The others rushed beside me and pounded the wall too. They couldn't get through either. Not even Rhys. Unshed tears burned behind my eyes as my nose tingled. My body threatened to overtake me in uncontrollable sobs. "Trapped! We're trapped!" I clenched and unclenched my hands and my teeth. My breath came in fragments. I had to collect myself.

Light in. Dark out.

Light in. Dark out.

It was no use. Not without Sakki. "Sakki... Where's Sakki?" I dashed about, tripping over burned roots, searching unsuccessfully in every direction. The panic I fought to contain would be restrained no longer. I screamed as I stomped my feet in an unqueenly tantrum.

"Sakki's gone!" I crumpled to the ground. Sobs racked my body as grief consumed my mind.

Someone grasped my shoulders. Liam. He shook me. "Get ahold of yourself, Colleen. We haven't been inside for five minutes yet. You can't lose yourself this quickly, or we'll never make it through."

"I c–can't..." I couldn't speak. What would I do if I'd lost Sakki? I couldn't do this without him.

You can't do this without Me.

I swallowed my sobs and straightened, searching for God. I heard Him so clearly—He must be close!

"What happened?" Liam forced me to face him. "Did you hear something?"

"G–God." I worked to find my voice. "God s–spoke to me."

Rhys slid beside me on his knees. "What did He say?"

"He said." More breaths. "I can't do this without *Him.*"

"That's good news, right?" Liam rubbed my upper arms. "If He spoke to you here, He must be here, right?"

I nodded, wiped my face, and chuffed a part sob, part laugh.

Sakki appeared midair inside the invisible wall in dragon form. As he broke through, a shimmer of light ran through everything—the invisible wall, the air, my friends, the dead plant matter, the ground—everything. He thudded his landing, sending up a cloud of ash, and everything was back to how it was.

"Did you see that?" I waved both hands over my head.

"That flare?" Liam released me, lurching side to side as though he hoped to glimpse it again. "Or whatever it was?"

"That was a disturbance in the magic saturating this place." Ruuta spun, studying everything around her, eyes wide in wonder.

"Did *Sakki* cause that?" Though I posed the question to the others, I looked at him.

Yes, Sakki caused the disturbance. Colleen will cause a disturbance too, once Colleen stops allowing the evil in this place to keep Colleen from trusting God.

Ouch. "So, God's presence did that?"

Liam hooked his thumb between me and Sakki. "What is he saying?"

"He's connected to God, so his presence affected whatever magic rules this place, I think. Is that what you're saying?"

Sakki jerked his head in a dragon form of a nod and puffed. Smoke blasted from his nostrils.

I took a deep breath. "And if I can keep it together and trust God, I'll do the same?"

Sakki nodded again.

"He spoke to me though. He's here. So why are we still affected? Why do we still look like this?"

God is here. Nothing can stop God. But Noita has cursed the land. Colleen and friends must destroy the witch to remove the curse.

"Destroy? As in kill? What happens if we can't kill her?"

Colleen and friends will never leave.

SIXTEEN

I sunk to the ground again. Ash smudged my torn pants. My mind transported me back to the little house in Bandia, hiding under the table from the monsters. As I spoke, I was stuck halfway between the present and the past. Both my nearly adult self stuck in the Divide and the little girl in hiding in Bandia uttered the words, both believing in our hearts we would never be free. "Never leave?"

The others converged on me.

Rhys scratched behind his ear and screwed up his face. "Never leave?"

Ruuta's yellowed eyes flashed as her snout flared. "What's Sakki saying, Colleen?"

"Are we to kill the witch?" Liam bared his fangs, making me flinch.

Fasgadair. Fasgadair had teeth like that.

While I simultaneously sat in the dirt and under the table, I closed my eyes to shut everything out.

Light in. Dark out.

Light in. Dark out.

Not real. None of this is real.

Breathe. Just breathe.

Something touched me, and I jerked, opening my eyes. Sakki. Just Sakki. I gathered his cat form to my chest, feeling his vibrations as I worked to steady my breathing. I hugged Sakki tighter, recoiling from my friends' monster forms, trying to see them beneath their cursed façades. "If we don't kill the witch, we'll be trapped here forever."

Liam kneaded the back of his head and blew out a breath.

Ruuta straightened and brushed off her pants. "Well, we'd best be on our way then, hadn't we?" She turned to Rhys. "Do you know where we might find this witch? You and Auberon found her before."

Rhys blanched. "This place has a way of twisting things—confusing the mind. It's easy to get lost."

"So, you've said." Liam sagged his shoulders and looked to the sky to deliver something more helpful.

"P—pohjola." I petted Sakki, digging my fingers in as I attempted to pull courage from his very fur. "That's where my father said he found her."

"Do you know where that is?" Ruuta pressed in closer to Rhys.

He squeezed his eyes shut and shook his head. If only that would help him arrange his memories in logical order. He wrinkled his nose, opened his mouth, then clamped it on the words. Seconds passed. "Everything in this place is distorted."

"What aren't you telling us?" Her hag eyes flared.

Rhys bit his inner cheek. "I feel—something. A connection?"

"To the witch?" Liam kicked up a cloud of ash as he rounded on Rhys.

"Because she created you?" Ruuta coughed and waved the cloud away.

Liam cut in front of Ruuta. "Does that mean you can find her?"

His hope almost revived me from my depressed stupor. Almost.

"Maybe?" Rhys pinched every pinchable muscle in his face. "But I feel many... *connections* coming from all over."

"How will we find her, then?" Liam swiveled to the rest of us.

"We follow the connections, see where they lead." When he gaped, sack-jawed, she continued, "Unless you have a better suggestion."

He rubbed his eyes, keeping them shut like he could forget he was trapped in a living nightmare with no clear direction for escape, as I was attempting to do. And failing.

Rhys hesitated. Then he moved deeper into the Divide, checking to ensure the others followed. They did. I didn't.

They felt far away from me and growing further still, like I was drowning and watching the sun sparkling on the surface drift further and further away.

"C'mon, Colleen." Liam motioned for me. "Don't you want to follow the black rabbit down the witch's rabbit hole?"

As I sat in the dirt in the witch's cursed lands, I huddled under the table in Bandia. While Sakki purred against my chest, my little brother Beagan slept on my lap. I was in both places at once. And nowhere at all. My sensations dulled. I no longer sensed Sakki's rumble. Perhaps he stopped. As I drifted further into the deep recesses of my mind, I felt less and less and less.

I was dimly aware of my friends converging on me. Their muffled words failed to connect.

Sakki pressed his face into my shoulder and shouted into my mind. *Sing.*

Sing? His odd suggestion pulled me partway from my stupor.

Colleen must sing! The volume rose, and his last word shocked me awake.

Anything to keep Colleen grounded. Something that reminds Colleen of God's love and power. Colleen knows such songs. Sakki has heard them in Colleen's head.

You... can hear? I drifted closer, almost reconnecting with my mind.

Songs, yes. Songs are powerful. Try it. Colleen's song will help Sakki too.

My mind slammed back to where it belonged. My legs hurt. I adjusted them as I considered his suggestion. He'd always helped me. Any time I panicked, he was there to calm me. That he might need *my* help? But what should I sing? Fallon's favorite. It helped her feel God's presence. Maybe it could help me too. And Sakki. So, I sang.

Great is Thy faithfulness. Great is Thy faithfulness.

It was weak... even without my real voice straining to find purchase. But I pressed on, strengthening as I went.

Morning by morning new mercies I see;
all I have needed Thy hand hath provided.
Great is Thy faithfulness, Lord, unto me.

As I sang the words in my mind, snippets of what God had done for me drifted in. Despite my feelings now, I was no longer the little girl in Bandia. He'd rescued me. Even better, He'd given me a family. A home. Then He returned me to my homeland. He gave me Sakki. My friends. Purpose. Even if I didn't know where I was going or what I was doing—or if I'd survive—God did. And He was with me.

I continued singing and remembering, choking back grateful tears. *Thank You, God.*

The others huddled around like they'd trapped a rabid animal, waiting to capture me without getting bitten. Their new features blinked in and out, and I caught glimpses of their natural faces and purple auras in between. I stared, hoping they'd return to normal for good, but the monsters returned, unblinking.

"Uh... Colleen?" Liam quirked one side of his face, revealing a fang. "Are you all right?"

I adjusted Sakki in my grip and steadied my feet as I stood. "I think I'm ready."

Their bodies relaxed while their distorted faces scrunched, but still no auras.

Rhys held up a finger. "Keep your fear under control and make every effort to stick together."

Liam smacked the back of Rhys's head, then motioned toward me while Ruuta focused intently like I might turn to dust like a dead fasgadair and blow away in the wind.

"I'm okay." I clutched Sakki tight. *You better not get separated from me.*

Only if Colleen loosens Colleen's grip. Even in my mind, his voice sounded strained.

Sorry. I eased up, and he took an exaggerated breath.

I gave Liam and Ruuta one last long look, then started after Rhys into the unknown.

Great is Thy faithfulness...

SEVENTEEN

We climbed over felled trees, blocking the path. Or was it a dry riverbed? Whatever it was, Rhys seemed to be following it. Either the sulfuric scent dissipated or I had become desensitized. My nose no longer burned, but it felt numb. Had I lost my sense of smell? The ashy ground grew soggy. Mud licked my boots, trying to suck them off my feet, and a new smell assaulted me—a rancid, decaying smell—like days-old dead bodies buried in a marsh.

It seemed my nose was working just fine.

I clung to Sakki, singing my song while I avoided looking at Liam and Ruuta. Both reminded me of how dangerous this place was. The dark magic here didn't just affect the land—it affected everything within, other than Sakki and Rhys. Even our minds. How else would they appear one way to me and I to them, but to ourselves, we looked the same?

My head started to pound just thinking about it.

The mud sucked my boot again. I pulled harder. This time, it wouldn't let go. I looked to see why I was stuck. A hand gripped me. I screamed and dropped Sakki, who landed in the mud with a squishy thud.

The others came running. Liam snatched a stick and stabbed the hand poking up through the mud until it released me.

The moment I was free, I ran to the nearest felled tree and climbed onto the base where the upended roots lifted it higher off the ground. "That was a–a *hand*? A *hand*! There are *hands* in the ground?"

Rhys clicked his tongue. "Remember, Noita feeds on fear. Do not feed her."

I laughed like a crazy person. "Don't feed her. Don't feed her! You think a hand can snatch my foot from under the ground and I'll just act like nothing happened? A *hand* reached up from the earth and grabbed me!"

Liam stood before me, his arms raised to help me down.

I smacked his hand away. I wasn't letting *any* hands grab me. "I am *not* setting foot down there again."

"Not touching the ground will make our task quite challenging." Ruuta crossed her arms, yet her gaze flickered to her feet.

"It was probably another illusion." Even Liam's brave face cracked. He didn't believe himself.

"An illusion. An illusion! Can illusions make it impossible for me to move? Do you have to stab an illusion with a stick to make it let go?" I shook an accusatory finger at the spot where I'd stood. "What if dead bodies are buried here and the witch has the power to reanimate them?"

"That's nonsense." Liam laughed. But a nervous quality hollowed the sound, and he eyed the area skeptically.

Rhys joined me on the tree. "Oh, it's possible. To be sure."

Ruuta gave up all pretense. She danced around to avoid getting snared.

Liam dragged his palm down his face. "It was a hand. Understood. That's scary, but if we don't pull ourselves together, we're never going to get out of here." He waved me down again. "Come on. We need to stick together."

Waffling, I inspected the tree. I couldn't stay here forever. Who knew what might come crawling out of its roots? That thought sent me jumping down, darting through the mud to a rock. But what if that morphed into something else? Anything could happen here.

Has Colleen forgotten to sing already? Colleen should be trusting God. Why isn't Colleen trusting God? It's very simple.

I groaned. "Sorry I'm not like you, Sakki. Sorry I'm not like the elves and being bonded to a part elf/part fae makes life so difficult for you."

Sakki snorted a smoky snort. *That is* not *what Sakki said.*

He was right. I had to trust God. God brought me here. There had to be a way through. But then, sometimes He called people to things they didn't survive. How many of His followers died in His service?

If that happens, Colleen will be with God. Won't that be better for Colleen?

Hey! I wasn't thinking that to you or to anyone else. How could you hear my thoughts... my private thoughts?

Again... Colleen's thoughts are leaking from thinking too hard.

I huffed while the others stood there staring at me, arms poised, ready to lunge should they need to restrain me.

Pull yourself together, Colleen. Sing. I chided myself. But the lyrics eluded me. *God, we haven't made it far at all, and I feel like I'm losing my mind already. The others don't seem as badly affected as I am, but I'm the one following You. Shouldn't I be the calmest of all? Aside from Sakki, that is.*

Silence.

Then the words returned. *Great is Thy faithfulness.*

I tiptoed from the rock, wary of the ground beneath my feet. But I sang as I placed one foot in front of the other. "Let's go."

Rhys twitched as if unsure what to do. Then he returned to his place in front, and the others followed. Sakki shifted into his dog form and heeled. I repeated the song over and over. Even so, the possibility that hands might grab my foot put a new skip in my step.

Eighteen

There was no real light here. The sky was gray. Not so much with discernable clouds, just... gray. And darkening from a dusty gray to a charcoal gray. Was night falling or a storm rolling in? If Noita could affect how we saw things—even hands coming out of the ground—why couldn't she affect the weather too?

Where was she? Did she know we were here?

And what was she capable of?

How, God? How are we supposed to kill something so powerful?

There was no thunder, no winds. Night must be falling. We'd traveled rather far. At least, we traveled for a long time. Or... so it seemed. Now that I was here, I could see how such a place would scramble one's brain. There was no sun to guide us. Something made Liam's navigation trinkets wonky. We had no object to aim for. Everything looked the same. Dead. For all I knew, we were walking in circles. Maybe the witch was already aware of our presence, already toying with us by shifting things around to make us think we were walking in a straight line.

We might've made no progress at all.

Great is Thy faithfulness...

My song wavered as despair pricked my heart.

Stop looking around, Colleen. Just sing. Though I spoke to myself, Sakki nodded his doggy head with a huff.

How long could I keep this up? Soon enough, despair would win, and I would be a useless puddle on the ground. "Are we going in circles?" I pointed to a spiky felled tree. "Didn't we pass that once before—or twice?"

Rhys shook his head. "Not that I recall."

"How should I know?" Liam threw up his furry arms. "They all look the same."

Ruuta pressed her haggish lips into a grim line.

I swear we passed that exact tree. The muddy puddle beneath it and the briars it had fallen into—all the same. But how was I the only one who noticed? Was Noita toying with my mind?

"You shouldn't be here," came a small voice.

With gasps, we jerked toward the sound. A young girl? A tattered hood obscured her face. But she was small, with tiny feet and no shoes. Wasn't she afraid of hands catching her bare feet?

"Are you alone?" Ruuta stooped before the girl with a smile that would have been compelling in her normal skin but was instead quite alarming. Her rotting teeth jutted out at odd angles.

The girl stepped back. "No."

I didn't see anyone else. A hideous hag smiles creepily and asks if she's alone and all she does is step back? She should run in terror. What was wrong with this girl?

She faced me. "You don't belong here."

"Just me? What about the others?"

"You and your dragon." She motioned toward Sakki.

Sakki, how does she know you're a dragon? You're in your dog form.

Sakki huddled beside me, his fur poking through the holes in my pants. *Perhaps the girl is a seer?*

Like Sully? Although the question sprang to mind, we didn't have time for that conversation. I shook the distraction away. "Why don't I belong?"

"You're an elf. Elves don't belong. Not anymore." The girl looked away. "Not since…"

"Not since what?" I prodded.

Her eyes snapped back to me. "Not since Noita the Witch."

"Does she not allow elves here?" The fear I tried so hard to stuff down began rising, shooting strands to every extremity.

"She will kill you as she killed all the others."

I sucked in a breath. "Noita killed the elves?"

"You must go!" She ran.

"Wait!" I chased her.

The others sprinted after us.

The girl plunged through a field of dead grass. Only her brown hood was visible across its tips. Then she disappeared.

"Where'd she go?" Pressing a hand to my throbbing side, I scanned the horizon and the path of broken grass. "Did she duck down under the grass?"

Liam grasped my arm. "Perhaps it's best to let her go."

I yanked free. "We're getting nowhere. Walking in circles. It's growing dark. That girl was the first thing to offer any hope of getting out of here. Or learning how to make our way through this place… or shelter for the night. We must find her."

"I agree." Ruuta glided along the broken grass and motioned us forward.

Her support bolstered me. And my desperation to find the girl squashed my fear. Mostly. The dead grass poked and scratched the exposed skin in my holey pants, making me itch. But I had to ignore it. We couldn't lose the girl.

As we neared where she'd disappeared, a hill dipped down, leading to a forest… the last place I wanted to go when the open sky grew dark. It must be pitch black in there.

We hesitated before shadowy woods.

"This is better than the burned trees, right? At least these trees don't look dead." I was reaching. At least where we'd been we'd seen sky without greenery blocking it. But the blackness before us wasn't better, not matter how I tried to convince myself.

Liam blocked my way with a stiff arm. "What if it's a trap?"

Sakki sniffed the ground. He snuffled every which way, nose to the ground. Then he perked up. *Sakki found the girl's scent.* He bounded into the woods, returned his nose to the ground, darted a little way, then sniffed again.

"We have no other leads." I pushed past Liam's outstretched arm to pursue Sakki. *Great is Thy faithfulness.*

His nose led us to a break in the woods and a cottage. Under normal conditions, I'd avoid such a dismal place with its caving-in roof and boarded-up windows. The house somehow rejected the siding, yet the shingles hung on for dear life. Though it seemed uninhabitable, dim light shone through cracks in the boards. Any light was good.

Like a moth, I approached. "Should we knock?"

Liam felt for the weapon beneath his coat. "Allow me."

He started off, me a step behind. The others trailed us. Then he held up a hand. "Just me. In case something goes wrong."

"All the more reason not to let you go alone." I pressed closer, holding my ground.

While Rhys scrunched his shoulders, Ruuta gave a firm nod.

Liam rolled his eyes and shook his head, then strode to the house and the rickety door.

Knock. Knock. Knock.

Heavy footsteps sounded inside. Not the little girl's.

NINETEEN

When I stepped back into Ruuta, she squeezed my arm.

The door cracked open, and an ogre-like shape appeared. The dim light at its back rendered its features indistinct, but a giant red eye blinked.

Ruuta and I both backed away into Rhys.

"Who goes there?" The gruff voice matched what we could see of the beast.

"Uh." Liam's hand hovered near his weapon. "We saw a girl come this way and hoped she might help us. We're traveling through Rotko."

The door burst open. The doorway framed the beast's outline, revealing a gargantuan head atop a massive neckless body. "No one travels *through* Rotko. It's a permanent destination—a graveyard."

I peeked around Liam. "*We* are."

The thing sniffed the air, then jerked to full height, smacking its head on the doorframe above, sending debris falling. "An elf?" It sniffed more. "And a dragon?"

Its gaze flittered off in every direction. Then he ducked inside, giving us space to enter as he ushered us forward. "Come in, come in. Quickly."

I wasn't sure I wanted to go into this thing's home, but it had to be better than the forest at night. Maybe. I scooted past Liam and into the cottage. The little girl sat on a dirty rug before the firelit hearth. She faced me.

I held my breath, forcing myself not to react to her piggish snout and floppy ears. No wonder she wore a hood.

Her eyes widened. Then she smiled. "I knew you'd come."

"You did?" I moved to sit beside her as the others entered.

The ogre locked the door, then spun. A jagged scar ran the length of its face, and a chunk of flesh was missing from its nose.

I bit back my gasp.

"Jumala wouldn't leave us here forever." The girl reclaimed my attention. "This place belongs to Him, not Noita the Witch."

"Who is Jumala?" I asked.

"The One. The Creator. Father of the heavens—of all."

Had another leader cursed the inhabitants into believing they were God? But if that were true, wouldn't Noita be the one? She supposedly ruled Rotko. She gave my father the curse to make the people believe he was God. Wouldn't she use it on these people to do the same for herself? To make herself God in their minds?

But what were these creatures? They weren't human. "Are you fae?"

She nodded.

"Unseelie fae." Ruuta snaggled up her lips like she was trying not to appear disgusted, but that was a permanent look on her new hag face.

"Does that make a difference?" The fae can't be cursed. No distinction had been made between seelie or unseelie... whatever that meant. And Ruuta's slight shrug didn't tell me anything. So, like the seelie fae, these people must not be able to be cursed. At least, not with the curse my father used. Did that mean... "Are you referring to the One True God?"

The girl nodded again.

Only time would tell if we spoke of the same God. For now, I'd assume it was the same. "This land is His?"

She beamed, making her appear beautiful despite the pig features. "Everything is His."

A warm sensation washed over me. *God, thank You for leading me here.*

I leaned in close to her as the others crowded around. "We're on a mission for God."

Her eyes grew so wide the whites shone all around. "What mission?"

I held up a hand by mouth to whisper. "We're to kill Noita."

"Shhh!" The ogre leaped to the windows, peeked through the slats, and pulled the poor excuse for drapes tight, then retrieved a wooden box from a cluttered table. It twisted a knob over and over, then set it down. The thing made a harsh sound that sent shivers up my spine. Was that supposed to be music?

"Choose your words with care." The ogre dropped into a padded chair, sending up a puff of dust. "There's no telling what Noita may hear."

I grimaced. "Is her hearing that good?"

"She knows things. I don't know how, but she does. Spies, maybe. Perhaps spells."

It—or was it a he?—thrust a hand out, splaying thick fingers. "Take care what you say."

Ruuta's haggish face drained of what little color she had. Or maybe that was just her new look. Liam's wolfy face wasn't capable of much expression.

"And it's not possible." The ogre sneered, showing rotting teeth. "She can't be killed. Not by any means anyone has tried."

"What have you tried?" Liam's hand brushed over the weapon beneath his shepherd's plaid as if to reassure himself it was still there.

"Let's see. She's been burned, drowned, buried." The ogre ticked off modes of murder on sausage fingers, pausing and tapping his fourth finger as he thought. "Oh, and stabbed with multiple objects in case a certain material is more successful than another."

"Has she ever been shot? With a bullet?" Liam asked.

"Of course. Are you familiar with King Auberon?"

I chuckled, but a pang from his recent death stabbed me, stripping away the coincidental question's humor. "Aye."

"He sent his men, defenders. They were armed with such weapons. But none stood against her." The ogre screwed up its face. "Nothing has worked."

Liam gripped his hair, fingers just missing his horns, and pulled his head down. "What happens? With each assassination attempt. Does she die and return?"

The ogre set his—yes, his—mouth in a grim line and shook his head. "She can be wounded. Her body is flesh, but it never lasts."

The so-called music box came to a screeching end, and the girl wound it up while everyone remained silent. She placed the box back on the table and released the key. The terrible sounds haunted the air and pained our ears.

The ogre continued. "No matter how badly her body is affected, she always returns seeming completely unaffected. Burns... nothing leaves even a scar. She can't die. From the stories I hear, she never even loses consciousness. Many believe she could be rendered nothing more than a skeleton and her flesh would grow back." He scratched at his scar. "I wish your plans would succeed. But they won't. Noita can't be killed."

The tinny cacophony came to another screeching end along with my hopes of ever escaping this nightmare.

TWENTY

There had to be a way. God wouldn't say that's what must be done if there weren't a way. Would He? Was the message from God at all? Or was it a trick to trap us here?

What if Sakki misunderstood something? He was the last of his kind. There was no way for him to learn what he was capable of... like me.

I wanted to ask more about killing the witch, but without the cover of the disturbing music, it seemed something we shouldn't talk about, even from my defeatist perspective.

The ogre pulled a covered pan from the flames and brought it to the table where he doled a meager amount into cups and bowls. There weren't enough seats, so we took our portions to the floor by the fire. An unidentifiable smell wafted up from my bowl. Onions? Mushrooms? Should I be concerned? Would a hand reach out to grab me? I scooped some onto the cusp of my spoon. It looked like chunky mud. Nothing identifiable.

Liam grasped my hand, keeping me from bringing the spoon to my lips. He cut a glance at the ogre still scooping, then shook his head. He released his hand and whispered, "Me first."

Eyes wide, I shook my head back with forced, yet hopefully unnoticeable-to-the-orge movements. If he was trying to poison us, I didn't want Liam to die. I pointed to the ogre and waited for Liam to get my meaning and let him eat first.

He quirked his lips and winked. Message received.

"May I ask your name?" I asked the ogre.

He scraped the pot and dumped the remains into his cup, then moved to his stuffed chair. "Petri." He groaned as he settled into his spot. "The young lady is Silja."

Silja smiled, revealing crooked rows of square baby teeth.

"How old are you, Silja?" I scooted to sit beside her.

She looked at the ogre. "Papa?"

"You're eleven. Now let's bless this food so we can eat."

I tried to focus on the prayer, but I couldn't. I would've guessed her to be six or seven. Then again, she was the first young fae I'd met. My father had explained that elves and fae aged differently from gachen and humans. Gachen didn't know that or that I was part elf, part fae, for that matter. They thought me to be three when I was six. I'd lost three years.

A chorus of amens rang out, and I added mine.

We watched as he ate. At Liam's discreet nod, I scooped a bite. Still uncertain I wanted to eat whatever this was, I sniffed at it, which failed to clue me in as to what I was about to consume, so I ate anyway. The thick gruel coated my tongue, and my gag reflex kicked in. I forced the stuff down and tried to cover my blunder with a cough. The next bites were easier. Then I found myself scraping the bottom, looking for more.

The place was dismal, but the food in my belly and the warm fire were oddly comforting.

Silja collected my dish along with the others, and I rose to help her clean them. She pumped water into a bucket, then dumped it into a basin to wash the dishes.

These people lived more like I was used to living in Ariboslia, except they had water indoors. Talamh Sí had come as quite a shock with their indoor plumbing, flameless lights, and all the conveniences keino brought with its artificial power. I'd grown accustomed to such things too quickly. Would I struggle to live as I had when I returned home? If I ever went home?

Nay. Don't let your mind go there, Colleen. Great is Thy faith-fulness...

I forced my sadness away and helped Silja dry the dishes. Then I placed one dried bowl on the rickety counter. "How long have you lived here?"

"All my life." She handed me another cup.

If she'd been here all her life, she wouldn't know if she'd ever looked like anything other than a pig girl or if her father looked like something other than an ogre. Maybe she didn't know the difference. After all, she didn't question whether Liam was a wolf man or if Ruuta was a horned hag or if I was a lizard. Could she somehow see through those things? Probably best not to ask, so I switched gears. "Where is your mother?"

"Gone since before I can remember."

"I'm so sorry. I don't remember my mother either."

She pulled her hands from the water and inspected them. Then, as if deciding she couldn't touch me with wet hands, she rubbed her face against my arm. My heart melted, and I gave her a little squeeze. We smiled at one another, then resumed our task.

"What happened to *your* mama?" she asked.

"I don't know. She brought me to another realm to rescue me from..." From what? My father? The humans? "From I don't even know what." I huffed. "Something happened to her, but I don't remember her or that time at all. I was three when I was rescued."

"That's sad." She held out the last cup, then hopped down from her stool once I took it. "My mama went to the village one day for food and never returned."

I hugged the poor girl again. "There's a village nearby?"

She crinkled one eye. "Not *close*. When Papa goes for supplies, he's gone all night."

My heart shuddered. I struggled to be in this place for one day with friends. This poor child lived her entire life here and sometimes had to spend the night alone?

Like storm clouds lifting, her gloomy expression changed. She grasped my hands in her tiny ones. "But now that you're here, all that will change when you kill that nasty ol'—"

"Silja!" Her father stood in the doorway, arms crossed, ogreish expression stern.

One side of her mouth turned down and seemed to pull her shoulders along with it. "Sorry, Papa." She maintained a low countenance as she walked past him back to her space on the rug.

I woke the next morning achy and stiff from lying on the floor. My nose seemed full of soot. It itched. We ate more of the same stuff we'd eaten the night before. While Petri drew us directions to the village, I rummaged through our supplies.

Liam's wolfy form appeared over my shoulder. "What are you looking for?"

"Food. I'd like to give them something for helping us." I pulled out some dried venison. "It doesn't appear they have much."

"We might need that. There doesn't seem to be much food around here."

"Exactly. But we'll have a better chance finding food in our travels than they will here. I'd hate for Petri to have to leave Silja to go to the village sooner because of us. Besides, we're on God's mission, right? He'll take care of us."

"Yeah." Liam kneaded the back of his neck. "I'm still unsure about all that."

I shrugged. "I suppose that's better than no faith at all."

After saying our goodbyes, we headed out. I felt better after meeting the ogre and the pig girl. I'd have to be careful not to judge things as they appear. Petri and Silja weren't as they appeared. Even the food turned out to be good. How I'd maneuver through this place without being able to rely on my eyes or my instincts, I didn't know. But if I was to survive, I needed to see in a way I'd never seen before.

God, give me eyes to see things as they really are.

TWENTY-ONE

The thick foliage blocking the sky crinkled and thinned until only a spattering of leaves clung on even in death. But no evidence of fallen leaves remained unless they decomposed long ago. As we walked along a crusty path, kicking up dust, the odd sensation that we were walking on the underside of the earth's surface struck me. As if a beautiful forest of trees lay beneath us and their roots shot out from the ground into the empty void surrounding us. There was no sun. Just that same gray we'd experienced the day before. How could this place get any worse? This was a fool's mission.

I stopped.

Liam, studying Petri's squiggly rendition of a map, ran into me. "Something wrong?"

I flopped my arms in defeat by my side. "What are we doing?"

"What do you mean?" Ruuta fidgeted with her sleeves.

"Why are we here—trapped in an unholy place we can never escape unless we kill an unkillable witch?" I didn't care if she overheard. I didn't care about anything.

"What choice do we have?" Ruuta's gaze flitted about every

which way as if the air was listening. "We're here. We have to find a way through."

How did nonbelievers have more hope than I did? *Great is Thy faithfulness...*

Liam handed the paper to me. "Keep this in case we're separated."

It looked like a treasure map with no words, just pictures. "But how will you find it if I have the directions?"

He tapped his temple. "I memorized it."

I frowned at the paper again. I'd have to consult these scribbles several times to make any sense of them, never mind find where I was going, and he had it memorized? Impressive.

I still walked with a suspicious eye on the lookout for grabby hands, but the eerie woods with potential for hands to reach out and grab me didn't sap my spirit as it had the day before. Though I struggled to understand the map, it bolstered my confidence—something tangible to show me where to go—even if it wasn't the final destination.

"Why do you keep looking at that thing?" Liam asked.

"I don't want to miss anything." To the north of the boxlike thing that I assumed to be Petri's cottage, a line led to triangles with circles inside over wavy lines. I thrust the map into Liam's face and poked it. "Are these eyes?"

"Could be." He shrugged.

Ruuta tore it from my hand, her brow furrowing under those horns as she bent over it. "If they're eyes, they look to be peering over the water."

"It may be krokotiili." Rhys shuddered and rubbed his arms.

"Krokotiili?" That sounded ominous. Then again, every new word in this place sounded bad.

He nodded, sending his black hair waving, then falling perfectly back into place. "It's a scaly beast, but neckless and low to the ground." He waved to Sakki. "Like if someone squished Sakki's dragon form."

Sakki bared one fang and snorted. Smoke flared from his nose, ending in wafting tendrils.

"Like an alligator?" We didn't have alligators in Ariboslia, but I'd read about them in human stories.

Rhys scrunched one side of his face. "I'm not familiar with alligators."

"Does it eat..." I gulped, then forced the word out. "People?" I was pretty sure alligators killed people.

"I don't know if it *eats* them. But they kill anything that gets too close. They have webbing between their front and back legs to snatch their prey"—he held his arms out and snapped them together in a hug—"then drag them down under the water."

"How do you know all this?" I grasped his sleeve, pulling Rhys to a stop. "I thought you'd forgotten everything about this place."

"I have flashes of what might be memories." He jabbed a thumb toward the map. "Krokotiili lying in wait look like that, with only their eyes appearing over the surface. Red eyes."

"If that's all you remember, how do you know about the webbing and whatnot?" *Please, God, let him be wrong.*

He raised a brow. "I *read*." His tone questioned whether I knew him at all.

"So you're saying you don't know." Liam cocked his wolfy head.

Rhys shot Liam an unimpressed look while Ruuta's snaggled lips curved into a crooked grin.

I sighed. "If we happen upon a swamp, we should avoi—"

A hairy beast leaped from behind a tree, snapping its jaws.

Gasps rang out. I sprang back, ready to flee, but where? Liam retrieved his weapon as the snarling beast stood, drool dripping from its fangs. It looked like a wolf. A much larger, much more menacing wolf than one found in nature. But not like Liam. It crouched on all fours, hackles raised like it might be an actual wolf.

"Who goes?" The wolf's rough voice was as threatening as its posture.

It could speak? And it was waiting for a reply. "W–we're trying to go to the village."

He wrinkled his muzzle and gnashed his teeth. "I said who, not where."

I teetered, my feet tripping despite the small movements. "I–I'm Colleen."

The wolf approached, sniffing the air. "You've elven blood."

"I–I'm part elf. Part fae."

He sniffed again, showing a yellow fang. "And you travel with a fae... and a *human*." He snorted as if to relieve his nose of a foul smell.

Could he see us? The real us? Or did his sense of smell allow him to see past the hideous glamors this place cast upon us? "What do you want?"

He snarled. "I'll ask the questions, half-elf. What purpose have you in Rotko?"

I couldn't tell him. I couldn't even speak the words aloud for fear something might overhear. How should I respond?

Ruuta stood tall, but her hand shook. "We're traveling to Seelie Clós."

Another snarl, this time accompanied by a growl that curled the hairs on my arms. "What fiends would have business in that wretched land?"

Ruuta and I exchanged a wide-eyed look that seemed to convey the same questions. Fiends? Wretched? What was wrong with Seelie Clós? Or was this creature so twisted as to think Rotko better than it was?

Liam gripped his weapon beneath his coat. I splayed a hand and gave my head a slight shake, hoping he'd get my message not to shoot the creature... yet. He released his grip but kept his hand at the ready. "If you're not here to help us, move along and let us pass."

The wolf laughed. Drool dripped from his jowl. "I'll allow you passage, once you answer me this—Why is a random jumble of intruders traveling together and *through* Rotko expecting to make it to Seelie Clós with no protective wards?"

We all eyed each other.

Sakki stepped between us. His legs and torso elongated as thick scales replaced soft fur. We gave him more space as he grew and grew until the wolf could have walked underneath without touching his belly. His mouth opened, and fire streamed from it, singeing an already burned-looking tree trunk.

A shimmer of light rippled through the atmosphere, and in the flicker, the landscape appeared entirely different. My friends looked like themselves again. Then it was gone. Was that Sakki's doing?

The wolf circled, studying his surroundings. Did he see it too? He lowered into a submissive posture. "Forgive me, Dragon."

Sakki touched the wolf's forehead with his lips—or whatever lines a dragon's mouth. Almost like a kiss. Then Sakki shriveled back up into his dog form and pawed at the wolf, inciting him to rise.

The wolf complied and sat on his haunches. "Are you to restore this land?"

That is Sakki's hope.

"What?" I relayed Sakki's message, then returned to my less-than-forthcoming dragon. "I thought we were just traveling through?"

Sakki and friends have work to do in Rotko. Colleen knows Colleen can't leave while the witch still lives.

"I know, but—"

If Sakki and friends kill the witch, Rotko will be restored.

Liam groaned. "Do you mind letting us in on your little conversation?"

"Sakki says killing the witch will restore the land."

"Shhh!" The wolf cowered, looking in every direction like a trapped animal seeking escape.

A chill breeze swept through. But it was no ordinary wind. It was as if a thousand evil spirits flowed past, attempting to siphon anything good from within me—peace, joy, hope—leaving me with nothing but sadness, fear... dread.

The wolf's yellow eyes went wide. He sucked air through his fangs. "Quick! Follow me!"

We chased him through the woods. Refuse crunched beneath our feet. Branches snapped. Liam, the only human and the slowest one among us, started to fall behind. Rhys noticed him, too, and morphed into a horse. Liam took a double take. Then, with the ease of a practiced expert, he mounted Rhys's bare horse back while in motion.

The wolf led us to a ramshackle cottage with boarded windows, and a door falling off the hinges clanged in the wind. Liam dismounted, and Rhys morphed back to his boy shape, clothes and all. When we entered the seemingly abandoned shack, the wolf lifted a tattered rug and opened a hatch.

"Quickly." He ushered us to enter.

I hesitated. Allowing a wolf in a scary world to trap me underneath his nightmare-inducing shack seemed like a bad idea.

Colleen is safe. Follow Sakki. He bounded down the stairs first.

I complied. The loose boards bowed under my weight, groaning, threatening to give out. I was almost offended.

The wolf grasped the carpet in his mouth, placing it so it would fall flat over the entryway behind him. He bit the string and lowered the hatch as he descended the stairs. Once the hatch was closed, a shimmering light, similar to when Sakki breathed fire at the wolf, swept over the cavern. But the reprieve from our cursed forms didn't come and go in a flash. It came and stayed.

Ruuta looked like herself again, minus the glamor face markings and slightly less flawless. A small scar puckered an indentation under her eyebrow, and bags beneath her eyes revealed her exhaustion. Her former perfect complexion must've been part of her glamor too. She still had nice skin, though it was somewhat blotchy. But she was no longer a hag. Liam, now as gorgeous as ever, dropped the masquerade as a goat-wolf hybrid.

I grabbed Ruuta's sleeve. "Do I still have scales?"

"No. You're back to your normal self." She scrunched her nose. "Perhaps a mite dirtier."

Our gazes shifted from one another to our surroundings, an occupied area well furnished and comfortable, despite the feeling of being in a cave. Women appeared caught in a private conversation. Teens lounging on pillows peered over the tops of their books. Children gathered together on a floor playing some kind of game. They appeared frozen in time, unblinking as they stared. The cavernous basement had sufficient lighting with some shadowy corners, though no visible source of light, other than the flickering candles on a table. Each gaze I met oozed unrelenting suspicion.

A man shoved back his chair with a shudder-inducing screech and approached. "Who've you brought into our sanctuary, Hadwin?"

We faced the wolf who brought us here. But the wolf was gone. A hairy man with a bulbous nose stood in his place. "A dragon."

Twenty-Two

Gasps and exclamations rang out. My heart slammed against my breastbone, seeking escape. What did they want with Sakki? I moved toward the exit, but Hadwin intercepted me. The other man emerged from the shadows, and I gasped.

He had pointy ears.

Hadwin gripped my arms, stilling me. "Where do you think you're going?"

He needn't have bothered. I wasn't going anywhere without talking to the elf. Despite the pointed evidence, I could scarcely believe a real live elf stood before me.

Liam raised his weapon, leveling it at Hadwin. "Unhand her."

"Do as he says." The elf gave a solemn nod.

Hadwin released me and raised his hands in defense, yet remained blocking the entrance. "I'm on your side. We, too, want to heal the land. Look at my friends." He gestured to the people surrounding the table, all in unnatural positions, ready to spring to his rescue. "Do you think they'd allow you to point a gun at me and live if we meant you harm? No, we're all friends here... assuming you want to kill the witch and heal the land."

I placed a hand over Liam's weapon. He glowered at Hadwin, then lowered it... slowly.

The tension holding Hadwin stiff left him as he turned to jelly. The elf squeezed his shoulder and led him to sit.

We followed the elf to the table where the others crammed together to make room, filling the quiet with rustles and screeches.

Was I seeing things? There were more with pointed ears, though not as pronounced as Samu's. "Are you all elves?"

Laughter erupted around the table.

One elf-looking man with brown hair pulled into a bun wiped his laughter away with a swipe of his hand. He pointed at the elf who'd led us to the table. "He's an elf." Then he motioned around the table. "The rest of us are fae."

"But your ears."

"Fae are partially descendants of elves, we have pointed ears too."

I looked at Ruuta. Her ears were always covered. I'd never seen them. In a daze, I lowered myself into my chair. How would I know the difference between elves and fae if everyone had pointed ears?

"May the sun shine upon you." Ruuta gave a small bow.

A fae woman with a more rounded human-looking features propped herself on her elbows. "Bah. Don't worry yourself with seelie graces here."

Ruuta flinched like she'd been struck.

"Allow me to introduce ourselves." The elf held a fist on his heart. "I'm Samu." He pointed to three men and two women and threw out names, which I promptly forgot. "And you've met Hadwin."

Ruuta, apparently the only one among us with manners, introduced us, calling me Colleen, not Princess Eerika. But her voice was unsteady.

Hadwin pressed his lips so they disappeared between his mustache and beard. Harsh stares softened, though the suspicion within them lingered. A woman set bowls before us, and a man doled out some sort of gruel more appetizing than what Petri fed us. Others gave us drinks. The scent of spices wafted up at me.

Yet again, Liam stayed my hand and waited for the others to eat before allowing me to partake. Would he do that forever? Once he released my hand, I tested a bite. Whatever it was, it tasted good. Like spicy cream with a grainy texture. My empty stomach rumbled a thanks.

"What is this place?" Had they built the dilapidated house atop this cave on purpose?

"A safe place." Samu sipped his water. "Free from Noita's magic."

"How?" Ruuta scooped a dainty spoonful of her mystery meal.

"When we were banished from Seelie Clós—"

The color drained from Ruuta's face, and her spoon slipped free and clattered into her bowl, splashing gunk. "You're unseelie?"

Guffaws came from those around the table.

"Unseelie." Another male fae with loose hair about his shoulders huffed a snort. "Do you even understand what that means?"

"Certainly. Unseelie fae oppose everything good—everything the seelie fae stand for. You're pakana." The way Ruuta said that last word, like a curse, jarred me.

I had to know what it meant. "What's pakana?"

Man Bun propelled his arm to block the fuming woman rising from her chair. "It's an incredibly unnecessary and unkind word. It essentially means heathen."

I widened my eyes at Ruuta and jutted my face at her in warning. She needed to collect herself before something bad happened.

"You're criminals." Ruuta's low voice quivered. She clasped her shaking hands in her lap.

I dragged a hand down my face.

"Of course you'd think that. You're Queen Rhiannon's minion." A woman tapped at her temple below threads of braids wrapping around her head. "Careful what you say around this one."

"Do I know you?" Ruuta narrowed her hate filled eyes.

"Of course not. Why would you remember one of the many accused? But I remember you sitting with Rhiannon's supporters as she banished me to Rotko."

"Are you all unseelie?" Ruuta paled. The harsh emotions fueling her seemed to have cooled as she recognized that we were outnumbered.

"Not all." Hadwin motioned toward Samu. "As we've already established, he's an elf. He found us and brought us here after the Divide darkened and fell under Noita's curse." He splayed a hand over his chest. "I'm a human."

"I'll be hanged." Liam gripped the back of his neck. "What's a human doing in the Divide?"

"God sent me to minister to the fae."

A missionary? Excitement rose within me like bubbles in a hot spring. I wanted to ask him about that, but just as I opened my mouth, the male fae spoke.

"The Seelie court has been exiling fae to Rotko for centuries. Many were born here. But unbeknownst to the fae who banished us, Rotko was a good place to live... before the Darkening."

"What's the Darkening?" I rested my spoon in my empty bowl.

"Do you know anything about Rotko?" The woman picked up her bowl to sip the last of her meal.

I fought my indignation at such an absurd question. Why should I know anything about Rotko? I braced my elbows on the table and leaned forward to see him better past Liam. "Only that it separates Talamh Sí and Seelie Clós, protecting the humans and elves from the fae."

"Do you know what the fae are? Where we come from?" As soon as she finished speaking, Ruuta let out a soft groan.

I shook my head.

"Time for a history lesson, then." Another male fae with brown hair pulled tight into a man bun reclined in his seat, lacing his fingers and resting them across his chest. Liam was kind enough to lean back too, so I could still see him. "I'll have to go back to the beginning... before the fae existed and only elves lived upon the land. The elves were peaceful. They cared for God's creation. God loved them and gave them dragons with which to bond to enjoy a deeper relationship and the skies. Then the angels fell from heaven."

The Bible talked about fallen angels. Had they landed in all the realms?

"According to God's Word as revealed from the humans"—he motioned toward Hadwin—"one-third of the angels fell. Once they were no longer in God's good graces, they became something else—demons. In the human realm, the demons mated with humans and created half-breeds called Nephilim. The angels who fell here mated with elves and created the fae."

"That's utter nonsense." Ruuta crossed her arms. "You're trying to apply human myths to our world."

"Your belief or lack thereof doesn't make it any more or less true," said the woman who disliked Ruuta.

Ruuta huffed a prim laugh. "That's the most preposterous thing I've ever heard. I can say the sky is green and argue your lack of belief doesn't make it more or less true. The simple fact that it's blue makes it true."

The woman sneered.

I had to stop Ruuta from making this worse. "Then what happened?"

Samu picked up the story. "God created the Divide, Rotko, to protect the remaining elves from the demon infestation. It was once a place of beauty, pure light. He assigned the dragons as its protector. But once they were killed, Rotko went dark. Noita seized her opportunity to curse the land, placing it under her control."

"But you said the seelie fae banished people to Rotko for centuries. The elves haven't been gone for that long. What happened to the fae banished here when the dragons were still protecting it?"

"I was banished before the elves were killed." Man Bun gripped the chair's arms and straightened. "Actually, I wasn't banished. My father was. My mother and I came with him. Back then, it looked like pure light. The seelie fae called it banishing—they thought it was a death penalty—that the light somehow ate us up. Which sometimes happened. I've heard tell of fae who came with others who didn't survive. The light burned them up so quickly they didn't have time to respond. But for those who made it through, once we enter, we can never return. Invisible barriers at all the borders trap us inside."

That couldn't be true. My father got out. Then again, he was an elf. Did that make a difference? I wanted to ask without giving myself away. I didn't know if I could trust them. My insides squeezed as I squirmed in my seat. "What about elves?"

Samu tugged the pointy tip of his ear. "The borders don't contain elves."

"But..." It trapped me, hadn't it? Was that my fae side? I blinked, losing focus on Samu's green eyes. "You're an elf. Why are you still here?"

He pursed his lips. "I chose to remain."

Huh. I didn't push him to elaborate though I would have loved to explore the reasoning behind *that* choice. "How do the fae cross the Divide with airships?"

Ruuta rolled her eyes at me. "As I've already said, they have protective wards."

"Yes, but many fae died before finding the right formula." Man Bun snarled. "Many a ship fell from the sky with few survivors."

Ruuta's enemy nodded. "But it was nicer then. The land was beautiful and plentiful. Or so I'm told." She slapped the table, and the fire in her eyes flared at Ruuta. What was with her? Ruuta hadn't caused the destruction and her fate. "When I was banished, this place had already darkened."

"It still is beautiful. Noita's curse has twisted it." Hadwin scraped his upper beard hairs with his teeth.

Now I was thoroughly confused. "What do you mean, it's still beautiful?"

"The beauty God created still exists." Hadwin's voice dipped to a low, almost reverent rumble. "The light was extinguished when the dragons died, and Noita twisted everything to appear ugly and frightening. She feeds off fear, and she's been feasting off us for decades. But those with eyes to see can still see it for how it truly is."

"Is that why our appearance changed when we crossed the border?" I gestured to Liam to offer an example though he no longer wore his goat-wolf façade.

"Exactly." Hadwin reached for his drink.

"But it didn't affect Rhys or Sakki... my dragon."

Samu's eyes glistened. "It wouldn't affect a dragon. They're impervious to magic. Plus, as they're shape-shifters, they have control over their form."

I wriggled in my seat, remaining in place but needing to pace as I worked it through. "Is that why Rhys didn't change? Because he's a shape-shifter too?"

Heads snapped to attention.

"What kind of shape-shifter?"

"A pooka." Rhys spoke for himself.

Gasps erupted. One woman gripped the table edge.

"Created by Noita?" Hadwin asked in a drawn-out tone.

"Y–yes..." Rhys's gaze whipped around the table.

Samu stood so abruptly his chair thudded to the floor. He thrust his arm toward the entryway in the ceiling. "Get him out of here!"

"What? Why?" Now I, too, clutched the table as everyone rose.

"He'll lead Noita straight to us!" Samu pulled bewildered Rhys's chair out from under him, spilling him from his seat. "She's connected to all her spawn. Do you know what pains we've taken all these years to keep this place hidden from her?"

Of course, we didn't.

Hadwin held up his hands. "This is bad, Samu. I know. But what good would it be to send him out now? While he's here where her magic can't reach, she can't find him."

Stomping back and forth, Samu fumed. "If she's been tracking him and he disappears, she'll investigate. She'll want to know how she lost connection."

Hadwin's skin took on the green hue mine probably had. All this time, we'd been following Rhys because he could sense Noita. It hadn't occurred to us the connection might go both ways.

"He must go now!" Samu pounded the table, making everyone jump. "If we send him out now, there's still a chance. Even if she sends her spirits out to find him, as long as her search is successful and it doesn't lead her here, she might not give his momentary disappearance any more thought. We might be safe."

"He's right." Hadwin rubbed his eyes, then lowered his hand to reveal the sorriest expression I'd ever seen. "You must go. I wish we could assist you in your quest, but we can't risk it. This is the only safe place. We have children to think of. You must go."

Twenty-Three

I'd forgotten how much Noita's magic—or whatever evil forces permeated the air—had affected me until we reemerged from the floorboards. The hatch rose with a screech, and the moment I popped my head out from the sanctuary, invisible leeches sucked what little peace I had. I fought the urge to duck back down and stay in the safe zone forever. But what good would I do there... paralyzed?

And I wouldn't risk causing them harm. Especially the children.

So, I steeled myself against the spiritual onslaught, and unlike the groundhog who sees his shadow, I emerged from my hole.

Great is Thy faithfulness...

I tensed more as I left the cabin, suspicious of everything... above *and* below ground. Attack would come... But what? When?

Then I noticed something I hadn't before. The complete absence of sound. No birds, insects, wind... nothing. It was as if the world lay in wait for a storm, or we stood in its eye.

Quick footsteps pounded behind us, and I spun like a spooked cat. A wolf! My heart caught in my throat. Then I saw Samu behind him, and my innards returned to their proper places as pent-up breath escaped like air from a leaky tire. It was only Hadwin. His satchel flopped across his back as he ran.

"Why don't you morph into a hideous creature like the rest of us?" I asked Samu when they were close enough.

He searched the area, perhaps expecting Noita to step out from behind a tree, then continued past me. "Because of what I am."

"An elf?" I whispered, falling into step beside him.

He held a finger to his lips, then nodded.

Though I wanted to know what affect Noita's magic had or didn't have on elves, I didn't press him since he was trying to keep it quiet.

"Decided to join us?" Liam adjusted Hadwin's bag to prevent it from slipping and sped up to match Samu's pace.

"Our services might come in handy." Samu gripped the strap stretching across his shoulder.

"You need someone who knows the land—a guide." Hadwin's speech sounded menacing, but then, he was a wolf speaking through menacing teeth. "Someone who knows how to live off this land—"

"And can see it for what it is." Samu fidgeted with his pack. He started to say something else but narrowed his eyes and pressed his lips together.

"And if you insist on keeping company with one of Noita's abominations"—Hadwin motioned toward Rhys—"you'll need extra protection."

Samu gave Rhys a full body scan with his gaze even as he walked at a brisk pace. "Are you Jaakko?"

Rhys was hoofing it trying to keep up, but his real name must've come as a surprise. He stumbled, then righted himself, and ran to catch up. "You know me?"

"I was a member of Auberon's guard. We flew to the Divide together as it darkened."

I gasped, my gaze pinging back and forth between them.

Rhys goggled, perhaps remembering something, then shook it away. "I don't remember."

"We think my—Auberon erased his memories." Oops. I'd nearly

revealed Auberon was my father. Until I knew where he stood, I didn't dare say anything.

"Whether he did or didn't..." Samu jabbed a thumb toward Rhys. "He can't be trusted."

I already knew I couldn't trust him. Not fully. Still, Rhys tried to be trustworthy, and I didn't like this stranger coming along telling me he couldn't. "He's our friend."

Rhys smiled, but his large, liquidy eyes betrayed his pain.

"That may be." Samu slowed, allowing Rhys and Liam to catch up. "But he's not just Noita's brainchild, she created him using part of her own soul. Her spirit lives in him. It's a struggle for anyone to fight Noita's power here. It's impossible for him."

What kind of fallacies did these people believe? "What do you mean, 'her spirit lives in him'?"

"Noita creates many things using God's breath, aether, but she's not God. She can't create a living soul. Some of her creatures are mindless beasts. But those who appear to have a soul"—he hooked a thumb toward Rhys—"do, indeed. Noita's."

Part of Noita's soul resided in Rhys? "But that's not possible."

"It makes more sense than a witch being able to create a living soul." Liam was huffing now. "Is that why she can't be killed? There's no soul within her to send to wherever it belongs in death?"

"That and the wards she's protected her body with to make her invincible." Hadwin nodded. "She's created several creatures with her soul as added security."

"Rhys?" Ruuta kept her smooth stride. She didn't seem troubled by our pace, but it wasn't natural for her to hurry. "Didn't you say you felt something when you arrived, like a connection to Noita but in different places? Is it possible you're sensing several creatures with pieces of her soul?"

Rhys swallowed hard, probably wishing to eat the words he'd spoken.

"Is there a way to return her soul to her body?" Liam panted. "Would we be able to kill her, then?"

Hadwin must've stepped on something. He shook his back left paw as he ran on all fours. "If a soul can be split apart and inserted in different creatures, I would think it could be returned to her. But all I've got is speculation."

"We'd probably have to..." Liam looked at Rhys as if he was dead already.

"Not another word." Hadwin growled, baring his teeth and surveying the area for eavesdroppers. "We've said too much already. It's not safe."

Rhys started falling behind. Since he looked ill, I slowed to walk beside him, nudged him with my elbow, and gave him what I hoped was a reassuring smile. No one would kill Rhys, especially not as an experiment. Not on my watch.

"What's your plan?"

To answer Hadwin, I stopped and pulled out the map. "We hoped to get to the village. Rhys seemed to be sensing Noita this way."

Liam bent over, bracing himself on his thighs as he caught his breath.

"We've put enough distance between us and the kids. Maybe we could lighten the pace, huh?" Hadwin smacked Samu's chest with the back of his paw. "The human seems to be struggling to keep up."

Watching a wolf teeter on hind legs, holding a map in his paws, made my head hurt. It was an illusion. Hadwin was standing before me in the form I'd met in the basement. I tried to envision it, but couldn't.

Did that mean my faith was weak?

"You're going through Synkkä?" Samu folded the map and handed it back to me. "You realize it's a swamp infested with krokotiili, right?"

So, our guesses were right. I'd hoped Rhys was wrong.

"It's on the way to the village." Liam stood straight and stretched.

"Kylä?" Samu asked.

"We weren't given a name." Ruuta smoothed back her grayed

hair, her chin held high as she spoke. Rather than looking regal, she merely put her horns and snaggled teeth into focus.

"For what purpose?" Hadwin's hackles rose, and he advanced a menacing step closer.

Liam grasped the back of his own neck. "Honestly, it's all we've got. Perhaps we'll find food, supplies, a lead... anything to help us figure out what to do next."

"Have you asked him?" Samu jerked his head toward Sakki, scampering along in dog form, stopping to sniff random objects or pee on them along the way.

"No." I questioned our decision. "But he volunteers information when it's pertinent. He didn't tell us not to go to the village."

Groaning, Samu slapped his forehead. "They have a direct link to God, and they haven't asked."

Sakki.

Sakki stopped mid-pee to look at me.

Do you know where we're supposed to go? What we're supposed to do?

Tell Samu if Sakki knew, Sakki would tell Colleen. Colleen should ask God. But if Colleen had tried, Colleen would know this place interferes with communication with God.

"What?" The blood drained from me and pooled in my gut. *We can't talk to God here? But He spoke to me.*

There is no place God can't reach, but something about this place is making it difficult for Sakki to reach God. God's voice is muffled.

That frightened me more than anything this place could throw at me. My stomach twisted, squeezing, threatening to expel the spicy cream as I fought to find words. "He doesn't know anything."

Liam's eyes were wide. He gripped my arm. "What's wrong? What'd he say?"

I swallowed the acid burning my throat, leaving a rancid taste in my mouth. "N–nothing. We just need to find a way out of this place as soon as possible."

Hadwin wrinkled his snout. "I wouldn't suggest going to the

village. Unless your pooka senses another of Noita's creations. Even so, maybe save that for last."

Rhys wriggled foot to foot, then held up both hands to wave away our unwanted attention. "I sense *something*—in many places."

"Are we heading toward any?" Liam asked.

"There's something in this direction, to be sure."

"Is it a bad idea to go to the village?" I edged closer to Hadwin and braved touching his furry hand.

Did I imagine it, or did his gaze soften? "Nowhere in Rotko is safe." He patted my fingers, his growly voice gentler. "But villages have more people. Some are on Noita's side and will give you over to her in hopes of gaining her favor."

"But you said—" I couldn't remember his exact words. "I thought the unworthy fae burned up when they entered the Divide?"

"The light. It was the light that burned them up."

"So, once the Divide darkened"—I gulped—"*all* fae could get through?"

"So it would seem. We never heard of a fae burning up since the darkening."

Liam blanched. "Let's avoid the village if we can. Instead, let's see where Rhys leads."

Rhys waved straight ahead. "This way."

Was it possible to feel any more depressed or tense? Despite Samu's desire to keep us away from the swamp, that's where we headed.

Fog thickened. Nothing was visible below our knees. The ground softened, then deepened until we were ankle-deep in water. The mud sucked my shoes, threatening to pull them off. I tried not to imagine a bed of hands reaching, grabbing, trying to trip me, steal my shoes, or hang on and never let go. Dead trees protruded from the murky earth like jagged spires, waiting to impale me should I fall.

With each step, a chill ran through me, inciting me to run for the nearest solid surface and never allow a toe to touch this ground again. But there was nothing.

Great is Thy faithfulness...

I couldn't feel God here. Was it because of Sakki's revelation? Or was I becoming aware of how dire our situation was? I'd never felt so hollow, so terrified. Not even as a child hiding under the table from the fasgadair, waiting, expecting a hand to snatch me and drain me of my blood. God had met me under that table. I didn't realize it then, but I knew it now. He had been there. He was always there.

Was He here now?

If He was, I couldn't sense Him.

Great is Thy faithfulness...

I wanted to scream or sob. Both at the same time. But nothing came out. The fog may as well have slithered up my body and wound around my neck, squeezing.

Light in. Dark out.

Light in. Dark out.

Breathe, Colleen. Just breathe.

The fog dissipated somewhat. Misty tendrils rose from the haze along the surface like steam, but it was bitterly cold.

Twin red lights shone in the mist.

Eyes. Red eyes. Glowing eyes.

I latched onto Liam, trying to climb him like a tree while hordes of crabs snapped at my toes. He tried to catch hold of me, but my squirming made it a challenge.

He grabbed hold and pushed me to arm's length. "What has gotten into you?"

My arm flailed toward the eyes as I fought to find my voice. "Eyes. Eyes! *Does no one see the eyes?*" Were they krokotiili? Would they eat me? Or Sakki? I wriggled from Liam's grip. "Sakki. Where's Sakki?"

Sakki appeared behind me as a dog.

Something's out there. Shift into a dragon. Fly away from here.

If Sakki takes on dragon form, the witch will know.

You did it earlier! If it keeps you safe, I don't care! Just do it! At least change into something bigger. Something inedible.

"...keep to the left. There's higher ground there."

I missed half of whatever Hadwin was saying. Sakki stood there *not* shifting into another form, and my heart ate away at itself. Stubborn animal. I wanted to pick him up and squeeze him into another shape myself.

"This way." Hadwin waved us forward and quickened his pace to the left.

I hurried to follow, wishing I could go fast enough to skim over the murky water. With a splash, something erupted like a volcano. An alligatory thing stretched to its full height, towering over us. Red eyes trained on me. The thing stretched its arms wide. Batlike wings cloaked the length of its body to the end of its stubby arms. Before I could move, it lunged, wrapping me in its wings.

Twenty-Four

I woke on a hard surface in a dark room smelling of musty herbs. *Sakki?* As I waited for his response, I strained to see... something. The harder I tried, the more complete the darkness seemed. No sliver of light peeked through dark curtains. Nothing. Then a terrible thought smacked me in the face—blind.

What if I'd gone blind?

Sakki? Rising panic thrummed through my mind's voice.

I held my breath and listened for a reply. Nothing. I couldn't sense his presence. Where was he? What happened?

The alligator!

My heart thundered. My throat closed as I remembered the beast wrapping me in its webbing. I clutched my legs, hugging them to my chest, making myself as small as possible, and tried pulling the air around myself.

Please hide me, please hide me, please hide me.

Was it even possible to make a veil in this twisted place?

Colleen, you fool. Why didn't you test it out when you had a chance?

Ruuta's illusions didn't work. We couldn't even control how our minds perceived what they saw. We had little control here and no reason to think my veil would have worked either.

I resisted running away. What if I ran into the beast? Was it here? Could it see in the dark? My heart beat faster, but I tried to stifle my hyperventilating and avoid moving in case it heard me. Without my vision, I needed to listen.

In the complete darkness, I could almost make out the tablecloth hanging above me as I imagined myself back under the table in Bandia, hiding. But I was alone. My kids weren't with me. I sniffed the air for the telltale fasgadair scent, expecting one to reach under the table and snatch me. My throat clogged, and my heart hammered like a crazed carpenter.

Oh God, oh God, oh God... Help me!

My ragged breathing sounded so loud, I clamped my hands over my mouth. Mustn't let them hear me. Mustn't be found.

Stop, Colleen, you're not in Bandia!

I pressed my hands to my chest and worked to slow my breathing and calm the tears and the screams under the surface, threatening to break free.

Light in. Dark out.

Light in. Dark out.

Breathe, Colleen. Just breathe.

Think, think, think. This isn't Bandia. There are no fasgadair.

Nay, but there are winged alligators that kidnap people.

It hasn't eaten me yet. I'm still alive.

Or am I?

If only I could see in this blasted darkness! Or was my worst fear true—that I'd gone blind? Facing all I'd faced was bad enough with vision, but without it?

What had become of my friends? Where was Sakki that he couldn't hear me? Or was something interfering with our connection?

I had to call out, even if it meant bringing unwanted attention. A strangled gurgle came out before I found my voice. I whispered, "Sakki? Are you here?"

I waited, barely breathing, to hear even the faintest reply.

Had I gone deaf too?

No reply, but no alligators either. At least, none that let their presence be known. "Liam? Ruuta? Rhys? Anyone?"

The panic welled with each unanswered name, tingling my cheeks, threatening to overwhelm me once more.

Light in. Dark out.

Light in. Dark out.

Great is Thy faithfulness...

They weren't here. Panicking wouldn't help. I had to do something—*anything*. If I was still alive, I couldn't sit here, hoping that reptile didn't return to eat me. What if my friends were in danger? I needed to find them, even if it meant fumbling about in the darkness and facing whatever might be in here with me.

I reached out a tentative hand, feeling the air to be sure nothing was there, ready to recoil at the slightest hint of anything questionable. But the surface was hard with slight splintering and grooves. Wood slats.

A striking match whisked out, and a flame burst into life. A cry escaped me, and I clamped my hand over my mouth. A small, yet hideous face appeared in the light for half a heartbeat. My heart skittered as I recoiled. Whatever the thing was, it nearly toppled the lantern. Claws scratched the wood floor as it scurried away, clattering objects in its path.

Light in. Dark out.

Light in. Dark out.

Great is Thy faithfulness...

Whatever that thing was, it eased my worst fears. I could see and hear. My breathing steadied as I searched the shadows for movement, listening for any sound. Nothing. All was quiet. The thing seemed to be gone. But I hadn't heard a door, and there were no windows. Unless there was a hole in a wall or that thing could move through solid objects, it was still in here with me. It must be scared, or it wouldn't have rushed off as it had. That bolstered my courage somewhat. I picked up the candle in its lantern and searched. The place was full of junk. A storage room. Crates heaped haphazardly lined two walls. Shelves laden with strange items and jars filled another.

I walked to the only door, grabbed the handle, and took a deep breath. As much as I wanted to escape this place, I wasn't sure I wanted to face whatever waited on the other side. I tried the handle, but the door didn't budge. I wiggled it as loudly as I dared, but it was no use. The door was locked.

Then where had that nasty little creature gone?

Maybe there was another way out of here. I lifted the lantern to peer through the items littering the shelves to the wall behind, pushing aside clay jars, wooden boxes, glass vials, a strange statue. The statue felt warm... pliable. I snatched my hand back as if I'd touched a hot stove.

Was it alive? The frozen face stared straight ahead as I closed in, then its eyes twitched my way, and it launched itself off the shelf, scrabbling away. A broom propped against the wall fell over. The handle crashed onto the floor.

Why was it so afraid of me? I scanned the clutter. There was nowhere he could go. I caught him in my light as he dove headfirst into a hole slightly larger than a mousehole.

Giving up on the creature, I swung my lantern toward the door once more. Maybe there was a key. Or something that could work as a key.

I searched the shelves and found a leather roll of tools. I could use those to tear a hole in the wall if I dared make that much noise. Another leather wrap held knives. I kept one should I need it to defend myself, but nothing fit the keyhole. Books, candles, cups, bowls... I peeked inside jars—herbs, salt, foul-smelling liquids.

Then I came to a wooden box. The lid was jammed. I clutched it to my chest and pried it open with the knife. The lid gave way, and the entire contents went airborne, then rained down on me.

I ducked to protect myself from the falling shards. When the onslaught ended, I inspected the fallout.

Bones.

My stomach lurched. Where had these come from? And why so many?

Although small, they'd belonged to something larger than a rodent... nothing as large as a human. Unless they were fingers. A full-body shudder swept through me, rekindling my need to flee. As much as I wanted to avoid the skeletal remains littering the floor, my gaze gravitated their way.

One might fit the keyhole.

Disgusting as it was, I had to try.

I picked one up and crunched others on my way to the door. I inserted it and jiggled the door handle. Nothing happened. I didn't know the inner working of a lock to know what I was feeling for.

"You safer here," came a gruff voice behind me.

I spun in the air, crunched more bones in my ungraceful landing, then clutched my chest to still my overexcited heart.

The tiny monster blinked black eyes like polished obsidian in a head somewhat flat, hairless. Giant fangs protruded from its lower jaw, hooking its upper lip. He hovered by his hole, ready to escape again.

I didn't trust this creepy thing, but I needed to get out of here. Perhaps it could help. I crouched. "Don't go."

"*You* don't go," the thing said. "Noita out there. Noita eat girls."

Blood drained from my face. "Th–this is—I'm in the witch's home?"

The thing nodded its sideways oblong head. It laced its spindly fingers and pressed its clasped hands to its chest. "Me Hiisi." It jutted its still-woven hands out to me. "You?"

"C–Colleen." Whatever it was, hopefully it didn't have any friends. And they weren't interested in feeding off me. "W–what are you?"

"Me Hiisi. No name. One of many Hiisi. What be you?"

"I–I'm a girl. A fae. And an elf."

Hiisi elongated as he straightened to his full height—still below my knees. His eerie black eyes widened. "Elf? Elf, elf, elf." He paced, throwing glances at me, apparently no longer afraid. "What Noita do?"

"What do you mean? Do you know what the witch plans to do with me?"

It stopped and stared. "Noita eat girls. But *no* elf." It shook its head and resumed pacing. "No, no, no. No elf. Noita never eat elf."

"Isn't that good? Can you help me get out of here?"

"No, no, no. Me no help. Not in here." Now it seemed agitated. It rushed to the pile of bones on the floor. "Elf see bones? Hiisi bones. No, no, no. Me hide. Stay safe." He patted himself. "Bones stay safe inside."

I flicked the bone in my hand away, sending it skittering to join the others, and wiped at my palm in hopes of stopping a spreading infection. "If you help me escape, I'll bring you with me." That might be a terrible idea. I didn't know what this thing was. It could secrete venom for all I knew. But I needed help.

The look the thing gave me was almost cute—in a hideous-creature kind of way. Its eyes shined with unshed tears. "Elf help me?"

I nodded.

"If me help elf?"

I braved another nod.

Hiisi marched over to me, spat in its hand, and held it out to me. Did he want me to shake it?

"Spit."

"Y–you want me to spit in my hand?"

Its mouth opened wide in a creepy smile, and its lopsided head bobbed.

I pretended to spit in my hand, then extended it out. The hiisi smacked his soggy palm against mine, and I nearly vomited. His hands, like bone wrapped in thin leather, slimed me with thick hiisi saliva. He released, and I held my hand away, wishing I could wash it.

The doorknob jiggled. A key turned in the lock. The hiisi dove back into its hole, and I frantically looked around, though there was no place for me to hide. Then I remembered the veil. I tried to pull the air.

God, please hide me, please hide me, please hide me.

The atmosphere felt different here. Was it working? The door opened. Light spilled in from the entryway, outlining what appeared to be a girl. She raised the lantern before her and smiled. "Hello, elf."

Twenty-Five

The girl beyond the doorjamb was the only pretty thing I'd seen in this cursed place. Everything about her shined. Her dark skin shimmered as if covered in diamond dust. Stunning green eyes peeked through strands of black hair. Like me, her large eyes took up most of her petite face. Unlike me, the tips of her ears poked through her hair.

My heart stilled in my chest, hardly daring to hope another elf existed. Or was she a fae? "Are you—?"

"An elf?" She laughed, and a joy I hadn't felt since entering this place yearned to rise. "I am."

She was so different from me—so free. I used my massive mane to cover my elfin ears. Not her. She styled her hair in such a way to flaunt them.

"My name is Eliina." She curtsied. "Pleased to meet you, Your Highness."

Highness? She knew who I was?

"You're an elf." In a robotic tone, I repeated what we'd already gathered. Clouds obscured my mind. I couldn't sift through the mist to think clearly. "Why are you here? Isn't this... Doesn't Noita live here?"

"Yes, she does." Eliina smiled an impossibly wide smile. It tugged me, urging me to smile back.

"But how? Why? Are you here... voluntarily?"

Her eyes widened as she nodded emphatically.

An echo of myself sent conflicting messages in my mind. Part urged me to flee, but another part wondered if Noita wasn't as bad as everyone made her out to be. What did she do? Sell my father a curse? He made the choice to use it.

A faint ringing in my ears carried a small voice telling me the witch ate humans.

Where had I heard that? Rumors. Vicious rumors.

"Are there any others?" I asked. "Elves, I mean."

"There are. Would you like to meet them?"

The split in my mind widened. Part of me screamed to run away, but her screams grew faint. I could hardly hear her anymore. The inquisitive side spoke over her, asking, *When will you have another opportunity to meet elves?*

Probably never. "Yes. I would love to meet them."

Something sounded behind me. A gasp? I turned to look, but nothing was there. Hadn't there been something? A storage room? A creature? Ho—Hi—What was it called?

Think, think, think! I shook my head in foolish hopes the movement could clear the fog. What was I just thinking? What was this place? How had I gotten here? And where had this girl come from?

Nothingness surrounded us. Nothing but darkness. And yet, the girl was as clear as if she stood in daylight. How was that possible? Who was she? She walked away. How she knew where to step in complete nothingness, I couldn't fathom, but I followed. As she moved, the space brightened. A room similar to a Folaím tree house formed around us.

"Oh no. No, no, no."

"What did you say?" Whatever had spoken, it sounded familiar, not like Eliina, but no one else was here.

"I said nothing." She spun around. "Did you hear something?"

Had I? I tried to think, but the haze obscured my thoughts. "I'm not sure."

She placed her lantern on the table, though the light no longer seemed necessary. The room was full of light, but where it came from, I couldn't tell. It seemed to emanate from everywhere and nowhere at the same time. Something about the light was wrong, artificial. Everything looked—off. But her broad smile yanked me from my negative thoughts. I hadn't realized how much I wanted to meet elves until I saw another, besides my father.

"Are you a full elf?" I'd never met a female elf.

"Yes, but you are not." Her small mouth barely moved as she spoke.

"How do you know?" I reached to ensure my ears were covered, an old habit, as I cringed at a sudden shame over my fae side.

"You are part fae. A descendant of a powerful fae line."

Did I imagine it, or was she impressed? "My mother?" I let my hands slide from my hair. "She's a princess—in the royal line. But she's the youngest of three—given away to my father to form an alliance."

"She is so much more than that." Something crossed Eliina's face, some twinge of—was it fear?—wriggling beneath her eager delight. "Noita will explain."

The cloud in my mind thinned and darkened. "Noita. How can you live here—with *her*? She cursed these lands."

Didn't she? Why was I no longer so sure? I'd been certain before, hadn't I?

But what had come before?

Eliina laughed. I fought the infectious merriment.

"Is that what you heard?" Her laughter continued, shaking her dark hair as her shoulders quaked. "Noita saved this place."

"Saved it?" I narrowed my eyes to intensify my gaze and see through her. If only that were possible. "How?"

"Let me introduce you to the others. Soon enough you'll understand." She blew out the lantern, and everything went black.

Seconds later, the space illuminated again. This time, we stood outside in a brightly lit forest with no shadows. That same unearthly light seemed to come from everywhere and nowhere. Birds sang and danced among the branches. Rabbits hopped across a tidy path. A mother and baby deer grazed on a patch of grass.

Was this real? A voice somewhere in the recesses of my mind screamed that it was all an illusion. But the screams grew faint until it was nothing but a nagging feeling.

Whatever this place was, it was warm and inviting, yet carried an intangible undercurrent of something ominous. I had nothing to compare it to. The closest sensation might be to stand on a great precipice, in awe of the impressive heights and surrounding beauty, but all too aware that one misstep would bring certain death.

The fawn sensed me staring and returned my gaze. It flicked its ear, then lowered its head, and sniffed. I crouched and held out a hand. The fawn took tentative steps, crossing the path. When it reached me, it snuffled my outstretched fingers, then pressed its nose to my palm, probably expecting a treat. Warm, wet breath moistened my hand. It gave me a quick lick, then backed away, perhaps saddened to find nothing but skin. The animal allowed me to stroke its neck. Its mother nuzzled the fawn to get it moving, and they pranced away.

Whatever void the fawn had filled felt emptier than before.

An image of a dragon broke through my foggy mind. Did I have a dragon?

Sakki.

Where was he? Was he alone? My heart cleaved like it'd been run through with a sword. I clutched my chest. But there was no stopping the bleeding.

I had to find him. The others too. "I need to find my friends. Can you help me?"

Her countenance darkened to such an extreme I feared she might strike me dead. But the moment passed. Had I imagined it? "First, let's meet the other elves."

There were more elves here?

"Would you like to meet them?"

"Would I? I'd love nothing more."

She brightened further. "I'd hoped you'd say that."

I followed her through the peaceful wood. But a nagging feeling tagged along. Like entering a room intent on doing something and forgetting upon arrival. But in that scenario, I knew I was forgetting something. Now, I had to question not what I'd forgotten, but if.

Twenty-Six

The panging in my heart, the desperate awareness something was amiss, didn't lessen as I followed the girl. My body might jump out of my skin at any moment. The lure to meet more elves was strong. But something was wrong.

Was it a dragon?

Had I ever seen a dragon?

My upper arm burned, and I lifted my sleeve, expecting to find an injury. But there were markings—a tattoo. I touched the ink burning me, and it cooled.

A dragon bond—socrú. Not only had I seen a dragon, I'd bonded to one.

But what was his name? Something that began with an S. Sam? Nay, that wasn't right. Sakki! That was it. Weren't there others? A man... Lee...? Liam! And Ruuta... Rhys. Hadn't others joined us? What were their names? Har—Hadwin. That was it—Hadwin. There was another, but I couldn't remember.

Why did my mind feel so fuzzy?

The trees flickered.

"What was that?" I ducked, half expecting them to come down around me.

"What was what?" Eliina's perfect hair swept over her shoulder as she spun to me, skipping backward now.

"The trees. They"—how to describe it?—"blinked out."

"You mean they swayed in the breeze?"

"Nay." I stifled the insult. I may be losing my mind, but I knew the difference between swaying trees and whatever had happened. Besides, there was no breeze. "They were gone for a moment."

She stopped and cocked her head, her large eyes scanning me for mental illness. "Trees don't disappear and reappear."

"I know that!" Ugh! Talking to her was no use. Trees in most places didn't blink in and out, but we weren't in a normal place, were we?

Where were we, exactly?

Wherever we were, these trees had done as I said. But I wasn't going to get anywhere with her. So, I dropped the matter.

She resumed her trek unperturbed.

Thundering water sounded up ahead, then, as we neared, rippling joined in. The trees cleared to reveal a crystalline lagoon. Three waterfalls delivered water to radiant rippling pools at differing heights before spilling into the lagoon. Flowers bloomed. Swans graced the water while singing birds swooped to bring the sky alive.

Everything beckoned me to be still, calm. But nothing could squelch the storm within. Sakki. I needed to find him. And my friends. Liam, Rhys, and... What was her name? My lady-in-waiting. Wait—Why did I have a lady-in-waiting? And why couldn't I remember her name?

"Your Highness, these are the other elves."

Four people stood before me—two women and two men. They weren't there moments ago. Were they? They each looked very different from one another, but they all had large luminous eyes almost too big for their narrow faces with petite features and prominent ears. Elves. Never could I have imagined being in a small crowd of elves.

The girl introduced them. I dipped my head in acknowledgment, then forgot their names. "Why do you keep calling me your highness?"

"You're Princess Eerika!" my guide responded.

The others bobbled their heads, their adoring gazes aimed at me.

"Daughter of Zorac," the dark-haired man said.

I'd been about to correct them that my name was Colleen. But that last comment confused me. I'd heard that somewhere else. But that was wrong, wasn't it? I didn't know any Zorac. What was my father's name? Aumicron? Aribon? Auberon? Yes, that sounded right. "My father was Auberon."

The blond stepped closer. "Was? Has Auberon passed?"

I couldn't recall the details, but somehow, I knew he was gone. I must've cared for him, for it saddened me. I nodded, squashing the rising emotions.

The five exchanged woeful glances.

"What?" I studied each solemn face. "Were you friends with my father?"

Eliina grimaced. "We didn't know King Auberon, but we know the prediction. If descendants of Zorac occupy the two thrones, the Divide separating them will fall."

I huffed a frustrated breath. "First of all, my father is Auberon, not whoever Zorac is. Second, wouldn't it be a good thing if the Divide fell?"

Now they all looked confused.

My guide gave me that look again. "If the Divide falls, nothing will protect the elves from the fae."

Weren't the elves gone? Yes, that's why I'd never seen any. "How long have you been here? There are no elves left in Talamh Sí. As far as I know, you're the only ones left. They're all dead."

They let out a collective gasp.

Tears slipped down one of the girls' cheeks. "How did they die?"

Think, think, think. I knew this, didn't I? Why couldn't I think? "My father? No, that can't be right. He would never do that."

One of the male elves, the blond one, looked at the others. "Might it have been Noita?"

Eliina spun on him. "Why would Noita get involved in affairs outside her realm?"

"Perhaps we should've left." The dark-skinned male wore no expression.

"Why didn't you?" I asked. "How did you end up in here?"

The blond male's shoulders sagged. "We were on a mission to seek the daughters of Zorac to ensure two never occupied the throne at the same time to keep the Divide from falling. You, your mother, your grandmother, and up the line for centuries, were all from Zorac's line. But never in all the time since God constructed the Divide had we come so close to having his descendants on both thrones. We heard of King Auberon's upcoming marriage to Princess Delyth. We were on our way to intercede, to ensure the marriage never took place."

My mind was still hazy, but Auberon married Delyth. Weren't they my parents? "But they did get married. My mother was queen of Talamh Sí while Queen Rhiannon ruled Seelie Clós. Both were on the throne at the same time, and the Divide is still here."

The blond guy shook his head. "No, Princess Delyth was queen by marriage. The crown was ruled by your father, an elf. The Divide won't fall until their offspring—*you*—take the crown while Rhiannon still rules."

"She's here now, so that won't happen." Eliina pressed her lips into a thin smile.

Why did the others look as if they might want to kill me just to be sure? I backed away. "If you've been here since before my parent's marriage, how do you know who I am?"

The blond guy spoke again. "Noita has been keeping us informed, assuring us the situation is handled. She has more to lose than we should the Divide fall."

"So you're staying with her willingly?" Dull warning bells pinged within me. Something more was going on here. This didn't add up. "If she cares so much, why wouldn't she let you fulfill your mission?"

A wave of shrugs swept across them.

"I mean, she can't *want* the Divide to fall." *Think, Colleen, think.* What did this mean?

Bouncing off her toes, Eliina clasped her hands together and gushed. "See? It's so good that you're here. As long as you remain, the Divide is secure. If you had to sacrifice yourself to keep the elves safe, is this the worst way to do it?" She spun around, arms wide, showing off the spectacular view. "It's not a terrible place to be."

Were they right? They were elves. Full elves didn't suffer separation from God as humans, fae, and gachen did, right? I still didn't understand that. But there were five of them and one of me. And I was part fae. Perhaps they knew better than I did.

Could God reach us in this place? What had God wanted from me? I couldn't remember, but it wasn't what the elves were saying. They couldn't both be right. What if the elves came here and lost their way?

Or what if they were here just for this, to share this with me and keep me here? Was it better for all if I stayed, ensuring the Divide remained secure?

But what about my friends? What were their names again?

TWENTY-SEVEN

I lounged beside the lagoon, eating some kind of tart fruit. Whatever it was, it was delicious. The waterfalls endlessly spilling their bounty soothed my mind. Still, the nagging feeling I needed to do something haunted me. But what? It swam around the periphery of my mind, but every time I came close to catching it, it swished away.

I sighed. Best give up and enjoy the scenery. Besides, whatever I was trying to remember would reveal itself once I stopped thinking about it. So, I studied the water flowing into the pool, then searched for the outlet. "Where does the water go?" I asked Eliina.

She took a swig from her carved mug. "What do you mean? When you drink it?"

"No." I laughed. "The water in the pool. How can so much water continuously fall into it without emptying? Wouldn't it overflow?"

Eliina, splayed out across a mossy rock, shrugged. "A lot about this place doesn't make sense. We're in the Divide. Things are different here."

"Because of Noita's magic?" I pressed a palm to my temple to ease the oncoming headache.

She rolled her shoulders again.

"Isn't that bad?" I fought through the pain to think.

"It's the price to pay." She lifted her mug toward the view. "And not a bad price at that."

But what was the price? *God, if You can hear me, please help me fight whatever is happening to me.* "Do you think God wants you to sit here, enjoying magic He doesn't approve of?"

Glaring now, she jerked and raised a hand to shield her glare. "How do you know He doesn't approve?"

I weighed my breaths, my chest hollow as it received them. Although unsure how I knew, I was right. "Would He ever approve of sitting idly by in paradise created by a witch's magic?" I continued to stare, but she continued to glower as if she wasn't unaware but didn't care to consider the truth. "It says so in His writings. Witchcraft is evil."

"Is this the human writings you speak of? Elves have no need for such writings. We can speak to God directly."

"Can you speak to Him here?"

Her scowl deepened.

My mind continued to clear as I worked it out aloud. "So, you're trapped here under a witch's curse without God's writings or any way to communicate with Him—and you're okay with that?"

She shuddered and flared her nostrils.

Sensing her resolve weakening, I pressed on, pushing her. "Don't you want to talk to Him again?"

As her shoulders drooped, she hung her head.

I leaned close. "Help me get out of here."

"Shhh!" She straightened, paranoid eyes searching in every direction. "You can't talk like that."

The scenery wavered with steamy wisps like the horizon on a hot day. Then it morphed and swirled the way a teleview lost connection. Having lost the seat to steady me, I toppled backward, landing on my rear. Whatever had trapped my mind in a haze released me. With a whoosh that blew my hair back, my memories returned, along with my desire to find my dragon... my friends.

"Now you've done it." Eliina's voice trembled.

A lantern lit, but revealed nothing beyond its dim light, and no one stood near it.

Eliina scooted away.

A hand reached into the darkness and lifted the lantern, illuminating a pretty creature. She looked elfin with her large eyes and slender face, but her ears were impossible to see through thick blonde hair. Purple markings similar to Ruuta's enhanced her features. Eyes like translucent amber, like tainted water turned to ice, surveyed me. "Eliina, you may go. It's time I properly introduced our new guest to the Divide."

This couldn't be the witch. Could it?

I searched the darkness for Eliina, but she was gone. Vanished. The lantern in the woman's grip blinked out, bathing us in complete darkness. Then moonlight streamed through a round window. The windowpane crossbars cast a warped crisscross of shadows over the table, floor, and us, giving the impression of being caged. Lit candles in candlesticks rose to my height from the floor and a candelabra on the table. More candles lined a beam hanging from chains overhead. The modest room seemed to serve as a kitchen, dining room, and living space. A massive stove with a ladder to what appeared to be bedding above faced a row of cupboards. A padded chair had been settled before a cozy nook of bookshelves, while a wardrobe and a well pump filled the rest of the space.

Where was the door?

Noita motioned to one of the wooden chairs at the table as she settled herself into the padded chair. Other than the long cape that appeared as shabby as her chair, she didn't match her environment. "Bring one of those so you can sit. I've only the one comfortable chair as I'm not in the habit of entertaining guests."

A guest? More like a hostage stolen from my friends by a winged alligator. Caught between her calling me a guest and her appearance, my mind whirred and came up short. She was not what I expected, not that I knew what that was.

"Come now." She clapped. "Let's not waste time."

I dragged the chair across a frayed carpet as close to her as I dared, then sat. "Where am I?"

"My home. As I'm sure even a dimwitted thing such as yourself has guessed by now, I'm Noita."

"The witch." That should have bothered me more than it did. Was she somehow manipulating my emotions?

She swung a dismissive hand. "If that's how you wish to see me."

"But you *are* a witch, right? You cast spells to make all this appear?" I flailed my hands to present the room about me.

"This is my home. There's nothing magical about it."

"But the waterfall—"

"I'm a fae. A powerful one. Gifted with illusion. I can make people see what I choose."

A gift. Right. I scoffed internally. I had to tread with care lest I find myself in another alligator's embrace. "Why am I here?"

"I'd appreciate an answer to that as well." She leaned forward, her resin-hard amber eyes boring into mine. "Why *are* you here?"

If I wasn't nervous enough before, I was now. "I–I—*You* brought me here."

She huffed. "You entered Rotko of your own free will."

"I was trying to get through to Seelie Clós. One of your alligators brought me here."

"No one travels through Rotko. It belongs to me. You're trespassing."

"You stole it!" Oops. Oh, how I regretted my words and my enthusiasm. My hands shook. I tucked them under my arms to still them.

She appeared unruffled. "When I found myself trapped in here, an opportunity to bend it to my will presented itself. So I took it. Think about that. It's better that I am here, keeping the Divide intact."

"Intact? This isn't how God designed it."

Her eyes narrowed to slits, wispy blonde eyelashes obscuring their glow. "No, but it serves His purpose."

That jolted me. I couldn't think of a response. Was she scrambling my brain? *Think, Colleen. Think.* "Why am I here? If you mean no harm, can't you let me go to Seelie Clós? That's all I want."

"You have this backward, dearie. I'm no threat to you. Rather, you are a threat to me."

"What?" This witch was off her broomstick. "How am I a threat to you?"

"Trapped in here, you're not. But out there." She flung an arm in a random direction, then resettled her hands on her lap. "By taking your father's throne, you will destroy the Divide. Therefore, I can never allow you to—"

She twitched, her back ramrod straight and her wide eyes filled with horror as she searched about the room. What was she checking for? An army of angels descending upon us? She looked ready to escape but unsure of which direction to flee.

Then I saw it—a shapeless cloud of silvery dust floating toward her.

"No." She gripped the arms of her chair and pressed her back as far as it would go.

In a blast of determined swiftness, the wraithlike cloud shot into her chest. Her back arched. Neck and legs extended, hands keeping a firm grip on the armchair. Her mouth hung open, and every muscle tensed like electricity jolted through her. Then she slumped, and her head lolled to one side.

Was she dead?

I twitched as I waffled between checking for signs of life and maintaining a safe distance.

She tensed again with a frightening gasp, and I jumped back. She sucked in air far longer than seemed necessary, then sat erect, pounding her chest as she looked about with wide, horror-filled eyes. She caught sight of me. "You!"

I stepped back, placing a protective hand on my chest. "Me? I haven't done anything."

She wagged a finger at me. "A descendant of Zorac appears, and now a piece of my soul returns? You had something to do with it. I don't know how, but I'll find out. You will rue the day you trifled with me."

With that, the witch blinked out—vanished.

Twenty-Eight

My heart thumped hard so hard my chest hurt. I spun around, looking for anyone, anything, but I was alone. I stood in the witch's eerily empty home, listening for anything in the deafening silence.

Tick. Tick. Tick.

A pendulum clock hung on the wall, reminding me of my father's castle full of clocks. What I wouldn't give to be back there. Better yet, to go home.

"Hello?" I called out, hoping for a reply yet fearful a winged alligator may respond.

Was I so pathetic that I preferred the witch's presence to being alone?

There had to be a way out of here. I had to find my friends, but where was the door?

There must be one. Noita was an illusionist. Maybe I just couldn't see it. Then again, the witch didn't seem to need one. She just blinked out.

My hammering heart slammed up into my throat as I groped along the walls for anything my eyes might not see. I heaved books to the floor and toppled the bookshelf, but no door hid behind it. I yanked the shabby carpet, but no trap door lay beneath it. There was nothing.

Except the windows.

I searched for a latch on the center window. Nothing but glass panes within the crisscross grille—no evidence the thing opened. Giving up, I moved to one of the two smaller windows. A latch! I jiggled it free. The circular glass swiveled open, forming a mini half-circle opening at odd angles. The hope bubbling within me flattened. Even with the glass gone, the window was too small for me to escape. Unable to see anything beyond the streaming moonlight outside, I pushed the circular glass and stuck my arm through. The sickening feeling that something on the other side might grab it sent a rush of shivers, like centipedes burrowing beneath my skin, racing one another. A vision of an alligator snapping at my arm made me jerk it back, snagging my arm in my haste, cutting it on a jagged edge.

"Ow!" Careful to avoid further damage, I withdrew my arm all the way and inspected the cut. A red stain spread along my ripped sleeve. I reached for a cloth napkin on the table, pressed it to the wound, then inspected it. It was minor. If only I could heal myself.

Blood dripped onto my useless hand, so I wiped it with the napkin, then unfolded it to tie it around my arm.

Refocusing on a way out, I rummaged through the drawers, and my hand stilled on a mallet. That would do. I smashed two of the glass panes in the large window, brushed away the jagged bits that might snag me, then tugged the grille. Iron. It might as well be a cage.

I was trapped.

This disaster of a room had no way out. My surroundings wavered, converting to the house I'd been trapped in as a child. But this time I was alone. My brothers and sister weren't here.

I was alone.

Alone. Alone. Alone.

I squeezed my eyes shut. *Hide me. Hide me. Hide me.*

Hide me from what?

I opened my eyes. I was back in the witch's lair, partway under a table. The rail between the legs didn't offer enough room for me to get all the way under. And no tablecloth concealed me. Plus, the witch already knew I was here.

So what was I hiding from?

God, help me!

Why did it always take me so long to call on God? Where was He? Was He even here? Why had He allowed me to come to this place? Why had He permitted the witch to trap me? Why had He left me—alone?

This was His fault. Everything was His fault.

A fury I didn't know I possessed rose from deep within. Fists shaking at my sides, I let out a scream of which I'd never thought myself capable. The wail died in my throat, and I slumped as if I'd just run farther and faster than I'd ever run before.

The ensuing silence reigned louder than ever. Other than the clock's incessant tick, tick, ticking.

"Why give me a family just to steal them from me? Why bond me to a dragon? Why give me so much only to take it all away?" I scraped my back on the table as I stood. Blood rushed to my clenched fists, and I pounded my feet on the floor. "Where are You? Why do You do so much for others and nothing for me? I've always been here, believing in You, being good. I'm not a liar. I don't cheat people. I'm not unkind. What is my crime? What have I done to make You turn your back on me? You took away my parents! You abandoned me and my siblings in Bandia! You left me in charge to protect them. That was *Your* job, not mine. How could You do that to me? I was only a child!"

My chest heaved. I could scarcely breathe as I fell to the floor. Sobs racked through me, stealing what breath remained as I pounded splintery wood. As much as I wanted to calm, to breathe, I couldn't bring myself to do my usual calming exercise. I wanted my anger more. I wanted God to feel my anger.

Nay, I wanted Him to feel my pain.

My anger ebbed, leaving me with profound sorrow. Grief over my lost dragon, lost friends. Grief over my lost childhood, lost family. Grief over the realization God had abandoned me long ago.

My sobs lessened to hitching breaths. As I calmed, I sensed a presence beside me. I jerked, wiping my eyes, struggling to see through the puffiness. A creature sat there, head bowed, spindly fingers on my leg.

"Hiisi?"

He blinked liquidy eyes at me, his grotesque face masked in deep sadness. "Me here for you, half-elf."

"My name is Colleen."

"Me fear you fell for Noita scheme."

"What are you talking about?" Irritated, I braced myself on the floor. "Why are you here?"

His hand fell from my leg. Then he spread his fingers. "Me promise. You forget?"

The memory of shaking his spit-covered hand made me shudder anew. I choked on another sob.

"Why you sad?" Was a tear falling down *his* cheek?

"I'm trapped. Alone."

"No, no, no. You no alone." He thumped his scrawny chest. "Me here."

I slumped. The tears I thought had dried up were lingering, ready to break forth another torrent. I waited to speak until doing so wouldn't open the floodgate. "Have you ever"—I lugged in a deep, shuddering breath—"felt alone?"

Hiisi nodded.

"Like everything you ever had was taken away from you?"

His head cocked. His fingers clenched. "You see hiisi bones?" A stony little Adam's apple bobbed in his throat. "Me family."

Something connected me to the little creature. "God took away your family too."

His statue-like eyebrows pinched together. "No, no, no. God no do evil. Noita do evil. Noita stole hiisi bones."

"But God allowed it."

Hiisi stood. Even on his feet with me on the floor, he couldn't look me eye to eye, though he tried. "God make you stronger."

"Do I look strong?" My voice cracked.

"You must break to be whole." He paced, waving arms too long for his body. "What you think? You good? God make you no good?"

"Of course not."

He wrapped himself in his oversized arms, giving the appearance of wearing a straitjacket as he jittered his foot. "Then what you think?" He thrust himself too close and tapped my head. "What happen in here?"

I brushed his hand away. "What do you mean?"

"God no evil. No, no, no. Noita evil."

I huffed. "Well, Noita may have taken me from my friends, but God allowed it. He took my family from me. He left me in charge of three little kids when I was a child myself, hiding from bloodsuckers that wanted to kill us!"

"Ah." His sour breath fanned me as he spread his long arms, apparently satisfied. "God with you."

"What are you saying?"

"When you alone?"

"When was I alone?" Sometimes it was hard to understand his broken speech.

With his mouth partway open, he grinned as if I understood, but I didn't. So I stared, waiting, seeking the understanding this creature thought I had.

In my earliest days, I'd been with my mother apparently. I might've spent some time alone before the Cael clan took me in, but I couldn't remember. From there, I'd been surrounded by people, the clan members, the other orphans. Until we fled to Bandia. Even then, I'd had my would-be siblings with me. Later, we were rescued and adopted. Had I ever been alone, or have I just always *felt* alone? "I guess I've never been alone—not until I came here."

"No, no, no. You no alone here." He thumped his chest again. "Me here."

"I suppose. But where's God?" My voice cracked on His name.

"God here. God no leave Colleen."

"You can't know that."

"Me can." He nodded, his squat body and oversized head reminding me of a bobblehead Aunt Stacy brought from America. "Hiisi can."

"But God isn't here. My dragon can barely hear Him in the Divide, though they're connected."

His oblong head tipped sideways, making him look off-balance. "God everywhere. Noita magic interfere with dragon. Dark, dark magic." He shuddered. "Hiisi immune to Noita magic. You see?"

Closing my eyes in a foolish attempt *not* to see this place, I rubbed my thrumming temples and forced my eyes open. "No, I don't." Maybe if he could form a complete sentence, I'd understand.

He scampered onto my lap, grasped my face in cold leathery fingers, and stared into my eyes to force his thoughts into my head. "Hiisi here all along. Before dragon. Before Noita. God put Hiisi here for elf to no fall for Noita scheme—you."

I pulled myself up, making him fall off me. "Are you saying God put the Hiisi here long ago to be the connection to God now?"

He smiled a wide, open-mouthed smile, his lower fangs hooking his upper lip, and nodded his extreme enthusiasm.

"For me?"

His wide smile spread to impossible new lengths as his nodding grew more wholehearted.

Warmth filled my chest as my head tried to keep up with what my heart already knew. "So, you can talk to God now?"

Another excited nod. "You stop fear. Trust God. You hear God."

"What does He want me to do?"

Now he vibrated with excitement. "You pass test! You no fall for Noita scheme."

"I passed Noita's test?"

His face darkened as he scowled. "No, no, no. You pass. In future. No yet."

"If this was all a test, can I find my friends and leave?"

He squinted and pressed his lips together so his lower fangs nearly hooked his wide nostrils. "That depend. You see door?"

I pivoted, but the room remained unchanged. "I've already searched for a door I might not see."

Smile gone. Hiisi sighed. "You no trust God, no see way out."

"So, there *is* a way out? I just don't see it because I'm not trusting God?"

He gave a sad nod.

"I trust you, God." I searched again. Still no door.

"No, no, no. Words no good." Hiisi poked my chest bone. "You *believe*. Here."

Yesterday, I would have been offended if someone suggested I didn't trust God. But today?

Well, no use denying what God and this Hiisi already knew. I'd said it myself. Spoken words I hadn't known were hidden in my heart. "How do I trust Him?"

Hiisi bounced on his feet, panting like a dog awaiting a bone. "Ask Him. He hear."

"God, help me trust You." I looked again for the door, waiting for something magical to happen. But nothing did. "Now what?"

Hiisi shrugged and slumped against me. "Me and you wait."

Twenty-Nine

"How long has it been?" I asked Hiisi as he crawled through the cupboards, knocking things onto the floor. "How can it still be night?"

"No, no, no. No night."

"What do you mean? Moonlight is streaming in the window."

A bottle dropped onto the countertop edge below. It shattered, spraying liquid everywhere.

"Creeping crabs, be careful!" Who knew what kind of potions or poisons the witch had stashed away.

"Where crab?" Hiisi clutched the shelf corner and searched below. "Me no see crab."

"No, there's no—" I rubbed my forehead to ease the inevitable headache. "It's an expression."

"Expression?" He tilted his oblong head, tipping over another bottle, sending it rolling toward the edge.

I ran and caught it before it spilled, forgetting the glass below. Thankfully, my boots had protected me. "Is there a broom?" All the stories from America involving witches riding brooms came to mind. I chuckled at the irony.

"Why you laugh?"

"Oh, nothing."

He pointed to the corner by the small window beyond the table. "There."

I chuffed another laugh, retrieved the broom, and set to work. "How is there moonlight if it's not night?"

"You new here? You never meet witch?" Hiisi hopped from the shelf and walked along the countertop. "Noita like night. Moonlight."

"So, it looks like this all the time?" I didn't know the little creature could be so sarcastic. "How am I supposed to know what time it is?"

Oh! The clock. I hurried to it.

There was no face. No numbers. No hands. Nothing. Just a pendulum. "What kind of clock is this?"

His hands twitched upward, and his head cocked with that confused look again. "Why you need time? Make wait harder."

"What am I waiting for, exactly?"

Hiisi sat on the countertop. Clutching the ledge, he leaned toward me. "God! You wait for God."

"What am I waiting for Him to do? Rescue me?"

He kicked his feet. "No, no, no. When you see, you leave."

"When I see? See what?"

"Way out!"

I searched the space, which was ridiculous as I'd done that a hundred times already. "If there's a way out, can't you just show me?"

He smacked his face, apparently unable to take one more minute of my ignorance. "You trust God. Then you see."

"How am I supposed to trust God while I sit here, trapped, doing nothing?"

He shrugged. "What you need?"

"I need to get out of here."

"No, no, no." He squeezed his eyes shut, then huffed. "When me see you, you sad. Very sad. Why you sad?"

Before Hiisi arrived, I'd felt... "I was... alone."

He started up with the exaggerated headshaking again.

"Why do you keep shaking your head at me?"

"You no alone." He banged a fist against his chest with a series of solid thwacks. "Me here."

"You're here now."

"No, no, no. Me here. You no see."

My frustration came out in a growl. What was he saying? "You were here all along?"

He nodded with extreme enthusiasm. Again with the open-mouthed smile.

"I couldn't see you?"

More nodding.

"But now I can."

Now panting accompanied his nods.

"Why?"

He slumped, appearing much shorter. "Why you no see?"

"See what?"

Hiisi slapped his face again. He twisted to stand on the countertop, then paced, shoulders down as he waved his long arms. "You call God for help. Yell at God. Blame God." He pivoted to me and thrust his arms out. "You no see? You believe God here. Why talk or yell or blame what not here? You trust God. You trust small." He pinched his fingers together and peered through the tiny gap. "Even with small trust, you see me."

"But I couldn't see you until I shouted at God?"

He shot up, stretching taller than I'd seen him before, nodding and smiling with more enthusiasm than ever.

I slumped onto the ground, laying the broom across my lap, speaking my thoughts aloud. "I was feeling so alone. It was the worst thing ever. But you were here the whole time. God was here. I was never truly alone."

Oh no, the tears were starting again. I sniffed, hoping to drive them away.

Hiisi slid from the counter, thudded to the floor, and hunkered beside me.

"I was never alone in Bandia either. I saw the kids as a burden to care for, but I had them with me. And God was there too?"

He patted my leg. "God *always* with you."

I tried to imagine what it might've been like hiding from the fasgadair under the table alone. Months of surviving in that hovel without my kids. Without God. And all that time, we had food. I don't even know how, but we never went hungry. Great. There was no stopping the tears now. I turned to Hiisi, though those tears blurred him. "He was with me there too, providing for me, providing for us all."

Hiisi frowned, his lips quivering. His gigantic eyes shone as he continued to pat my leg.

"He's always been with me."

"God everywhere. Nowhere He no reach. Even here. Noita magic no stop God."

A profound sadness overwhelmed me. I clutched my knees, burying my face in them as sobs racked my body. All this time, I'd been so angry at God for failing me. But He'd been with me all along. *Forgive me, God. Forgive me for not trusting You.*

While I cried, Hiisi patted my back. *Thank You, Father. Thank You for always giving me comfort, even when I didn't know it.*

My tears changed from sadness to gratitude. I felt light. As if a heavy cloud weighing me down lifted. I wasn't in this alone. I never was.

I gripped Hiisi's leathery shoulder. "Thank you, my friend."

He beamed a giant, closed-mouthed grin, nearly picking his nose with his teeth again.

Wow. We'd sure made a mess. "We should clean this up." Who knew how long I'd sat there, but my muscles had gotten used to the position. They groaned as I used the table to heave myself off the ground. What was that? Flat round disks formed a pile on the table. "Was this here before?"

"You see?"

"Aye." I picked one up. "What is it?"

After climbing onto the table, he poked the pile. "Bread. Now me and you eat."

I tore off a piece.

Just as I was about to pop it in my mouth, he yanked on my arm. "No, no, no. God gave bread. Thank God, then eat."

"Right." I'd forgotten my manners since being in this realm. And never had food miraculously appeared like manna. "Thank You, God, for providing this. And Hiisi."

His infectious smile spreading, he grew tall again.

I plopped the piece in my mouth. "Oh, how heavenly." I mumbled around the bite, my manners forgotten again. "Sweet, like honey."

We devoured the pile. As I chewed my last bite, I stilled. Was that? On the far wall. "A door!"

"You see door?" He stood on the table and clapped. Then he reached for my hand and hopped off the table with it. On the ground, he pulled me to my feet. "We leave now."

As much as I wanted to leave, I hesitated. "We can just... go?"

"Yes, yes, yes!" He tugged harder.

"But what's out there? Will we run into the witch? What about the other elves? Should I rescue them?"

Hiisi blew out a breath, deflating, and released my hand. "Elf no leave if elf no see, like you."

"So what should I do?"

"Me and you go."

Hiisi and I walked through the door where an otherworldly land-scape surrounded us. The giant moon that streamed into the window was much larger than any natural moon. Moonlight bathed the house on either side, but we stood in the hut's shadow, everything before us obscured. Wooden planks squealed with each step. We must be on some sort of decking. Afraid of falling down rickety steps I couldn't see, I turned right to walk alongside the hut in the moonlight.

"Where you go?" Hiisi's impatient voice floated around the corner.

"I want to be able to see where I'm going. Where are the steps?" I whispered in case the witch was near.

The decking wrapped around the hut. There was no railing, and beneath the wood was dark.

"No, no, no. No steps that way. Follow me." He returned to the front door and charged down something in the darkness, his bare feet slapping against shaky boards.

I felt for steps the way he'd gone, dangling a foot over the side, feeling for anything, but there was nothing. My feet tingled as I wavered. Then I lurched back before losing my balance.

Hiisi's hushed voice penetrated the darkness. "Why you no follow?"

"Where are you? How did you get down there?"

"Bridge. Walk on bridge."

"What bridge?" And why was there a need for one? Were we up in the sky? Was there a pit below us—filled with those alligator things?

Even from this distance, I could hear Hiisi's frustrated sigh. "Trust. You will see."

We hadn't even left the witch's grounds, and already I was failing to trust—again?

God, I can't see anything. How am I supposed to get out of here?

Step out in faith.

I sucked in a breath. Tingles raced throughout my body. That was God. No doubt about it.

The thrill didn't subside as I neared the edge. The itching intensified. My heart raced. God told me to step out in faith. So I must.

I stared into the blackness. What if I stepped in the wrong spot? What if the bridge wasn't beneath me *here*. What if I needed to step more to the right or to the left? What if one misstep sent me careening over the edge, plummeting to my death or into the jaws of those winged gators?

This would not end well for me.

My heart rate and itching reached agonizing levels.

Okay, Colleen. Stop trying to control everything. You're not in control. You never were. And how would it be a step of faith if you could see where you were going, assured of safety? Time to put your faith in action. Trust God. He wouldn't lead you wrong. Take a step. Go on, do it. Step out in faith. Prove you trust God.

I took a deep breath, everything within me prickling, warning me not to do this foolish thing. I raised my leg and allowed it to drop.

THIRTY

My foot landed on something solid. As it shook beneath me, I nearly lost my balance, but it held. My breath escaped in a whoosh, and my heart rate took time to realize I hadn't fallen as every part of my being had expected. My muscles relaxed, and the intense itch subsided. I couldn't see the entire bridge, but I saw where I stepped and the next board. I moved to it. With each step forward, the board appeared until I came to a grassy area where Hiisi hopped from one foot to the other, almost clapping, keeping his hands from connecting, probably so as not to make noise, with his wide mouth smile.

"Good, good, good. You do good," he spoke in a hushed voice. "Now we leave."

"Do you know the way out?"

He gave me his sideways look. "No, no, no. Me follow you."

"Follow me? But I don't know the way."

"God show you."

Hiisi wasn't going to keep leading me? The elated feeling filling me died, and I deflated. "But how?"

"King's Road. Only elf see King's Road to leave Rotko."

"But I can't leave yet. I have to find my friends."

"Trust God. Follow King's Road."

"Where is it?"

"Hiisi no see. Only elf see."

Fake moonlight streaming behind the witch's lair revealed the hut was built on a branch jutting from a cliffside tree. I shuddered. If I'd jumped out of the window or fallen off the deck, I'd be dead. Why didn't she have a railing? To kill anyone who managed to get outside? There couldn't be a road in that direction. But this side of the hut was nothing but skeletal trees, fallen leaves, tangled grass, dirt patches, and jagged rocks. "I don't see a road. I'm not a full elf. What if only full elves can see the road?"

"You see door. You see bridge. You see road."

Creeping crabs, was my faith already waning? God just led me across a bridge I couldn't see. Why didn't I continue to trust Him? Why was it so easy to forget God and revert to seeking answers anywhere else—within mere seconds? So infuriating. Why He bothered with us at all, I'd never know. Not if everyone was as slow-witted as me.

God, give me faith like Hiisi's. Help me find my friends and get out of this place.

Something sparked just off the cliff. Please, no. Not that way. I moved to inspect it, slowing as I neared. A white rock, glowing in the night. I stepped on it and another rock lit.

Hiisi hyperventilated behind me. "Good, good, good. You find King's Road."

Each rock varied in size but was at least the size of my foot. The moment I stepped on one, the next stone lit. Hiisi hopped from rock to rock behind me. After he left his spot, the light dimmed until we appeared to stand in the middle of the cliff, unable to see the path ahead or behind, so going back wasn't an option. As we descended the cliff, some footholds had big spaces between them. I felt for anything to hold, but encountered nothing but solid rock or crumbling dirt.

Our descent seemed to take hours. If only I had a timepiece to know for certain. The unnatural moon remained in its spot, offering no clues as to the elapsed time. But the ground finally leveled. I still took care to step on the glowing rocks only for they appeared to be surrounded by blackness. Still water perhaps? I didn't want to find out. I focused on each rock as it presented itself.

"If you can't see the stones for yourself, how did you know they were here? How did you know of the King's Road?" I hopped to the next landing.

"Hiisi no need road. Hiisi guide elves. Elves need road."

"Do Hiisi live anywhere else? Or just in Rotko."

"Me know only Rotko."

"Are there any others here besides you?"

"Me only Hiisi left."

"Did Noita kill them?"

Hiisi blew out a breath, and I took that to mean that she had. Poor Hiisi. Lost all his family. But I'd thought I was the only elf left, only to find more under Noita's spell. Perhaps Hiisi wasn't the only one of his kind left either. Just how much did he know about the witch? She sold the curse to my father in exchange for his soul. Was she responsible for the rumors that he'd killed all the elves too?

"Do you know how the elves died?"

"Hiisi know nothing outside Rotko."

"My father made a deal with her here. She sold him a curse."

"Hiisi know nothing."

I sighed. As much as I'd like answers, they wouldn't change anything. And they wouldn't bring my father back. After everything he'd done, there was no restoring his reputation anyway. I might as well let it go. For now, I had to keep following these rocks and hope they led me to my friends and helped us escape Rotko. I wouldn't leave without them. But then, was that just me taking control again? Failing to trust God? What if it was God's plan for me to leave them behind? God loved them as much as He loved me, right? If I was to trust God fully, then I'd have to go wherever He led and trust that He watched over my friends too.

God, help me do as You ask and trust You with everything... even my friends. Even Sakki. I blew out a breath. That one was especially hard. *But I hope You'll lead me to them so we can all leave together.*

As much as I wanted to trust God, what would I do if I found myself at the end of the Divide, able to leave, without my dragon and the others?

But then, God told Sakki we couldn't leave without killing the witch. Unless, that message was meant for Sakki, not me. Only the end of this path would tell.

Hiisi and I carried on, stepping on rocks one at a time, and I wished we'd had more food. Traveling like this was exhausting and making me hungry. I kept a wary eye out for the witch. Perhaps we'd left at the right moment to slip away unnoticed. But who knew what she'd do when she returned to find me gone. Would she search for me? I was on a faith journey now, following God's lead. I had to trust He'd protect me from the witch and provide food. I just hoped my definition of need was the same as His. Judging by the lack of food and the ever-lighting rocks before me, God didn't think I needed food like I did.

So we continued on, across whatever still waters appeared like blackness surrounding the stepping stones, through a muddy bog to a dry wasteland where we kicked up dust from dirt-covered stones. My lips were cracked. Forget food, I needed water. My tongue scraped the roof of my mouth like sandpaper.

The fake moon was no longer visible. Light extinguished the dark in unnatural increments as I hopped from rock to rock. Not because the sun had risen but because this desert was lit with a fake sunlight and no sun. Just a hot, reddish-colored sky.

How much time had passed?

I should've taken one of my father's timepieces.

God, where are we going? How long must we travel? Are You leading us out of Rotko or to Sakki and the others? Are they all right?

God didn't seem to have any interest in answering my questions. But I'd never experienced such thirst. This dry heat made it so much worse. I glanced back at Hiisi leaping across the stones, long arms swinging to increase momentum, solid feet slapping as he landed. His mouth hung open, and his forked tongue lolled to one side. Was he panting? Was it my imagination, or did his leathery skin have cracks running through it?

Okay, God. If not for me, for Hiisi. He needs a break. We need water. Please?

I was about to step on the next rock, but it wasn't there. I lurched forward, teetering in my spot as I righted myself. Hiisi jumped into me, sending me tottering again.

"Why you no move?" He peered around my legs. "Where next stone?"

Several stones peeked out from the sand, but none were lit. Which one was part of King's Road? It couldn't end here, could it?

"Where do we go now, God?" I yelled at the sky.

"Shhh!" Hiisi held a finger to his cracked lips.

A flock of blackbirds squabbled, flitting about overhead. Were they in the witch's service? I shouldn't have shouted and given us away. One of the birds flew straight at us. I ducked, protecting my head with my arms, ready for the attack. But it didn't come. The bird landed on the dirt and began pecking away at a rock. Hiisi and I shared a shocked glance, then returned our attention to the bird's strange behavior. After several strikes, water bubbled up from the rock.

We drew in sharp breaths at the miracle unfolding. The bird flew off, but a pool rippled within the rock that had been flat and dry. Hiisi squeezed past me and dragged water through his cupped hand. Most of the water filtered through his spindly fingers. So he used both hands to minimize leakage, slipping them between his fangs to slurp up the water.

He dragged more and more water. The supply never seemed to deplete. After he'd drank his fill, he sighed, face to the sky. His skin no longer cracked.

I cupped my hand to draw out water from the pool. It tasted so good. I could almost feel my dry skin plump up with moisture as I drank. My tongue no longer scraped my mouth, and the splits in my lip healed. This was no ordinary water. If only I had something to carry more. But as the thought hit me, the stone seemed to suck up what remained, leaving nothing but dry rock.

I guess that means we've had enough water, huh, God? What now? No more stones are lit.

With that, the squabbling birds returned. Three swooped down. Two plopped something at our feet. The other jabbed its beak into the dirt. As they returned to the sky, something poked through the dirt from the hole the bird had made. A sprout. It dropped its husk, and the first leaves unfolded. Then it continued to grow. More leaves emerged, and the stem thickened, sending off new shoots with more leaves until a tree with a leafy canopy shaded us.

I stared at Hiisi, my jaw hung as slack as his. Then I remembered the other birds had left something too. I stooped to pick it up. A cluster of some strange-looking thing. Fruit? It looked like a flower with thick petals and fat seeds within.

"What is it?" I asked.

"Outo." Drool dribbled from Hiisi's lip. He swiped at it with his forked tongue as he plucked one of the seed things into his mouth. "Outo taste good. Try." He scraped more seeds into his mouth.

I picked up the fruits before me and followed his example. The plump black seed tasted like nothing itself, but the moment I bit into it, a burst of juicy sweetness coated my tongue. "Oh, this is good." I plucked more seeds and shoved a bunch in my mouth. Several at once was even better. Once the juice was gone, I chewed the fleshy part. They tasted like apple.

"If fruit no open, no eat. Poison." Juice ran down his jaw, he swiped at it with the back of his hand before it slid to his neck.

I chewed, pressing down the thick flower petals to conceal the seeds to form a ball. "So, it opens on its own when it's ready to eat, but before that, it's poisonous?"

Hiisi nodded as he slurped more fruit.

We ate our fill and discarded the peels. They sank in the sand surrounding our stone seats. I sucked in a breath. "Could we sink in that sand?"

He shrugged.

"I'm glad we stayed on the stones."

"Stones sucked water."

Good point. God had made that happen. He probably disposed of the peels too. I had to stop worrying about everything and start trusting more.

"No leave King's Road." As he spoke, a new rock lit up.

"I guess it's time to be on our way again." What would we face next?

THIRTY-ONE

The sands and dry air didn't bother me as they had. Although refreshed and energized, after seeing the sand swallow our fruit peels, though I knew it was probably God and I had nothing to fear, I was afraid of slipping off the rocks. "Hiisi, when you said not to leave King's Road, did you mean something bad could happen if I left the rock for even a second?"

Hiisi shrugged. "Stay on road. No find out."

That didn't make me feel better. But I had to trust God. He made the way clear. He'd help me stay the course.

Thank You for feeding us, God. And giving us water.

Colleen is speaking to God, trusting God? That gleeful voice with a sarcastic edge in my head was *not* God, and yet I was just as thrilled to hear it.

"Sakki!" I didn't see anyone in the desert. *Where are you?*

Sakki and friends will come to Colleen.

"Nay!" I didn't want them risking getting sucked under by this unholy sand, and I couldn't leave King's Road. Not even to look for them. *Can you fly?*

Hiisi craned around me. "Is someone here?"

I held up a finger for him to wait.

No, Sakki already told Colleen. If Sakki switches into dragon form, Witch will know. Sakki will not risk Witch finding Colleen.

I groaned. *God, what should I do?*

Colleen is talking to God and following God too? Sakki's dragony laugh came through our connection.

Even though he couldn't see me, I rolled my eyes. *I'm glad you find this so amusing.*

Sakki is amused... and happy.

"My friends are somewhere nearby," I told Hiisi. Eager to reconnect with them, I raced along the King's Road as fast as the stones would light up. I nearly slipped, righted myself, then continued at my fast pace.

"Why you hurry?" Hiisi huffed, losing his breath. "No go fast."

My fear of falling made me slow, but my equally motivating fear of missing my friends spurred me on. Mountains loomed ahead. With the rocky slope in my sights, I moved as quickly as I dared. Once we landed the mountain ledge, the King's Road seemed to stop. Nothing lit up.

"Is this the end of the road?"

"No, no, no." Hiisi shook his head, looking disgusted. "King's Road leave Rotko. We still in Rotko."

Sakki, can you still hear me?

Sakki is here. Colleen sounds closer. Keep talking to Sakki. Sakki will lead friends to Colleen.

Why was it I had no trouble with words until someone wanted me to speak? Then I had nothing to say. *Uh, where are you?*

Good, Colleen sounds closer. Even in his mind, he seemed breathless. He must be moving quickly. *Sakki and friends are on a mountain.*

We just reached a mountain, I said.

Sakki sees Colleen! He sounded so close. But where was he?

Up ahead, Sakki's dog body peered over a ledge. I wanted to run to him, but I couldn't leave the King's Road.

Come to Sakki.

I can't!

Why not?

I'm on the King's Road. God is leading us out of Rotko.

Where? Sakki doesn't see a road.

It's not lit up now, but I can't move until it does.

But Colleen must. Sakki passed a piece of Noita's soul. Friends must go back.

I'd forgotten about that. But that was what we thought before we knew about the King's Road. Now that God was showing me the way, maybe we could just leave. The sinking sands were gone from around my feet. We stood on solid rock. But I still didn't dare move until the next step was made clear.

God, what are we supposed to do? Should I stay here until You light up the next step? Are You done showing me the way? Should we try to find Noita's soul and release it?

I waited, listening. But I heard nothing from God or Sakki. And no part of any path made itself clear.

Sakki's heavy sigh rang in my head. *Sakki and friends will come to Colleen.*

He disappeared over the ledge, then appeared off to the right, climbing down a path with the others behind him. They sent pebbles pinging off the cliff as they made their painstaking way toward us. I felt awkward standing there, failing to meet them partway.

He bounded at me, turning to a cat and leaping into my arms. I snuggled his warm body and felt like a missing piece of me had returned. I felt whole again. Liam, Ruuta, and Rhys jostled into a group hug while Hadwin and Samu waited on the outskirts.

"These you friend?" Hiisi asked.

We peeled apart. Sakki dropped to the ground, returning to his preferred travel form, a dog. I introduced everyone to my new little friend. "He helped me escape the witch's lair. We're following the King's Road." I gestured to the dark stone surrounding me. "Well, we were."

Ruuta rammed her hands to her hips. "Are you all in on some little joke? Why are you pretending to see her invisible friend?"

Liam's thick eyebrows, thicker in his wolf form, mashed together as he thrust an arm out to Hiisi. "What are you playing at? You don't see him?"

She bent toward Hiisi and swung an arm, just missing him. "There's nothing there."

I was about to express my confusion when it became clear. "You can't see him because you don't have eyes to see. Isn't that right, Hiisi?"

Hiisi nodded emphatically with his open-mouthed smile. "You see. Friends see. This one"—he pointed to her—"no see."

How could Liam see him? Or Rhys? Everyone else made sense. I gave a quick explanation everyone seemed to grasp, except Ruuta who looked perturbed. Then I described the King's Road. But there was still no evidence of its existence. "So now I don't know what to do."

"We wait for King Road." Hiisi sat with a thud, crossed his long arms, and pressed his lips into a thin line like a petulant child refusing to eat his vegetables.

If Colleen doesn't destroy the witch, how will Colleen return to Talamh Sí?

I relayed Sakki's message to Hiisi.

Hiisi leaped to his feet. "Same way. King Road!" He unraveled his arms and flailed them about.

Sakki huffed, sending a puff of smoke at him. *Colleen must end the witch. God said so.*

I should stop translating to end this debate, but neither one had steered me wrong so far. Both were attuned to God.

Liam raised a hand. "Hang tight. The only reason we entered this dump was to seek Queen Rhiannon's help. Then we're to return to Talamh Sí so Colleen can become queen and the Divide will fall, right?"

"Yes!" Ruuta spoke, her wide eyes showing her frustration that it took so long to grasp this simple concept and her relief that it had sunk in.

"To be sure. To be sure," Rhys said.

She eyed me, waiting for me to agree.

But did I? That was the original plan. But was I certain I should be queen? All I wanted right then was to get out of the Divide, away from the witch, to some place safe. Then again, after the promises I'd made, didn't I have to try to undo some of the damage my father had caused... that *I* had caused?

"Colleen?" Ruuta demanded an answer. At my hesitant nod, she scanned my face, then quirked her lips, satisfied.

"Okay." Liam now held up both his hands. "So the question is do we destroy this place now by killing the witch or do it later by following the King's Road, *if* it reappears."

Hadwin brought a finger to his lips. "Shhh!"

Samu pressed a palm downward like a foot pumping a brake.

The locals held our attention for a second. Then Ruuta returned to the conversation. "Thank you for spelling it out for us." She tucked a tuft of gray hairs behind her thick ear.

Liam dragged his unimpressed gaze away from her. Giving Hadwin and Samu a sidelong glance, he spoke in a hushed voice. "We should bring it down now." He moved both hands in a weighing motion as silence ensued. "Think about it. What guarantee is there we'll get through on the way back?"

"Human logic is all well and good." Ruuta's lips snaggled up. Clearly, she didn't think so. "But what of the prophecy that Colleen will bring down the Divide by claiming the throne?"

"By all means, ignore us. Don't worry about the witch," Hadwin interjected.

"Prophecy is the prophetic word of God, right? Where does this prophecy come from?" Keeping my foot on the stone, I turned to Rhys, Mr. Encyclopedia.

He hopped back. "Don't look at me. The prophecy comes from the fae."

"The fae believe in God?" I asked.

"Not to my knowledge." He shook his black hair, then every strand fell back into its exact spot.

Ruuta straightened her spine and looked down her nose at me. "We believe in Zorac. He gave us the prophecy."

"Zorac?" Was that another name for God? Nay, Ruuta claimed I was a descendant. "Who is he?"

Her haggish face lit up, even in this place. "Zorac is an angel."

"An angel?" Several of us spoke in unison.

I rubbed my temple, fighting the oncoming headache. "How can I be a descendant of an angel?"

"You're not." Rhys's hair swung again. "The angels who were banished from heaven are demons. The fae were created when elves mated with fallen angels... demons. You're a descendant of a demon."

Thirty-Two

"A demon?" If words were capable of causing physical pain, those were it. Clutching my stomach, I staggered back. Then realized I'd probably stepped off the King's Road and scrambled to my spot. "I'm a demon?"

Hiisi's mouth dropped, and he dragged his spindly fingers down his face, pulling his eyes into a ghastly look.

"Technically, all the fae are demon's offspring," Rhys said unhelpfully.

"We're not demons!" Ruuta's personality was matching her appearance, but she tried to collect herself. "And not all fae are descendants of Zorac."

Rhys held up a finger. "I didn't say you were demons. I said you are the *offspring* of demons, to be sure."

"Zorac is no demon." Ruuta sneered at Rhys, giving me pause. "Zorac and several other angels came to earth. He is their leader. There is no one greater."

My intestines twisted and kinked like a heap of tangled necklaces. I wanted to vomit her words to keep them from settling in and becoming true. "You believe Zorac is like God?"

Hiisi's gripped his head and stared, slack-jawed.

"No." She wrinkled her hag expression at the lunacy of such a statement. "But he is immortal—the highest angel. He watches over us—protects us."

After clamping his mouth closed so hard his fangs might've pierced his skin, Hiisi paced with dramatic headshakes and arm swings, muttering all the while.

Good thing Ruuta couldn't see him. She was already growing angry. His antics at her reply might've sent her into a rage.

"Does that make him God?" Her wonder seemed genuine.

"Nay! It doesn't! And if he's a fallen angel, he's *not* protecting you." I couldn't be hearing this. It was one thing not to believe in God, but quite another to replace Him with a demon. "What about Queen Rhiannon?"

"She is our queen." Ruuta's expression flickered. "She serves Zorac, if that's what you're after. We all do."

"I'll be hanged! We're seeking help from a bunch of Satan worshipers?" Liam scrubbed his wolfy jaw.

Ruuta's haggish face snapped to Liam. "Who is Satan?"

"A fallen angel—" I began.

"A demon. Like your Zorac." Liam huffed.

I warned him with my eyes before continuing. "He was God's second-in-command. He fell from heaven and brought a third of the angels with him."

"Yeah, and he aims to destroy humanity," Liam interrupted again.

I locked my hands to my hips and spun to him. "How do you know all this? You sound like you believe in God."

"My mad uncle spouted off a thing or two about it. I thought he was insane, but..." He waved both hands before his face, palms out. "You shouldn't worship that thing or serve him in any way."

I plopped onto my butt, landing on the hard rock, wanting to purge this from my mind. I'd allowed her into my home. I'd followed her... *trusted* her. And all this time she served a *demon?*

God, what do I do? I'm a demon's spawn? Is that why all those terrible things happened to me... why they're happening now? I deserve this? Am I unintentionally serving a demon?

Sakki's cat form climbed onto my body. *No! Colleen was trusting God. Do not let errant thoughts make Colleen fall away. Colleen must trust.*

"I'm demon spawn." The words escaping my mouth didn't feel like my own.

Hiisi sat beside me and patted my leg. "You no demon. You trust God. Remember? You see."

His words sounded far away, and I couldn't feel him or Sakki. I felt even further away from myself. Present, yet not.

Ruuta's voice warbled through the haze. "Zorac said that when his descendants laid claim to the throne in both kingdoms, the Divide would fall. The only descendants that remain now are Queen Rhiannon and you. Obviously, Queen Rhiannon cannot occupy both thrones."

I covered my ears, not caring how childish it appeared. It didn't matter. All that mattered was shutting out her words. Her lies. How had I so blindly followed someone who served a demon? To travel to a queen who serves a demon?

Colleen was not following Ruuta, but God. God said to cross Divide to Queen Rhiannon.

How did he keep reading my mind?

Colleen is emotional. Projecting thoughts.

"I don't understand what I'm supposed to do," I whined. "Am I supposed to take down the Divide? What does Zorac plan to do if it falls?"

Ruuta shrugged. "That's none of my concern. My only concern is in ensuring that happens."

"I thought your only job was being my friend. Isn't that what you said?" As I spat the words at her, an unfamiliar anger seared my heart. I thought she was my friend. As I thought Taneli was my friend before he tried to kill me to keep me from becoming a queen. But Ruuta worked for the opposite side and sought to ensure I became queen. I couldn't trust either side. Should I tell her to leave us now? *God, I beg You, please tell me what to do!*

Sakki's voice infiltrated my prayer. *Colleen shouldn't trust Ruuta.*

But, Sakki, how well are you hearing from God in this place? You're suggesting the same thing she is—to take down the Divide. After listening to her, I think we should do the opposite. We should wait for the King's Road.

He chuffed a smoky breath. *Sakki doesn't hear God well now. But Sakki doesn't forget like Colleen. God told Colleen to go to Rhiannon. Maybe not for the same reason Ruuta wants to go to Rhiannon. But go to Rhiannon Colleen must. God also told Sakki that Colleen must kill the witch. Liam killed krokotiili and released a piece of the witch's soul. When the witch's soul left krokotiili, Sakki felt a rift. God's presence strengthened. Witch's power lessened. Sometimes what people want and what God wants aligns, but not for the same purpose. Sakki and friends must kill Noita the Witch. If Colleen should be queen is a question for another day.*

I heaved a heavy sigh as I weighed his arguments.

"Since we're throwing caution asunder..."

My gaze floated to the unfamiliar voice. Then I remembered Hadwin and Samu were among us. Samu had stepped forward.

"...by having these sensitive conversations in the open. Please allow me to interject." He motioned between Hadwin and himself. "We've been here for nearly twenty years, and we've learned a thing or two. What's happening right now, while understandable, is of the witch's design. Her goal is to keep you fearful and divide you. And it's working. You each have your beliefs and goals. You're fearful of those who seem to oppose you. So, rather than argue about the many things we disagree on, we must focus on where we agree. And we all agree we must leave this place. Am I correct?"

I felt more connected to my body with each nod.

"Then let's focus on that—our unified goal. How do you propose we leave?"

"What did you say before?" I squeezed my eyes shut to help me focus. "God put you here as a guide?"

Hiisi pressed a splayed hand over his chest. "Me or all hiisi?"

"For all hiisi. You're here for God, right?"

He hopped back and forth from one foot to the other. "Yes! Hiisi guide. Lead elf out."

"But Sakki also hears from God. He says we must stay and kill the witch." How was I supposed to know what to do when the two who listened to God disagreed?

"Is it possible"—Liam reached out to me to help me stand—"they're both right?"

Once I wobbled to my feet, he crouched to Hiisi. "We can kill the witch. *Then* you can lead us out?"

Hiisi frowned and shrugged on one side, making it appear as if half his lip and one shoulder were being sewn together by an invisible string. "Hiisi no know. Hiisi no more. Only me left."

I tapped my boot on the last stone that lit up and glanced around my feet, still holding out hope something would show us the way before we made the wrong move. *God, please give us wisdom to make the right choice. Show us the way.*

When nothing happened, I touched Sakki's furry head and spoke aloud for everyone's benefit. "You're certain we must kill the witch before leaving the Divide?"

With a puff of smoke, Sakki gave his dog head a firm nod, bumping my palm.

If I trusted anyone, it was my dragon. "Then that's what we do. Rhys, lead us to the next piece of Noita's soul."

"We passed one on our way to you." He waved back the way they'd come and up the incline as if using antennae to hunt his prey. "It's still there, to be sure."

Ruuta fell in line behind him. Sakki and Hiisi appraised one another. My two most trusted advisors, outside of God Himself, sizing each other up. Sakki bowed low, offering Hiisi a ride.

Hiisi splayed a spindly hand over his chest, dipped his head in respect, then climbed aboard. He gripped Sakki's hackles in two fisted tufts, and his body swayed as Sakki sauntered off.

Liam sidled up to me. He nodded to Ruuta like he expected her to go into full demon mode and attack. "We need to get rid of her."

And just when he'd been warming up to her. I huffed as I climbed the steep slope. "I don't trust her either. But... I don't know. She's here for a reason. And at least we see her for what she is now. Who knows? Maybe we can help her."

Liam blew out a frustrated breath. "What if she turns on you?"

"If she believes everything she said, she'd never turn on me."

He looked at me as if he thought I'd lost all mental capacity. Then he softened. "I don't like it. We should be following God, not some demon worshiper."

"I'm not—" No need to defend myself. But I did need to find out what was going on with him. "When did you become a believer?"

"Am I?" He raked a hand through his black hair, gripping it before letting go, leaving it disheveled... befitting a wolf. But I could almost see his true self. His ocean eyes hadn't changed. They shone with intensity, yet something about them made me melt under their stare.

"I've been remembering things...."

He was going to need some help pulling this out. "What kind of things?"

"My uncle. He used to tell me about God and His Son. One day, before I turned thirteen, he brought me to an underground church service. Afterward, he begged me not to atone. He didn't say, but he knew it was a curse. My parents found out and lost their minds. I never saw him again." His voice thickened, and he tensed his jaw. "Wherever he is, I'm betting his memories were erased."

I touched his arm. The life force within him roared to my hand, and I let go as if it had stung me. I'd forgotten about what happened when we touched. What did it mean?

"He was right." His musings pulled me from my thoughts. "About all of it."

Whatever I felt at our contact, he must not notice it. And how could I be thinking about that when he was on the verge of a breakthrough? That mattered more... much more. "So, you believe him? You believe in God?"

"When that reptile released Noita's spirit, something happened." Liam massaged the back of his neck as he tended to do. I easily imagined I was seeing his true self, dark hair spilling into his oceanic eyes. "I think... I think God's been there all along. From the beginning. Working on me, showing me little miracles... one after another. Then, when I thought we'd lost you forever, I begged Him to bring you back to us. He did."

We reached the ledge where I'd spotted Sakki, and I paused to catch my breath. But we were falling away from the others. We hurried to catch up.

"Do you believe what your uncle told you about God's Son? That He's your Savior? Do you believe in Him enough to follow Him?"

He gripped my shoulder, sending my energy whirring. "I think—no, I *know*—I do."

Then I felt something. A tear in the atmosphere. Clouds of light rippled overhead, then dissipated.

Sakki lurched, nearly spilling Hiisi. *Did Colleen feel that?*

I did. I turned to Liam and gasped.

"What?" He stopped, pulling me to stop too.

"You—You're—" I couldn't believe what I was seeing. "You're *you*. No more wolf. Though you do have a shaggy beard growing in."

Hiisi danced on Sakki's back. "You *see*."

"Does anyone else see? Liam's no longer a wolf?"

I've always seen, Sakki said.

Ruuta shook her hag head, looking bored. "He still looks like a wolf to me."

"And you're still a hag," he retorted.

"You mean she *looks* like a hag," I corrected.

"Think whatever you want." Liam shrugged. "Sadly, you still look like a reptile."

"You no see." Hiisi shook his head at Liam with sad eyes, then beamed at me. "*You* see!"

"Hopefully, soon, you'll both see." Samu smiled over his shoulder at us.

I laughed, and unexpected tears of joy escaped. Liam was a believer, and the witch's curse was losing its hold on me. "Welcome to the family, brother."

"Brother?" His newly bearded face looked alarmed. "I'm your brother now?"

My face warmed. "Only in spirit. We're all God's children now."

"Okay." His expression relaxed as the others walked away. After waiting a beat to give them distance, he followed, playing with his scruff. "What do you think of the beard?"

"I don't know..." I tilted my head and squinted. "It kind of looks good on you."

He studied me, then seemed to decide that my response was acceptable. "Good."

What was that about? Did he have feelings for me? Something stirred within, excited bubbles swirling from my stomach to my heart.

THIRTY-THREE

We walked through rocky terrain to another steep slope. My calves and thighs were angry with me for exerting them so. "How much further?"

"It's close," Rhys said. "I can feel—"

A giant rodent-looking thing leaped from the ledge above, landing on Rhys. Its buckteeth gnashed close to Rhys's strained face. He tried to fight the thing off as drool dripped far too close to his mouth. Liam aimed his rifle. A blast rang out, echoing off the rock wall. Blood sprayed from the thing's head, and it fell limp, suffocating Rhys. We all ran to push the beast off him. As the thing rolled, pink feet twitching while the life left its eyes, Rhys remained frozen, drenched in blood and drool, petrified.

Liam helped him to his feet, and the silvery thing I'd seen return to the witch before now left the ratlike carcass. It floated away, presumably toward its rightful host.

"What was that?" Shivers coursed over me.

"J–j–jyrsijä," Rhys stammered.

"Are there any more?" Ruuta tipped her head back, surveying the ledge above.

Rhys covered his hand with his sleeve to swipe at the rodent's drool, grimacing all the while. "If there are, they don't have part of Ruuta's soul. I don't sense any more nearby."

"Where's Hiisi?" I pivoted. Ah, there. Peering around a boulder, trembling. I ran to him. "Are you okay?"

He stepped out. "Me no fight. Me guide."

"That's okay." I stroked his leathery back. "We'll protect you."

Liam reached out to Hiisi. "Would you like to ride on my shoulders?"

After getting my confident nod, Hiisi accepted Liam's proffered hand and let Liam swing him up onto his shoulders.

"Where now?"

At Liam's question, Rhys squinted, spinning, studying the air for who knew what. Then he pointed east of where we'd come. "That way."

As we all set off, I fell into step with him. "Do you have any idea what kind of creature is hosting her soul?"

"No, I only sense a piece of her soul. But the remaining pieces seem to get stronger as more are returned."

"I saw her soul return to her."

"You did?" He stopped.

"Aye. She disappeared seconds later. I'm sure she was looking for you. Did she find you?"

He rubbed his forehead. "She doesn't know where the creature is after it's lost its soul. She only knows the general area."

"But she knows what we're doing now, right?" Liam asked. "Won't she protect the creatures with her soul?"

"We'll need to be on guard." Samu sidled up beside us. "She could use the other containers as a trap."

Hiisi whimpered like a sad pup.

"Probably." Rhys gulped. "Nothing's changed. We still must proceed with caution."

"Right." Hadwin mumbled under his breath. "'Cause you've all been so cautious up till now."

Samu gave Hadwin an approving chuckle.

We descended the cliffs in silence. At least going down was easier. And my surroundings didn't look as dire as they had upon first entering this place. Did that have something to do with Noita's soul returning to her? Maybe we were diminishing the curse. Or maybe her magic wasn't working as it had on me. I was starting to see this place for what it was.

Thunder roaring from the cliffs above broke me from my thoughts. The ground shook. We gaped at one another.

"Stampede!" Rhys shouted.

Everything seemed to slow as I ran. My feet struggled to keep up with my racing heart. Blood rushed in my ears, dulling the roar at my back. Sakki and I matched speed ahead of the group. But what was that up ahead? A ledge? I skidded to a stop, sending pebbles raining. Arms windmilling, I teetered, the rocky surface cubits below.

Sakki jumped. My heart pounded as he dropped. He landed safely.

Liam caught up. Eyes wild, he looked below, then to the rest of us. "Jump!"

Hiisi's mouth stretched into the widest grimace possible as he clung to Liam's head careening over the edge.

It wasn't that far. It might hurt, but not more than the stampede. I sucked in a breath and jumped. A shock jolted from my feet up my legs, but I stuck the landing. I flattened myself against the vibrating rock wall between Liam and Sakki. Debris clattered on my head as the others jumped, then claimed their place among us against the wall as crashing feet roared. Creatures thundered overhead, landing on the ground before us, then continuing without pause. I cowered, covering my head in my arms to protect myself. I peeked through the gap in my arms at the rush of giant rodents like the one we'd killed.

The vibrating wall at my back slowed with the beasts. We remained crouched as one. Then two more, slower beasts raced to catch up with their mischief.

Liam dared emerge first. He backed away from the wall to peer over the edge. "I think we're safe."

"I don't think we are." Rhys dusted the dirt from his sleeves and pant legs. "Though there was an entire herd of jyrsijä, the one with Noita's soul attacked me. She must've activated it to seek me out and kill me. Since I can sense them, they can sense me too."

"Why doesn't the witch come after you directly?" I asked, not that I wanted *that* to happen.

"She's searching for me. To be sure. The more of her soul is returned, the easier it will be for her to find me. And if that jyrsijä found me, she's not far behind."

I searched, almost expecting to see her standing among us. "We should move, then."

We continued following Rhys at a more hurried pace.

"What will we do if she finds us?" I asked. "We have no weapons against her."

"I do." Liam tapped the gun across his back, sticking out from his other shoulder, then the pistol at his side. Hiisi eyed the rifle and made a strange hissing sound. Was he shaking his head at me?

"She can't be killed." Hadwin reminded us. "We've tried everything, including bullets."

"And I feel like my abilities are returning," Ruuta said. "I may not be able to compel anyone just yet, but perhaps with a few more souls?"

I felt different too, but I couldn't manipulate the air to gather it around myself or anyone else. Not yet.

"And we've got Sakki," Rhys said. "He may not be able to shift into a dragon now lest the witch find us sooner, but once she has, there will be no reason for him to hold back."

Something in all this didn't feel right. The witch was evil. Her reign needed to end. But I hated all this killing. So far, the creatures had attacked. At least the rodent was killed in self-defense. But what happened when we neared the end? Were they all heinous creatures?

Or were some of them like Rhys? And what would we do when Rhys was the only one left?

WE DESCENDED the mountain back down to a desert. Still, there was no sun, yet the air was sweltering. Sweat dampened the hair by my temples in a wasted effort to cool me down. Everything else was dry. Bone dry.

Light shimmered across seemingly endless dunes of reddish sand. What if this sand swallowed us up like the fruit peels? "I'm not walking across that."

Rhys pointed ahead. "But I sense a piece of Noita's soul this way, and we must keep moving." He took tentative steps onto the sand, paused, then walked further out. "It's safe."

"Do you know that because you've been here before?" I asked. "Or are you assuming because nothing bad has happened... yet."

Rhys shrugged and continued walking.

"That wasn't an answer." I hesitated until the others followed. Then I went too.

Trudging through the sand made me sweat more. Each step seemed more laborious than the last.

"Why you say you no weapon?" Hiisi bounced along Liam's shoulder, frowning at me.

His question startled me. Liam had guns. Hiisi knew that now. Then I realized what he was asking. "Because we have nothing that can kill the witch."

"Ha! Ha! Ha!" Hiisi nearly slipped from Liam. He scrambled to readjust his grip, watching the barrel of the rifle warily.

"Are you laughing at me?" I raised my palms and screwed up my face. Now I was getting annoyed.

"God. God you weapon. Why you forget?"

He was right. God was our weapon. And hadn't I read that, if God was for us, no one could stand against us? Nothing was more powerful than God. Was my faith so small? My trust so lacking? "Should I have stayed and waited for the King's Road?"

Hiisi scratched his temple. "God help Colleen, mistake or no... *if* Colleen trust."

The ground shook beneath us. I splayed my arms to steady myself. Something rippled under the sand. Something big, like a train cutting a curvy path beneath the surface. The sands settled back in place behind it as it passed. It headed straight for us, faster and faster, then burst through the sands. An enormous worm-looking thing leaped into the air, aimed straight for me with an open, toothless mouth. I pushed Liam out of the way and the beast swallowed me whole.

THIRTY-FOUR

I woke to a horrendous odor burning my nose. What was that? Like sewage tossed in a barrel of acid. And why was it so dark? I tried blinking. Was I even opening my eyes? Why couldn't I see? I tried to sit up and slipped. Everything was slimy. The soft surface... me.

I clutched my stomach. *I'm going to vomit.*

Breathe, Colleen. Just breathe.

Light in. Dark out.

Light in. Dark out.

Great is Thy faithfulness.

Where was I? What happened? That giant wormy thing. Was I in its stomach? Is that what that stench was? Was I close to some other undigested food? A sensation of maggots wriggling their way in and around my body made me want to jump up, scratch off the offending sludge. Vomit them. But I didn't dare move. What was around me? What might I touch?

Another wave of nausea swept over me.

I'm going to freak out. I'm going to freak out. How can I not freak out?

Light in. Dark out.

Light in. Dark out.

I couldn't calm my breathing. The rapid breaths worsened.

Oh God, get me out of here! Kill me if You must. Just get. Me. Out!

Light in. Dark out.

Light in. Dark out.

My rapid breaths continued.

I'm going to pass out. I'm going to pass out.

A dim light ignited. A lantern? What was that face?

I choked on my breath. "Hiisi?"

He gave me a solemn nod. No big smile.

"But how? I pushed you and Liam away." I glanced around me at the squishy insides, and another wave of nausea nearly made me faint. Only Hiisi's inexplicable presence grounded me now.

"Me told you. Me guide. You trust small. Me help until you trust big."

"So you can just... *appear* wherever I am? And where'd you get that lantern?"

He smacked himself, gripping his face. His long fingers tapped the top of his head. Still resting his chin in his palm, he turned his hand away so I could see his face. "Me appear twice. Three times now."

"I thought you just happened to be there."

"No, no, no. God send me."

"So, God's still with me?" I choked on a sob.

He patted my hand. "He never leave you. Never."

When I sobbed, he kept rubbing my hand. "No time for tear. You and me must escape."

"How?" I tried to see him through blurry eyes.

Slipping on the mucky surface, he fought to stand and carry his lantern. He yanked the glass off the lantern and raised it to the squishy ceiling, running it along the surface.

"Are you looking for something?" I hugged my arms around myself, unable to stand and help him.

"No, no, no. Must irritate käärme."

The fleshy insides twitched, contracting and expanding, leaving less and less room with each contraction. Was I sliding?

He reached out to me. "Hold me hand. No move to käärme gizzard. You and me no food."

Was that what was happening? Was the worm digesting us? "Stop! You're making it worse!"

"You stop." He continued running the flame along the serpent's interior. "Trust."

I scrambled onto my knees, clinging to him, bending as the space grew smaller. "God, help us. God, help us. God, help us."

A gust of wind blasted us, extinguishing the light. Then a brutal force erupted from the opposite direction, firing at my back, pushing us along a slimy tunnel, spewing us from the serpent's mouth into the sand. The worm dove back into the ground and disappeared. The vibrations continued, leaving an echo of the sensation.

I tried to stand and brush myself off, but it was no use. The sand glued to my slimy body. Now I was wet and gritty all over. I spat sand from my mouth, but the more I tried to expel it, the more I found.

But I was alive. "Thank you for saving me, Hiisi."

"Thank God. God saved you."

"But He used you. You don't have to serve Him." Even as I spoke the words, a pang slammed my gut. I needed to remember to thank God. It wasn't wrong to thank Hiisi as long as I remembered God. *Thank You, God. Help me remember to thank You more. But thank You for Hiisi too.*

Hiisi remained silent. Did he know I'd gotten the message? Could he hear my communication with God like Sakki?

Sakki! I spun around, seeing nothing but sand in every direction. *Sakki!*

He didn't respond. We couldn't have gotten that far from each other—Could we?

"I have to get back to the others. Do you know where we are? How do we get back?"

His snakelike hissing sound whisked over me. Not a good sign. "Hiekka."

"Yay–gah? What's that?"

"Hiekka Desert. Confuse traveler."

"It's meant to confuse travelers? What, because nothing indicates where we are or in what direction we're going? Especially with no sun, just this odd light?"

He nodded. "All Rotko confuse traveler. Need King's Road."

So we were back to that again. I should have waited.

Nay, we made a decision, and I would stick by it. No one said destroying the witch would be easy. It was a so-called impossible task. But nothing was impossible with God. I wouldn't back down now. "You're a guide. Can you get me back to my friends?"

His stout body slumped. "No, no, no." He flung his long arms up in the air. "When you stop following *you*? Follow *God!*"

"Doesn't God want me to find my friends?"

He swung those arms into a dramatic shrug. "Yes? No? Me no know. No ask me! Ask God!"

I circled, noting the absolute lack of anything but sand. *God, where should we go?*

My question was met with absolute silence. No sound. Not even a cricket chirp. No wind. No ripples in the sand. Nothing.

Did I die? Did that creature eat me and spit out my soul into this wasteland? This sandy void. Was this hell?

I dropped into the sand. Let it eat me up. I didn't care.

Then I eyed it with suspicion. The thought of sinking soured my stomach and made me itch. Okay, maybe I cared. But why didn't God? A growl rose from within me. "What do You want me to do!"

More nothingness. Except for Hiisi. I hadn't noticed him sidled up to me, pressing against my leg.

I took a deep breath. At least I wasn't alone. *Thank You for Hiisi.*

What was that speck in the sky? "Do you see that?"

Hiisi stood and looked everywhere except at the speck.

"Up there." I pointed.

Could it be? *Sakki? Is that you?*

Colleen? Even in our mind-link, his voice sounded strained. *What are you doing in dragon form? The witch will find you. Run!* Witch already found Sakki. Colleen should run. Run now!

THIRTY-FIVE

My heart raced as I searched everywhere. There was nowhere to run. Nowhere to hide.

Hide!

Could I hide?

I grabbed Hiisi's shoulders. "Stay close."

God, please hide us! You gave me this ability. You're more powerful than the witch no matter where we are or what spells she's put on us. So, please. Hide us! I felt the air and pulled it around us like a cloak. It felt like it was working, but there was only one way to be sure—to stand still as the witch passed by and hope she didn't see us. But what about Sakki and the others? How would they escape the witch now that she was after them? Sakki's shape grew as he neared. I could almost make out Liam and Ruuta on his back. Rhys must be behind them. But where was the witch?

God, help me hide them too.

I reached out into the air in Sakki's trajectory. I was being greedy now. Trying to hide everyone would probably expose us all, but I had to try.

Sakki, I'm going to try to hide you. Do you see me?

Silent pause. *No.*

I released a pent-up breath. *Good. It's working. Keep flying toward my voice, but lower your altitude.*

You want Sakki to land? The witch will see.

If she's following you, she'll find you wherever you go. But if you land now, at least we'll be together.

More silence.

We have a better chance together, I added.

Sakki dipped lower in the sky.

I stretched the cloak surrounding me and Hiisi into the sky like a net until it spread to Sakki's altitude. I hoped. This place had a way of confusing my depth perception. Sakki flew somewhat to the right of my net, so I pushed it that way. Then a little higher. *You're almost there, drop a little lower and prepare to land. God, I hope this works.*

Sakki too.

The moment he flew into my cloak, I wrapped it around them. *I've got you!*

Sakki sees Colleen! Relief pushed the strain from his mental voice.

Land! But land softly. We don't need a sand spray giving up your location. I'd learned *that* lesson when our location was spotted by the matted grass beneath us.

Sakki will need to circle, then.

Do whatever you need to do. I turned, hoping I wasn't disturbing the sand too much as I kept him in my cloak while he circled above, lowering each time.

He landed. There was no way his large body wasn't upsetting the sand. The witch would find us, anyway.

As soon as Liam and Ruuta dismounted, Sakki shifted into his dog form.

Where are the others? I asked as we huddled together, easing the burden of keeping us hidden, but the sand was sure to give away our location. Without any wind, the sand was smooth everywhere but at our feet. Still, I held us within the cloak.

In the sky... somewhere.

My gaze followed his. "Where's the witch?"

"She was right behind—"

Laughter interrupted Liam. The witch materialized. She was the same person I'd met before, but taller, more menacing, with treelike antlers sprouting from her head. "Did you think you could escape me in my realm?"

"It's not yours. You stole it." I kept the veil around us. She knew our general location, but if she couldn't see us individually, we might keep an advantage. Somehow.

"I don't take kindly to trespassers, particularly those who dare rise up against me." She poised her arms in the air, motioning with her hands.

The sands around us stirred, swirling in the air. By the time I realized what she was doing, a sandstorm vortex surrounded us.

Sakki shifted into his dragon form while I fought the winds to maintain the veil that seemed increasingly pointless. With my attention fixed on the witch, I hadn't noticed the other dragon in the sky. It looked like Sakki, but with Samu and Hadwin on his back.

Rhys.

He dove, flying into the witch and disturbing my veil. The sand vortex died as Noita leaped out of the way. A shot rang out, and the witch jerked. Blood splattered from her left shoulder, and she staggered backward. She grasped the wound, then glanced at her hand. Incredulous awe masked her face as she gazed upon the blood. She pressed her hand against the wound again, then gaped at Liam with the gun still poised. A fierce scowl overtook her shock, and she disappeared in a puff of smoke.

None of us moved nor said a word. If Noita didn't want us dead before, she would now. Especially Liam.

"We need to get out of here. Now," I said.

Ruuta moved to climb on Sakki's back as I picked up Hiisi, ready to hoist him up behind her. She paused, scanned my sticky body coated with sand, and wrinkled her nose. "Just try not to touch me."

After rolling my eyes, I thought better of judging her. I reeked.

Hiisi scrambled up Sakki's back behind Ruuta. Even though she couldn't see him, she cringed when he touched her—so she must feel him. When I sandwiched him between us, she threw an annoyed look oozing with repulsion over her shoulder.

Rhys looked just like Sakki, but bigger. Samu and Hadwin were settling into saddles and grasping reins.

Too bad you can't morph complete with riding gear like Rhys.

Sakki turned as far back toward me as he could and blasted a flame. *Ask Rhys if he can do that.*

I didn't bother. Something told me he couldn't or he would've ignited Noita instead of tackling her.

Liam was about to climb onto Sakki's back when I worried about Sakki tiring with too much weight.

"Go with them." I tipped my chin toward Rhys.

"No way. Make her go." Liam motioned to Ruuta. "She'll be safer in a saddle, anyway."

While Liam was still talking, Ruuta was already dismounting. On the ground, she swiped at her back. "I'd rather not get coated with grime."

Samu held a hand out to help her up, then positioned her in front. I cradled Hiisi in my lap, and my back lit up at Liam's chest pressed against it. He wrapped his arms around me, and I feared I might spontaneously combust. How could he not feel that?

He backed away. Maybe he *had* felt it? "You know"—he lifted a hand toward my face—"you got a little something—"

"I know!" I smacked his hand away.

He laughed. "I hope there's a lake wherever we're going. You need a bath."

Good feelings gone. But he was right. I could barely stand being near myself... or touching Hiisi. I didn't know how he could stand to be so close.

The dragons took flight over the endless desert. Though the torturous feeling of my energy reacting to Liam had evaporated, I couldn't escape the feeling of his presence while I prayed we weren't going in circles. The rippling sand looked the same. There was nothing, no cactus, no tumbleweeds—*nothing* to clue us in to the right direction. I sensed Sakki tiring. Rhys must be too.

You can't keep this up, Sakki. We should land.

Sakki senses something... just up ahead.

I strained to see anything other than dunes. Then, along the horizon, something different appeared. Rocks rose from the ground, and the smooth horizon turned jagged. Hopefully, we'd be able to hide from Noita there.

Sakki shifted his weight like a person adjusting to a child on their back, giving us a jolt. Hiisi cried out as we scrambled to hold on.

Sakki, bring us down. We can walk from here.

Just... a little... further. Sakki... senses... something. He gave us all another push. Hiisi screamed and clamped his long arms around my waist, squishing his face into my stomach.

Stop doing that, Sakki. You're freaking out Hiisi. Just bring us down.

Sakki continued over the craggy surface and another peak. Then the ground leveled. We all sucked in a collective breath at the image that lay beyond—an ornately carved building face appeared in the rock. Everything was the same reddish-brown color—the mountains, the rocky sand, and the building. Sakki seemed more energetic. With a sudden burst, he charged for the building.

The building grew larger—fast.

Uh, Sakki? Maybe you should slow down?

Hiisi snuck a peek, then shrieked, and buried his face again. Sakki maintained his trajectory as if I hadn't spoken. The two-story building had no openings. The carved windows and doorway were all stone. He headed straight for it.

Sakki, slow down!

Liam shouted in my ear. "Make him slow down!"

"I'm trying!"

Sakki! You're going to kill us!

Should I jump and take my chances with the fall? But the ground rushing past... It was too far. The fall would kill me. And Sakki wouldn't intentionally kill us.

As the building advanced, I clung to Hiisi, and Liam tightened his grip around me. Sakki folded his wings and dove.

Thirty-Six

We plunged into the rock-face window and continued through the other side into a cavern glistening with brilliant stalactites dripping over railed walkways forming a cross. Light streamed through the windows that had appeared to be nothing but rock on the outside. Sakki curved, gliding down past the walkways to the polished floor. When we landed, he shifted into dog form, depositing us in a heap. Rhys came skidding in, swerving at the last minute to avoid hitting us. Clearly, he didn't have Sakki's skills.

I disentangled myself from Hiisi and Liam and fumbled to stand. *Sakki! Couldn't you wait for us to dismount?*

He leaned back, stretching out his front paws, then shifted to stretch his hind legs and raised his head to look at me upside down. *Sakki's back couldn't take another minute.*

I softened. How could I fault him for that? *Thanks for saving our hides.*

"I can't believe we made it." I spun to include Rhys in my thank you, then fell silent. Ruuta and Hadwin were back to themselves. No more old goat-hag or wolf. But she didn't look as beautiful as I remembered. With the illusion of face paint gone, the bags under her eyes made her look tired. Which, in all fairness, she probably was. Was I seeing everyone for who they were because I was seeing even more now, or was there something about this place?

I tilted my head back, taking in the massive room—a circular building with columns supporting the crossbeams. Dragons were carved into the pillars. The walls were painted floor to ceiling with dragons and elves. "What is this place? Are you all seeing the dragons too?"

"I see it." Ruuta brushed something off my shoulder. "Noita's magic must not reach this place. You look like you again." Her nose wrinkled at Hiisi. "And I see your little friend too."

Well, that answered that question. If Ruuta saw it too, something was special here.

"How did we just fly through stone?" Liam asked.

"It's an illusion," she answered. "Did a fae build this? In the Divide?"

Not fae, Sakki said. *Dragons. This is a dragon lair. Sakki can sense God here.*

I relayed the message.

"A temple, actually," Samu corrected him. "And I painted these."

Questions filled the silence, and Samu squashed them with a waving hand. "It was nearly twenty years ago when the Divide darkened. After your mother escaped your father with you."

Now I goggled. How had I spent so much time in his presence only to learn this now? And had we ever told him who I was? "How do you know who I am?"

"You're her exact likeness." He looked upon me with such warmth, he must've cared for her. Then a twinkle appeared with a laugh. "And the others told me after you'd been kidnaped."

"What happened... with my mother?"

"I wish I knew." He shrugged. "So much happened at once. The humans turned on the elves. Your mother left with you. The Divide grew dark. The dragon eggs were destroyed. I've had years to think it over. And I can only assume that, somehow, Noita planned it all. She had the humans kill the elves because she couldn't do it herself. She had it pinned on your father to force his hand into subduing the humans to keep them from becoming a threat. And she had the eggs destroyed so she could curse this place and make it hers."

He approached a painted wall and ran his fingers over it. "When Taavi, my dragon, was receiving all the memories of the dragons who'd shared before him, I entered a trance and painted all this. I've never been able to find this place again, without Taavi...."

His pain was palpable. "You had a dragon?"

He pressed his lips together and nodded. How he carried on without his dragon, I couldn't guess. I didn't dare ask any more and widen the wound.

"But I'm glad to know the last dragon egg survived and you received him."

I stood there, my mind racing, yet going blank all at once, like running through an empty void.

"When Taavi and I came to rescue the eggs, we found only one remaining." He pointed to Sakki. "Yours. I'd given up all hope when we found it stolen."

"Sakki's egg was stolen?" I gasped. "By who?"

"By your pooka—Jaakko. Your father's servant."

"What?" I jumped away from Rhys as if he'd caught fire and I didn't want to get burned. "You *stole* Sakki's egg? Every time I convince myself I can trust you despite the evidence, I learn *another* reason why I can't!"

Rhys shook his head, sending his black hair waving. It, too, probably wanted to escape his presence. "I did what I was supposed to do. You have a dragon. You're here."

"I wish the witch made it so your nose would grow with each lie."

I lost everyone with that comment. I shrugged at their confused expressions or blank stares.

"Pinocchio? It's a story about a—" I waved a hand. "Never mind. Doesn't matter. The point is you're a liar and I can't trust you. I knew this! Yet I trusted you anyway. Again and again and again. So stupid."

"You can't be blamed." Hadwin placed an arm around my back and squeezed my shoulder. "This is where God wants us now. Question is... why? What are we to do now that we're here?"

"Best place to start is for Sakki to enter the chamber and receive his ancestor's memories." Samu scratched Sakki's achy back.

Sakki can do that? He practically vibrated with excitement. His tail wagged so fast, his butt wiggled too.

Liam looked skeptical. "How long will that take?"

"Are we safe here, then? From Noita?" I rubbed the goose bumps from my arms, grinding in slimy sand. Yuck.

"Yes. After I painted these, Taavi told me they would protect us from the witch."

"Maybe we should stay here forever, then." I huffed a laugh.

Sakki imitated my laugh, punctuating it with twin puffs of smoke. *Sakki wants dragons' memories.*

I pivoted, taking in the enormous space. "Where's the chamber?"

We followed Samu to the framed entryway with no door. The room opened up to more paintings of dragons and elves. The far wall was framed, like the entryway we'd just come through, but it had a red stone face like the building's exterior. Sakki moved toward it, then shifted into his dragon form, and walked through the wall.

I tried to follow, but I smacked myself on solid stone. "I can't get through." *Sakki?*

No response.

"What is this? A giant dragon trap? I can't feel him." My heart raced as I pounded on the wall. *Sakki? Sakki!* "Sakki!"

Samu gripped my shoulders and pulled me away. "He's safe in there. Only dragons can enter."

"Have you read these paintings?" Rhys asked.

"You can read them?" Samu released me and joined him.

I scoffed. "I wouldn't trust anything he says unless someone else can confirm it."

No one stepped up, but Samu didn't seem capable of squelching his curiosity. "Read them? There are no words."

Rhys laughed. "Are words the only way to communicate? Do you think only in words? Or do you think sometimes in pictures?"

"What are you saying? These pictures tell a story?" Samu looked more closely at them, but unless he saw something I didn't, they looked like just that, paintings—nothing more.

"Look here." Rhys pointed to books scattered along one depiction's floor. "These symbolize knowledge or wisdom." His finger trailed over a dragon clutching a book. "The dragon is wearing a green scarf, symbolizing blood, as it protects the book."

I followed his finger to several dragon skulls.

"The skulls mean death."

"So what's it mean?" Samu's voice came out thin, as if he barely breathed.

"This confirms what Samu has said. Dragons contain the wisdom and knowledge of every dragon who has ever lived. They died protecting the knowledge stored in this place. Sakki can retrieve it."

"Well, Encyclopedia, thanks for sharing what we already knew." Liam's sarcasm was showing again, but this time, I approved. "Let's hope their collective wisdom can help us kill the witch."

"If their knowledge could have saved them, shouldn't it have done so whilst more of them lived?" Ruuta found a puddle on the floor. She eyed her reflection and smoothed her hair.

"There's water? Where—" White light flashed across my vision, blinding me. A current ran through me, tightening every muscle. Pain burst from the back of my head, rushing through in waves. My friends' panicked voices sounded distant—incomprehensible—as though I was underwater. More voices bombarded me, but they came from within, pounding my head, speaking in a foreign tongue. So many voices, slithering and tangling like snakes in a cluster.

Then it stopped.

Thirty-Seven

My muscles relaxed, though my head continued to pound. I tried to open my eyes, but my lids merely stretched as I raised my eyebrows. The most I could get from them was a flutter. I was so tired I could sleep for a week. I groaned.

"She's waking." Ruuta's eager voice neared.

A cool hand touched my face. Footsteps hurried my way. Why couldn't I open my eyes? My eyelids felt so heavy. *Everything* felt heavy.

"Colleen?" Liam's voice. The electric shock of his hand as he grasped mine couldn't even make me move. But the initial shock dissipated, settling into a comforting warmth.

"Allow me," came a strange woman's voice.

The bedding tightened as the unknown presence sat beside me. Light brightened beyond my closed lids. A warming sensation emanated from my chest and spread throughout my body. My blood tingled as it did after I gave energy but in reverse. Whoever this person was, she was sharing her energy with me, and she had so much more than I could ever imagine. I drank it with greed.

The flood of energy and accompanying light shut off as some invisible door or barrier slammed shut.

I opened my eyes, ready to leap from the bed, run to the witch, and take her down in one fell swoop. A woman who looked eerily like me but with barely perceptible gray hairs mingling with the blonde sat beside me. "Who are you?"

"Sakki," she said.

I scrambled to sit. Hiisi sat by my feet on the bed. Or was it a table? It was hard as a rock, softened by their shepherd's plaids. Liam, Ruuta, Rhys, Samu, and Hadwin stood around it. They all shrugged or gave uncertain smiles. Hiisi climbed closer with his wide, open-mouthed smile.

"Sakki?" I inspected his feminine form. "You can talk? Even when you shifted into King Eerikki, you couldn't talk."

"There is much Sakki didn't know. Sakki knows now."

"Prove it's you." *Speak to my mind.*

Sakki has nothing to prove. Colleen and Sakki are bonded. Colleen would know.

"It *is* you. Why do you look like this? Whose form is it?" I asked, though I already knew from the portraits in my father's castle.

"Queen Delyth, Colleen's mother. Sakki didn't know what better form to choose. Sakki can only speak out loud and heal in human form. Sakki needs hands. But Sakki is tired now. Sakki must rest." He shifted into a cat and kneaded the plaid for a fraction of his usual time, circled once, and plunked down, apparently too tired to take one more turn.

"What happened?" I asked the others.

Ruuta sat beside Sakki. "As Samu said, when Sakki went into that room, all the wisdom of the dragons entered his mind."

"Is that why I heard all those voices?" I grasped my head at the remembered pain.

"The bond affected you, to be sure. To be sure." Rhys flashed a crooked smile.

Hiisi crawled over to Sakki's sleeping form and plopped down.

Sakki lifted his head, squinty-eyed, and let out an annoyed grunt. Hiisi held a hand in the air, poised and ready to pet, waiting for Sakki to relax. Once he did, Hiisi petted Sakki who responded with a chirp, then purred. Hiisi continued to pet Sakki whose purr grew louder. Hiisi grinned at me.

Liam squeezed my hand. "We were so worried when you fell. You were petrified. Literally. Your body was stiff as a statue. You barely breathed."

I moved to rub my sore muscles, remembering the pain all too well. But it was gone. Sakki's energy had restored me. "I feel great now. I've never felt such incredible energy from anything." Then I noticed the sand was gone. I no longer reeked. "I'm clean. How am I clean?"

Liam pointed to Ruuta. "She did it."

"It had to be done." Ruuta wrinkled her nose like she still smelled me. "It was a public service to everyone." Then she nodded to Sakki's sleeping form. "He received far more than wisdom in that chamber." The way she eyed him, she'd probably reach inside him to take whatever he'd gained if she could.

"He was buzzing from so much energy when he left that room, he had plenty to restore each of us as well," Liam said.

Sakki's chest rose and fell, Hiisi now curled up beside him.

"He seems to have used some up."

"Giving it to you." Liam squeezed my hand.

"How long was I out?"

"Three days."

"Three days!" I leaped from the makeshift bed, half afraid restraints might shoot from it, ensnaring my limbs to tie me down, forcing me into another lengthy rest. Sakki and Hiisi floundered in my wake, aiming their grumpy faces at me.

"Same as me." Samu laughed. "At least you didn't wake up with a paintbrush in your hands."

"That's how long Sakki was in that chamber." Liam scooted back on his stool, giving me more space. "If you ask me, three days seems fast to absorb knowledge from the beginning of dragons."

"But I'm not even hungry or thirsty. I feel great."

"We all do. Sakki's energy did that for us all, to be sure," Rhys said.

"Then it's time to go. We need to take down the witch and get to Queen Rhiannon. Who knows what kind of damage the people are doing to my father's kingdom? We need to end it."

Ruuta dipped a nod. "Spoken like a true queen."

I hated her reasons for wanting me to be queen. But I felt too good to scoff.

"Sakki needs time to recover. To be sure, to be sure." Rhys's black hair dangled in his eyes. He needed a haircut. Couldn't he control the length of his hair?

"Here." Liam scooped Sakki's limp form from the bed while Hiisi sneered. "Let me take him."

"Take him where?" I followed him through the massive chamber to the room I couldn't enter. My throat squeezed, making my voice shrill. "You're putting him in there?"

"He went here himself after energizing each of us. It restores him."

"But it knocks me out... for days."

"There's no harm in staying put a little longer, is there? Let the dragon rest." Liam jostled me, trying to step around Ruuta. Then he pushed Rhys aside and slid Sakki across the floor through the sealed entrance, and I steeled myself for another onslaught of voices.

Seconds ticked by. The assault didn't come.

Sakki strutted from the chamber in his cat body looking like he'd eaten a large mouse. *Sakki's ready to go catch a witch.*

Thirty-Eight

I walked through the false wall from our cool sanctuary empowered to take on anything that witch could dream of throwing at me. Then I stepped into blistering desert heat. I broke out into an instant sweat, and the invincible feeling vanished. Was Noita turning up the heat, trying to sweat us out? No wind cooled us. The air didn't move at all. Only our steps kicked up the mounds of sand. Misery and oppression weighed down my bones as if I'd never been refreshed. Each step was more laborious than the last.

Sakki was right. The witch needed to go. Not just for our sakes, but for all the souls trapped here. A place like this shouldn't exist. Particularly since God created it to protect the elves. But that witch stole it from Him and turned it into something evil.

As much as it angered me, I didn't have their confidence to face more of Noita's schemes or the creatures she entrusted to protect her soul. "How many more creatures do we have to kill?"

Rhys's feet squeaked across the sand. "Two or twenty, who can tell?"

"You can." Liam glowered, wiping damp hair from his forehead. "You're the only one who can."

Sakki pranced beside Liam, looking up at him as if speaking to him. *Sakki can too. Sakki had a minor sense of them before, but now, since Sakki entered the Chamber of Wisdom, Sakki's senses are stronger.*

I shook out my shirt to fan myself. *Did the previous dragons know where the witch hid her soul?*

No. The previous dragons existed before Noita took control of the Divide. But now that Sakki is powered by their spirits, Noita's veil has no power over Sakki. Sakki can sense her spirit, like Rhys. Better than Rhys.

My heart skipped. *Then you know how many are left?*

Sakki senses five—Rhys, Noita, and three others.

Lovely.

Sakki cocked his head at me. *You think so?*

I thought you were supposed to be smart now. Or did the dragons know nothing of sarcasm?

Gathering dragon memories, being smart, and understanding Colleen are all very different things. Besides, three is a good number. Better than twenty.

I suppose. Zero would be even better.

Sakki chuffed.

So, where's the nearest one... aside from Rhys?

Not far, but Colleen and friends should fly.

What about the witch?

Sakki isn't afraid of Noita. Colleen shouldn't be afraid either. Colleen can manipulate air to hide us if necessary.

Aye, that worked out so well last time.

"Do you two mind sharing with the rest of the class?" Ruuta crossed her arms and scowled, then realized she needed her arms to trudge across the sand.

"Sakki says we should fly. Especially since Rhys can carry some."

So, we assembled ourselves as we had before. Liam's presence didn't affect me as strongly as before, but my body was still hypersensitive to his touch. I tried to ignore it as we flew up and out of the blistering desert heat and over a forest. A green canopy covered the forest floor. Was this a nicer forest? One Noita forgot to horrorize? Or was I seeing things as they were, not as she wanted me to see them? I hoped for the latter. I wanted to be out from under her influence.

Keep your eyes on Me.

I breathed in God's words, letting them wash over me and cleanse my spirit like a long-overdue bath. Hearing God's life-giving words and being in the air, closer to heaven and away from Noita's influence, soothed my soul like nothing else. *Thank You, God. Great is Thy faithfulness!*

As we soared, I sang. Sakki's voice joined mine, and we soared higher, freer, than ever. He undulated through the sky to the song's melody. I'd never felt so connected to him. Hiisi pressed into my stomach while Liam clung to my back, shouting out his glee. With renewed energy, we circled Rhys who eyed us with his giant, luminescent eye as we passed. He looked like a dragon, but that eye was all Rhys in its unnatural blue, and he was unimpressed with our antics. Ruuta too. But Hadwin and Samu appeared pleased. Samu shot a fist through the air and shouted, spurring us on.

But all good things had to come to an end. Sakki interrupted my praises.

Sakki senses Noita's soul below.

Let's hope it's not Noita.

Yes. Colleen should hide us.

As we dipped, I checked to ensure Rhys followed, then pulled the air around us. It was much easier now, like tossing on a light cloak. Sakki found a break in the trees and aimed for it. Like a diver swimming out of the way to make room for the next jumper, he shuffled away under the trees so Rhys could land through the same spot. When we slid from Sakki's back, I was still vibrating with joyous energy. As much as I wanted to leap and dance, Noita's soul was nearby. I had to contain myself, keep us cloaked. Sakki morphed into his doggy traveling form as Rhys shrank back into his boy self, making them both easier to hide without their excessive bulk. We followed them to Noita's soul along the forest floor littered with strange spiky balls. Hiisi seemed especially aggravated by them, grunting and kicking them with more force than necessary.

"What are those things?" I whispered.

"Makea purukumi," Hadwin whispered back. "They contain the seeds for these trees."

Pods. Just pods.

As we walked, more and more of the pointy things littered the ground. They were unavoidable. We crunched them beneath our feet. Hiisi's grumbling escalated as he plowed through them.

"Would you like to get on my shoulders?" Liam asked him.

Hiisi gazed at Liam with adoration. His shoulders relaxed, and he gave an open-mouthed nod.

When Liam reached down for him, his face strained. "How are you so heavy? You're tiny."

My guide's open-mouth smile never faltered. His adoring eyes tracked Liam as he swung him over his shoulders. Apparently elated, he settled in and wrapped spindly fingers over Liam's head, matting his hair.

Sakki and Rhys slowed. Sakki sniffed the air all over while Rhys seemed to use his invisible antennae again. Sakki nosed along the ground with Rhys close behind.

Then Rhys stopped and splayed his hands for us to stop as well. "Noita's spirit is close. I can feel it."

I crouched and scanned the area, expecting her to pop out from behind a tree. Small rattling, scraping sounded around us.

"What's that sound?" It didn't sound like forest critters. Unless an army of them came in every direction. And it was constant, unlike spastic rodent movements.

Everyone stopped. The spiky balls were moving. Each little point acted as an arm or a foot.

"The makea purukumi?" Hadwin stepped back.

"The pods!" I whirled on my tiptoes to take stock of those closing in on me.

As if my shout invigorated them, the freaky things moved faster, pressing at our feet. I danced to avoid them, crushing them.

"Run!" Liam yelled.

But they were everywhere. There was nowhere to run.

"One of these has Noita's soul." Rhys picked one off his pant leg and threw it to the ground, then squashed it beneath his feet. "Step on them!"

I crunched one under my foot and another, then spotted one climbing my riding pants. I tried shaking it off, but it stuck like Velcro. Nay... worse. I tried not to hurt myself on its barbs or puke as it writhed. The unholy thing came free, and I launched it as far from me as I could, but others were climbing my leg, clinging to me. I plucked as many as I could, but they were gaining ground. Climbing higher. I snagged one nearing my tunic, then another, no longer caring as I pricked my fingers and pierced my hands.

Panic gripped my heart. We were being overrun. Eventually, they'd cover me completely. Would they suffocate me? Choke me? The idea of them entering my mouth made me pluck the nasty things off my tunic with new abandon, but for each one I launched, ten more appeared. My pants were covered. "They're going to kill us!"

Sakki shifted into his dragon form, stretching the boundary of my veil. He blasted several with his flame. *Stay by Sakki! Sakki will shield Colleen!*

Sakki's fire disturbed the air I used to hide us, and I dropped the veil. His energy took its place, pushing through to form a shield. Spiked orbs coming at us hit the invisible wall. They tried and failed to scale it, then climbed on top of one another, forming a pile at the base of the shield. A few more sneaked in before the shield closed around us. Then stopped. While the freakish orbs swarmed each other, seeking a way in, the ones inside no longer moved. Some fell, but most remained lodged in our clothes. And we were coated as if we'd bathed, fully clothed, in a pool of burrs.

A flurry of activity ensued inside Sakki's shelter as we scrambled to pick the prickly sacs from our clothes before they reanimated. As I plucked away, no longer caring about my shredded hands, I stomped the fallen pods for good measure. Something caught my attention in the corner of my eye. Another spiky ball making its way up my shoulder.

"Wah–ah–uh–ah!" Revulsion wiggled through me, and I squirmed as I picked the thing off and propelled it into the barrier.

Kinked spikes wriggling, looking for anything to cling to. It bounced off and fell at Liam's feet. He crushed it under his shoe, grinding it into the dirt.

I held my breath as he lifted his shoe. The barbed appendages unfolded as the forces cramming it lifted. But the anathema remained still... dead.

A silvery fog slithered from the crushed spiky hide. What escaped the pod seemed to have more mass than its former host. It expanded in the air, then shot off, presumably in Noita's direction, but slammed against Sakki's shield. It bucked, rebounding in the opposite direction, finding no escape. I sensed it growing desperate. It hovered in the center of the enclosure, pulsing with mercurial ribbons, then slammed into Ruuta, and disappeared. She recoiled, head lolled back, mouth hung open in an unbecoming way, eyes wide.

"Nay. Nay, nay, nay, nay." That thing did *not* just enter Ruuta. It couldn't have.

But it had.

She dropped her chin back to where it belonged and closed her mouth, but her bewildered stare remained the same. Everyone turned solemn. Even Liam looked upon her like she was dead already and he was sad to see her go.

THIRTY-NINE

"How are we going to get it out of her?" I asked Samu, hoping he'd have an answer.

Liam pressed his lips together, probably to keep his words from escaping, but they came out in a rush. "How were we planning to get it out of Rhys?"

I slumped my shoulders and caught every other sad gaze, feeling like we were at their funerals already. Then I noticed the activity outside Sakki's shield. The vile burrs were climbing each other and had piled about knee-high around the entire thing. And Sakki's back.

"Sakki!" *They're on you!*

Sakki rotated his head to see, then huffed a breath, making our enclosure slightly smoky. He shook his back down to his rear like a dog freeing his coat of water, and the revolting things went airborne. *Noita's pods can't stick to Sakki's scales.*

Ruuta's misfortune had distracted me from the nauseating burrs. I resumed picking them off me while the others did the same.

"At least we know we can trap Noita's spirit." Hadwin plucked the last pod he could see by his ankle with his bleeding hands, then crushed those by his feet.

"There are more on your back." Free of burrs, Rhys helped Hadwin rid himself of those he couldn't see.

While Liam twisted to pluck the pods from his lower back, Hiisi relieved him of those within his reach. "But what good is that if it enters one of us?"

"Oh, just say it. We all know." Ruuta, more disheveled than I'd ever seen her, heaved an annoyed sigh that couldn't cover up her fear. "You'll have to kill us both so Noita's soul will return to her body and we can kill her."

Liam lowered Hiisi onto the ground where he set to work removing pods we'd missed.

"I'm not certain we'll be able to kill her once her soul returns." Hadwin rubbed a red scratch on his neck.

A chorus of "huh?" and "why?" rebounded within Sakki's barrier.

Hadwin scraped the hairs on his lower lip with his front teeth. "She has wards protecting her body, remember?"

"But she bled." I spread out my hands. "We all saw it, right? She was bleeding."

"And she's in her lair right now, reinforcing her wards." Hadwin dropped another ball at his feet and squashed it with a satisfying crunch. "When she's wounded, she blinks away to heal herself."

"Perhaps it wasn't God's timing." Samu freed Liam's back from the last pod and gave his back three sharp downward swipes. "God told you to kill the witch, so there has to be a way."

Aye. Hopefully, a way that didn't involve killing Rhys and Ruuta. God wouldn't require two of my friends to die, would He? Not that I could consider either one a friend. I still couldn't trust Rhys. He didn't understand why lying and stealing weren't okay. And Ruuta... She'd admitted to serving a demon! Were they destined to die? Was this God's judgment upon them?

But would we make it to Queen Rhiannon without Ruuta's help?

Shivering, I chided myself. *How can you even think such things, Colleen? This is a life we're talking about. And you're worried about how it will affect you?*

"It's okay." Rhys's small voice pulled me from my thoughts. "I've known Noita's spirit resided within me all along. If I have to die, I have to die."

His words, shrinking demeanor, and faltering smile were a jagged knife coring my heart.

Ruuta, staring at Rhys as if attempting to murder him with her mind, obviously didn't share his sentiment. On this, I was with her.

There had to be another way. *God, please help me find another way.*

"We'll deal with that another time." Samu laid a hand on Rhys's shoulder and pointed outside Sakki's barrier. "Right now, we have other problems."

The squirming pods, continuing their climb, had grown to about waist-high, covering more of the sphere as they sought a way in.

Sakki shook his back, sending the spiky balls climbing it flying in all directions. Some landed on the barrier and slid down, making others tumble. The boundary shifted as he quaked, and the orb piles collapsed to about knee height.

"What are we going to do? We still need to find two more creatures with pieces of Noita's soul. How are we going to do that with these things surrounding us?" The idea of those things climbing me again sent a full-body shudder coursing through me.

Sakki has an idea. Tell friends to press in near Sakki's belly, walking where Sakki walks. Quickly.

I relayed the message, and we all moved in tandem. The nasty orbs to our right writhed as the invisible barrier pushed them out of the way. On the other sides, they fought to catch up. Within moments, we were clear of them, but it wouldn't last long unless Sakki planned to shuffle like this all the way to the next Noita-filled creature.

What are you—

With a whoosh, Sakki lowered the barrier and blasted the pods with his fire. The heat warmed my skin. But, pressed in close to him, we stayed under the sweeping flames. The balls that didn't burn continued their relentless pursuit, their programming for one thing and one thing only—attack. But there were far fewer of them now. As they neared, we stomped on them without being overrun. Soon, crunched and scorched pods carpeted the ground. Not one alive. My whole body slumped as relief washed over me.

Thank You, God. And Sakki.

Sakki's appendages recoiled, and fur sprouted as he shifted into his dog form. *Time to find the next spirit.*

As we walked through the forest, lush greenery blinked like bad reception on a teleview, switching to dead trees with lifeless limbs. A wave of dizziness washed over me, and I splayed my arms.

"Everything okay?" For less than a second, Liam's wolf form contorted his true image. Then it returned and blinked out again—replaced by the witch's twisted version.

I squeezed my eyes and shook my head, willing my vision to stabilize. *God, help me continue to see things as they truly are. Don't let me doubt. Don't let me fall under Noita's curse.*

I paused, half expecting my vision to blip again, hoping it wouldn't. It didn't. I took a deep breath and continued following the others, who carried on without noticing me while Liam waited.

"You good?"

Hiisi did a double take from Hadwin's retreating shoulders but must've decided Liam could handle me. He faced forward and allowed Hadwin to carry on without a word.

"I hope so. I just started seeing things the way Noita wants me to again, I think. What about you? What do you see?"

"Around here?" He waved his arms at the foliage. "Just trees."

"Dead... or alive?"

"Alive." He squinted at me. "Just like you're you and no longer Sakki's humanoid twin." He huffed and cocked his head at me. "I thought we were over that."

"Apparently not. It depends on how much you're trusting God." I eyed him with extreme skepticism. "How is it I've believed in God my whole life and I'm struggling under Noita's curse and you're a believer for all of two minutes and you're unaffected?"

He shrugged. "I don't know. Maybe I trust God more than you do."

I jabbed his shoulder, hating the truth in his words.

He laughed and rubbed the spot like I'd actually hurt him, then grew serious. "Maybe it's because I spent my life wrestling with the idea before accepting."

"You couldn't have spent your life wrestling it. You were under my father's curse. You believed He was God."

"Yeah." He tipped his head, only half-heartedly agreeing with me. "But I grew up confused. The people around me all believed the same thing without question, and I couldn't understand how. I mean, they didn't argue about anything. Did people change so much the moment they atoned? Something was wrong. My uncle must've recognized my doubt. When I was old enough to be trusted not to blab to those under the curse, he began sharing all he knew. He even gave me a Bible. I kept it hidden under my bed. I wanted to believe those words. But I also wanted to make my parents proud and get atoned with my friends. I remember thinking my uncle was confused. That somehow, both were right. But I was wrong. Very wrong. And now I know. With all of my being, I just know."

Did his wrestling with the existence of God make the difference? I grew up with believers, and I never questioned what they taught. God was always real to me. Was God putting me through this now to test my faith and get me to finally wrestle with it as Liam had?

He kicked a spiky ball from our path. It skittered between Ruuta's legs, and she squashed it with excessive force.

He returned her glare with a shrug. "When I came out from under the curse and knew without question how wrong we'd all been, I wanted to reject the idea of any god. But I couldn't shake what I'd learned from my uncle... from God's Word. And then, going through all this with you and seeing miracle after miracle? How could I doubt Him?"

"Apparently, I can." I slumped my shoulders as I trudged on, kicking debris, hoping nothing at my feet would spring to life. What was wrong with me? I'd always wanted faith like Fallon. She assured me it would come with practice. But Liam had it without having to practice.

Nay. I *was* getting better. My faith and trust *were* growing stronger. I could see now what I couldn't before. Wasn't that evidence of my growth? I had to stop comparing my walk with God with anyone else's. We were unique, and so was our journey. *I trust You, God. I trust Your plans for me.*

Maybe if I keep saying it, it will come true.

Help me trust You more.

Something sparkled between the trees up ahead. Water. A lake. We continued until we reached the shoreline. When Hadwin placed Hiisi on the ground, the creature scrambled away from the water's edge.

Sakki sniffed the wavering surface. *Noita's spirit is in there.*

FORTY

"In there?" My stomach sank. How would we defeat whatever lay in wait for us down there? Underwater, Noita's creature, whatever it was, would have the advantage. Big or small didn't matter. If it was large, it might be able to overpower us and hold us down. Or a gazillion tiny creatures, like the pods, could overwhelm us. Either way, we'd drown.

Despite my thoughts, I heard myself saying, "I can swim."

I was a good swimmer. Since being adopted, I'd spent most of my life in the water. But I wasn't *that* good of a swimmer. I could hold my breath for a long time, but long enough to find and kill whatever hosted Noita's soul down there? Nay. Not possible.

"I can too." Samu rolled up his sleeves. "Most elves are good swimmers."

What was he doing, getting ready to jump in without a plan? Did he take my comment to mean I had no concerns?

Ruuta stepped away from the shore. "I can't."

Hiisi clung to a tree like he expected the dirt embankment to fall away and plunge him into the watery depths. "Me no swim. Hiisi sink."

"I can't swim either." Liam scowled at the water.

"You grew up in an ocean-side city and never learned to swim?" Who could see the ocean day after day and never dive in?

He held up his arms. "There were always other things to do. School. Work. No one swam."

"That leaves me out too." Hadwin shook his head. "Like Liam, I never had such luxuries as free time to frolic in the sea."

How sad.

If only we had my adopted dad or the selkie here. Or Carr, Fiske, or anyone from their village. Wait. I clutched Rhys's arm and twisted him toward me. "You're a shape-shifter. You can shift into a dolphin. So can Sakki."

The minute the words came out of my mouth, I regretted them. I turned to Sakki sitting on the shore, scratching his chin with his hind leg. *I don't want you to go down there.*

He stopped scratching, his leg poised midair. *Sakki must.*

Then I'm going with you.

His leg lowered oh-so slowly. *Colleen isn't coming. Sakki and Rhys can handle this.*

I widened my stand and crossed my arms. *I'm not letting you go without me.*

Sakki blew smoke from his nose. *Colleen is stubborn.*

So, you've said.

"How thoroughly annoying." Ruuta tried smoothing the hair that escaped her updo, but it was a wasted effort. For every out-of-place strand she noticed, there were a hundred more. "Do you mind sharing your conversation with the rest of us?"

"I was telling Sakki I'm not letting him go alone. I'm going with him."

"You can't!" Liam grasped my wrist, igniting the spot. "You don't know what's out there. You may be able to swim, but unless I missed something, you don't have gills. You can't breathe underwater." At my unmoving expression, he scrubbed a hand down his face. "For the love of Betören, would you please let Sakki and Rhys check it out first?"

I cocked my head, hands jamming on my hips. "What if they come upon something and need us?"

"They can get away and seek help. But then we'll know what we're up against and come up with a plan to face it." He leaned in as if to share a secret. "You tend to get into trouble."

"Like when?"

"When you were captured by the krokotiili"—he started counting off on his fingers—"swallowed by the giant worm, attacked by the rodent, trapped by the witch—"

"I'm on a mission to kill a witch! Of course she's going to attack!" I balked.

"You wouldn't have survived without us." He faced the sky as if imploring God to back him up. Veins protruded from his neck. He took a deep breath, perhaps working to calm his voice. "You can't do this. Wait for Sakki and Rhys to find out what we're up against. Please."

His intensity gave me pause, but I'd rather die with Sakki than let him do this alone and have something happen to him when I could have helped. "Nay. I can't take that chance."

"Ugh!" Liam yanked at his hair in both fists. "Stubborn! You're so infuriatingly stubborn!"

Sakki chuffed. *As Sakki said.*

I chose to ignore them both. "Samu can ride with Rhys, and I'll ride with Sakki."

Liam let out a series of huffs while clawing his hair. I threw him an apologetic look as I removed my shoes.

Still holding onto the tree, Hiisi reached out and tugged my pant leg. Then he looked up at me with the most pitiful face I'd ever seen, like he knew he'd never see me again.

"I'll be okay, Hiisi. Don't worry."

He released me, his wide mouth scrunched into a frown.

Sakki jumped into the water, splashing as he bounded through until he lost ground and doggy-paddled. His body elongated as his fur smoothed to rubbery dolphin skin. He charged, then leaped up, catching air before diving back down. He reemerged upright, standing on his tail, letting out squeaks and trills until he fell sideways with a splash.

Being a dolphin suited him.

I kicked off my other shoe, then shuffled into the water with Samu and Rhys. The squishy feel of whatever decaying substances formed the lake bed oozing between my toes made me squirm. I tried walking lightly. It didn't help. Cool water encircled my waist, stealing my breath. Sakki's antics sent waves crashing into me, splashing me more as I sucked in hitched breaths.

Better to get it over with. I dove and swam out until the nasty lake bottom fell away. The initial shock faded, and my body adjusted to the comforting weightlessness. Sakki swam underneath me, and I clutched his fin. Together, we broke the surface. I clung to his body, and he raced through the water. How I'd missed doing this with my dad. It was the closest I'd ever come to flying.

I missed my family. Would I ever see them again?

Rhys surfaced beside us with Samu. He looked comfortable in the water.

"Ready to hunt a witch's soul?" he asked.

Nay. Never. Definitely not underwater. But I nodded.

Sakki senses Noita's spirit below. Tell Samu to prepare to dive.

I relayed the message and filled my lungs before we went under. Floaties danced in the water in the light filtering through. The water grew darker and colder as we descended. I swallowed to relieve the pressure building in my ears.

We neared the lake bed where everything looked brown. The rocks and even the plants. Brown sludge coated everything. A school of fish flitted away. Rhys got ahead of us. His tail kicked up a cloud of sediment. Sakki and Rhys swam straight for an outcropping of rocks.

Something odd took shape as we neared. An eye? A gray haze obscured it, reminding me of Sully's cloudy eyes. Was it blind too?

I could only hope, especially if that's what we came for. The eye blinked. Two eyelids. When both lifted, a large iridescent eye expanded and contracted as it trained itself on us.

Sakki! Swim up! Now!

With a powerful thrust of his tail, Sakki charged for the surface as the staring creature lunged. Rows of teeth snapped at his tail fin, barely missing him.

What is that thing?

Ankerias.

My hammering heart made it harder to hold my breath. My lungs begged for air, threatening to force my mouth open without my say-so.

Rhys slapped the attacker with his tail, stunning it, then darted off behind us.

Sakki continued to the surface.

What are you doing? Go back! We need to kill that thing.

Colleen needs air.

If we have to resurface every three minutes, we'll never kill it.

What did Colleen expect?

That thing, ankerias, looked like an eel. Only much larger than any eel I'd ever seen. If I pulled it straight, the thing might be as long as Sakki's outstretched dragon body head to tail. The creature faded and disappeared in the murky water.

By the time we broke the surface, my lungs were screaming at me. I gulped in air as if it might be my last.

Hold on!

Sakki dove and used his echolocation to spot the ankerias and the others. I searched the brackish waters for any signs of life.

The beast snaked straight ahead.

Sakki slowed as the thing came into view. It slithered with impressive speed through the water after Rhys.

Colleen must let go. Sakki needs speed.

I released his fin, and Sakki charged. He rammed the ankerias's gills. The monster went limp, turning over as the force of Sakki's hit carried it away. Then it recovered, shook its fish head, and blinked its dual eyelids. It spotted me floating all alone and charged straight for me.

FORTY-ONE

I nearly sucked in a mouthful of water in my shock, then kicked for the surface. No way could I outswim that thing. Its jaw opened, ready to strike. I tucked my feet up. Sakki circled back and bit the end of its tail as the beast was about to strike, yanking it away from me.

The ankerias's eyes bulged as it gnashed its rows of menacing teeth, then turned to strike Sakki. Rhys appeared with another powerful kick to its head. He seemed to have knocked the thing unconscious. But then the sharpness returned to its eyes, and it retreated, slithering back to its hiding place.

My lungs burned. I fought to keep my mouth from opening and taking in water. I swam for the surface. When Sakki came up beneath me, I grabbed his fin, and he flew, making my ears pop. The moment my mouth was free, it opened, taking in air and a little water. I coughed between gasps, clinging to Sakki.

"We survived." Samu coughed out the words.

I wiped the water dripping into my eyes. *Does that thing have Noita's soul?*

Sakki blasted air from his spout. *Yes.*

Of course, it did. If only Samu could speak into our minds too. Or at least with Rhys.

"We have to go back. It has Noita's soul."

"I suspected." Samu slicked his soaking hair back. "Any thoughts on how to get it?"

"Nay. None whatsoever."

"Sakki and Rhys fought well." Samu swiped the water from his face. "I don't think the ankerias will stand a chance against another attack now that we know what we're up against."

How could he be so confident? "But it's wary of us now. What if we can't get it out of hiding?"

"I have an idea. Let's go back to shore and regroup. The beast will still be here tomorrow."

"Aye. But will the witch find us in the meantime?" I peeled hair from my face.

"We'll have to take that chance. If we hope to kill the ankerias or prod it from hiding if necessary, we'll need spears."

Spears. As eager as I was to get this over with. His plan was better since it was... an actual plan. So, we swam ashore to make spears.

God, please don't let the witch stop us.

As soon as it was too shallow for the dolphin, Sakki and Rhys shifted. Sakki doggy-paddled ahead, planted his legs, and shook himself, showering anyone who got too close. The others greeted us as if they hadn't expected to see us alive again. At least, Hiisi and Liam did.

"You made it!" Liam passed the others, stepped into the water, and pulled me into a tight embrace, lifting my feet from the slimy lake bed. His energy connected with mine and pulsed everywhere within me. He smelled like his soap—rosemary and lemon. He must've bathed.

I tried to calm my racing pulse as we peeled apart. His ocean eyes looking at me with such intensity, I struggled to meet them. So, I focused on the mission. "We need to go back."

"You can't be serious." His eyes flashed.

"Aye. We need to make spears first. But the longer we delay, the more likely the witch will stop us."

"I feel the same, Colleen." Samu shook out his hair, sending lake-water drips raining. "But night is falling. We can't go out in the dark. We'll be blind."

Once my feet were both planted on the shore, Hiisi lunged at my legs and wrapped his long arms around them. "Me glad you safe!"

I patted his back and smiled at his happy face, then frowned at the sky. "How is it growing dark? Has that ever happened here before? I've never seen the sun. And I've only seen the moon outside Noita's hut."

"Time works differently here. Night and day are unpredictable." Hadwin moved to a campfire and turned something on a spit. "But we should see day and night as they are, just like seeing through all her other illusions, as our faith strengthens and her power dwindles."

What could I do? Despite my desperation to get killing the anke-rias over with, I'd die out there alone. And they were right. It was hard enough to see when it was light out. As it grew darker, it would be impossible.

Ruuta sat beside the fire. She didn't have anything to say, which wasn't a surprise. She didn't talk much anymore. Not since... receiving a death sentence. Hiisi was just glad to have me back. He seemed to live forever in the moment. Rhys was already at work helping Samu find sticks that would make good spears.

Liam appeared beside me with my pack. "Change into dry clothes and get something to eat."

I grumbled, accepted the bag, and retreated to a thick copse of trees. Part of the lake wound its way back there, so I could bathe privately. I found my bar of soap, and as I was bathing, I remembered Fallon's story of bathing in a hot spring when fasgadair happened upon her. And here I was, alone. I searched the trees as if expecting a fasgadair to emerge from the shadows. When nothing moved, I hurried to finish up, stepping with clean bare feet through the dirt and debris, making them dirty again.

As much as I wanted to finish our work and leave this place, I was relieved to be back with my friends again. Dry and clean, except for my dirty feet and damp hair. The fire warmed me, and the meat, kani, filled the hole in my belly. Still, I couldn't help but worry about the witch. "What might Noita do to us while we wait for light?"

Hadwin licked the juice dripping from his meat down his palm. "We should take turns keeping watch in twos."

"Everyone else should sleep under the protection of Sakki's wing." Samu spoke like an elf who had a dragon once.

"That leaves five sleeping under Sakki's wing. Is there enough room?" Liam asked.

"Me small." Hiisi jabbed himself in the chest.

"Maybe we should watch in threes." Hadwin scraped the hairs on his lower lip with his teeth again. I was beginning to detest the habit.

"Samu." I hesitated to ask, but I couldn't stop myself. I had to know. "What happened to your dragon, Taavi?"

Sakki lifted his blocky dog head off his paws, and his ears perked up.

Samu poked the kindling with a stick, and his eyes shined with unshed tears in the firelight. "The witch happened." When we continued to watch him, waiting for him to elaborate, he heaved a heavy sigh and twisted his lips. "Elves and dragons—especially dragons—are a threat to her curse. The mere presence of a dragon causes a disruption in her illusions."

"Why is that?" I asked.

"Dragons were the keepers. The protectors from the fae."

"Humph." Ruuta rolled her eyes. "This again?"

Samu gave her a sad, sidelong glance. "You're aware fallen angels began taking female elves as their wives, creating the fae, and God constructed the Divide to stop the spread of demon blood, yes?"

"I've had enough of this." She stood and brushed the grass bits from her pants. "Fae aren't demons."

She started to walk off when Samu's words stopped her. "No, they're not."

She spun around on him. "Then what's all this business about demon blood and the Divide being constructed by *your* God to protect you from *us*?" She poked her breastbone and leaned closer to him. "From *us*! As if we're some evil atrocity."

Samu threw his stick into the fire, sprang to his feet, and gripped her hands, pulling her to sit, but she refused. He sat anyway and looked up at her. "You suffer the same malady as the humans. You have sin that separates you from God."

"First, I don't believe in your God. But if I did, how is it that the humans and the fae have this so-called *sin* and the elves don't? Are the elves somehow superior?"

"By no means! However, the humans allowed a fallen angel to tempt them into disobeying God. Some elves did the same by wedding fallen angels. Unfortunately, any child ever born in the line of the first fallen human, Adam, or a fallen angel will also have the same malady... sin that separates them from God. It's not an insult to overcome but a problem to work through. Thankfully, God makes a way."

"How? The humans have the only way, right? God's only Son? What of the fae?"

"The same. God's Son died once for all." When no one responded, he added more emphasis. "For *all*."

"And I'm supposed to believe this? He gave His word to the humans, not fae."

"Colleen, you're part elf, part fae. Do you believe God's Son has saved you?"

Until Samu spelled it out like this, it never occurred to me that my faith wasn't given to my kind. But I remember when I was first saved, the feeling of floating. And all that happened in my life since. God had been with me... even in Bandia when I feared for my life. He'd never left my side. I gave a firm nod. "Aye, I do. And if God's Son can save me, He can save you too."

Ruuta's eyes twitched, then flashed. She spun on her heel and stormed off into the darkness.

Samu followed. "I'll keep an eye on her. No one should be alone."

"I'll take first watch." I wouldn't sleep anyway, and I was concerned about Ruuta.

"I'll watch with you." Something in the way Liam looked at me sent shivers racing through me. The good kind. The I'm-about-to-go-on-the-adventure-of-my-life-and-I'm-a-little-scared kind. Not the bad, I'm-about-to-be-eaten-by-a-fasgadair kind.

"Me too." Hiisi smiled at me with his wide opened-mouth smile.

Liam and I placed ourselves beside the fire, leaning on each other's back. Hiisi sat beside me, hanging on my leg. And Hadwin and Rhys curled up under Sakki's wing. Liam took up a stick and set to work, carving one side to a point. I wanted to snatch one from the pile and dive in to kill the ankerias. The longer we sat around, the more likely the witch would stop us. But I was outnumbered and couldn't go alone.

And it was dark. Too dark.

"I don't think you should go back." Liam's voice vibrated through my back, making me hyperaware of his presence.

I had to squash my feelings and focus on the mission. I grabbed a stick from the to-be-done pile. "Do you have another knife?"

"Me agree. Me no want you to go underwater." Hiisi gave me his sad-eyed look.

Liam pulled a knife out of his pocket, unfolded it, and placed it in my awaiting palm.

I began carving out the tip. It was harder than I expected. "What other choice do I have, stay here forever?"

"Leave it to Rhys, Samu, and Sakki."

"No. No way. I'm not letting Sakki go down there without me."

I could feel Liam's groan through my back, but he didn't press further. We made our spears in silence and waited for whatever horror the witch would bring.

Forty-Two

I woke feeling cramped. Hiisi was pressed against my back with an arm draped over my shoulder. And another hand. Two hands? I pushed on Sakki's wing so I could sit. Dim light spilled into the opening as Hiisi adjusted without me supporting him anymore. The other hand belonged to Liam. He smacked his lips and readjusted too. Both of them had their hand on my shoulder, and now, without me there, Liam cuddled Hiisi like a gargoyle stuffed animal.

Liam looked even more beautiful as he slept. Long lashes brushed his high cheeks. Dark hair spilled away from his face, offering a rare view of his forehead. And hugging the little gargoyle?

Adorable. Downright adorable.

I scooted out from under Sakki's wing, trying not to wake the others. Hadwin and Rhys kept watch by the fire.

I stretched and yawned. "Where are Ruuta and Samu?"

Hadwin and Rhys gave each other a look. Then Hadwin flattened his lips into a thin line, making the red hairs on his lower lip stick out. "They haven't come back."

I jerked in the direction they'd disappeared last night. "They're not—They've been gone all night! We have to look for them!"

"What were we supposed to do, take off into the woods at night not knowing in which direction they'd gone?" Hadwin scraped his bearded lip with his teeth. I better never find a razor around him, or I'd shave that thing off. "We had to keep watch."

"To be sure." Rhys nodded.

My fault. This was all my fault. I should have gone after them last night. Wasn't this what Rhys warned us about? What *everyone* warned us about? The witch would try to separate us. I dropped near the fire. "I kept watching and waiting for another one of Noita's creatures to attack us. But this? I should've known better."

"What's going on?" Liam appeared with squinty eyes. He rubbed one eye, yawned, and stretched all at once.

Hiisi and Sakki came up behind him. Sakki morphed into a cat and crawled onto my lap while Hiisi sat beside me and patted my leg.

"Ruuta and Samu"—I didn't want to say the words and make them real—"never returned."

"Oh?" Liam ran a hand through his hair, scanned in every direction like we hadn't already done that, then sat beside me.

"What are we going to do?" I spread my empty hands, hating their uselessness.

Hadwin did his grating teeth-beard scrape thing several times. Just as I was about to ask him to stop, he spoke. "We have to keep going. Wherever they are, whatever trouble they're in, the only way we can help them is to continue with our mission. We can't stop now."

When I opened my mouth to object, Liam gripped my shoulder. "He's right. This is what Noita wants... to distract us. Our best chances of finding them again, of helping them, is to stop her and break her spell over this place."

They were right. I knew it, but not scouring the woods for our friends felt like such a betrayal.

"You have your spears." Hadwin motioned to the pile.

I wouldn't need all those. "But without Samu..."

"I'll be with you, to be sure." The confidence in Rhys's eyes bolstered me.

I stood before I lost heart. "Let's do it. Now."

Liam sprang to his feet, but I held out a hand to stop his arguments.

"It's now or never, Liam."

He scowled.

"Rhys, it's best for you to go as a dolphin again. But I'll carry two spears in case you need one."

Rhys brushed off his pants and made his way to the bank.

All too soon, I was riding Sakki next to Rhys in search of the ankerias harboring Noita's soul. And all too soon, Sakki found it.

Time to die.

I couldn't have heard Sakki right. I was about to say something before I replayed his words and caught my mistake. Right, time to *dive.*

Still, the other sounded accurate. I clutched the spears under one arm and held a deep breath as Sakki dove into the murky waters.

The slimy ground looked the same, yet different from the day before. There were more plants and grungy branches. Broken limbs from trees had settled down here. We passed multiple rock outcroppings.

Ankerias is close.

I tried arming myself with the spear. But I had two, and I needed to hold on to Sakki's fin.

This was a bad idea.

I motioned to Rhys, and his fins elongated into arms as he transformed into something between a human and a fish. A merman? He could do that? Why hadn't he done that yesterday?

Samu. He needed to carry Samu.

Today, he didn't need to carry anyone.

I couldn't think about that now. We needed to kill this beast. I had to focus.

Rhys reached out for a spear, and I handed it to him. Both armed, we searched for evidence of the eel.

Ankerias is in there. Sakki jerked his head toward a pile of rocks with a dark space where the creature must be sleeping. Or lying in wait.

Rhys caught Sakki's motion and cut in front of us. He rammed his spear into the hole. The beast came charging. Rhys tried to pull the spear back, but he dropped it in his haste. With powerful swipes of his merman tail, he bolted toward the surface, kicking up sediment, obscuring our vision.

Sakki swam upward, too, but away from Rhys. The water cleared, and the eel surged through the cloud, ramming Sakki and making me lose my grip. Sakki tried swimming back to me, but the beast turned and slithered our way, forcing us further apart.

Ice in its eyes, the beast came after me. Jaws open.

With nowhere to go, I armed myself, ready to jab the thing, but Sakki came flying up at it and bit its tail.

The beast spun around to counterstrike. Its massive tail smacked me.

I flew toward the rocky outcropping. Plants scratched at me, slowing me before I collided. Something shiny floated before me, then fell.

Was that?

I felt around my neck. The chain was gone. My mother's ring was falling. My chest tightened, begging for air. But if I went up for a breath now, I'd lose the ring forever. Swimming after it, I caught a glimpse as it landed, disturbing the scum. I rooted around the dregs until I felt the smooth metal. My hammering heart calmed.

Oh, thank God!

As I kicked for the surface, desperate for air, certain I wouldn't make it to the top, I placed the ring on my finger for safekeeping. My surroundings wavered, and the pain, the need for air—to breathe— was gone.

What happened? Had I drowned and didn't realize it? I looked below me for my body, afraid I'd find it lying in the muck. But nay. No bodies.

What's happened to Colleen and Sakki?

What do you mean? I would have thought he was asking where I went, but why ask about himself as well?

Rhys had retrieved his spear and was swimming toward the monster as it trained itself on Sakki.

I could see their auras.

But Sakki was distracted. He stared at me, not seeing the beast coming at him.

Sakki! Look out!

The ankerias attacked, mouth wide open. Its aura blipped black and red as if opposing emotions warred within. I winced at the inevitable bite. At least, I think I winced. My heart wasn't hammering. I couldn't feel my body at all. And the beast swam straight through Sakki!

Now I was seeing things for sure. I had to be passed out somewhere having strange air-deprived visions.

Does Colleen see this? Sakki spun his dolphin body to watch the ankerias, but his body defied the natural laws by moving without the use of his tail or flippers.

Rhys let his spear fall, and we all stared—dumbfounded. The ankerias looked equally confused. It shook its head and blinked its dual eyelids. As Sakki swam toward me and I went to meet him, the ankerias hurled itself at Sakki again. Sakki wasn't even paying attention until he saw the beast slip through him and end up in front of him.

I closed in on them. *Raise your shield!*

Sakki faced me. His wordless confusion came through our mind-link loud and clear.

Do it! Get me and the ankerias inside.

Even I didn't understand what was happening to explain what I was doing. I just knew what needed to be done—somehow. Sakki stretched, and scales sprouted along his body as he shifted into his dragon form underwater. His clawed feet pawed through the water, helping him remain in place, then stopped. Though he didn't move, he remained unnaturally still. His otherwise invisible shield disturbed the lake as it emerged and closed in around us.

The ankerias's gaze flipped back and forth between Sakki and me as we closed in on it. It snapped its jaws and shot off, away from us, and collided with Sakki's invisible shield. The hit made the water ripple outward, away from the shield. The eel shook its head, blinking its eyelids as its puny brain tried to make sense of what was happening.

It charged again, slicing through the water between me and Sakki, and collided with the other side. Then again and again. The thing ricocheted off Sakki's shield until it turned on us. The fight had left its eyes. Instead, they looked pleading, desperate for an explanation... an escape.

"I won't hurt you." I stretched out a tentative hand, ready to snatch it back should the thing strike.

It jerked away from me, but the moment I touched it, the beast stilled. My energy felt different, but I summoned it as I'd done before. This time, my entire body seemed to glow, not just my hand. My energy surged from me to the ankerias, feeling for the life force within, and sensed opposing spirits—the energy God had breathed into the ankerias, giving it life, and Noita's. My energy reached for hers. Though it fought to remain where it was, it couldn't prevail against me. The energy that belonged pushed out what didn't, assisting me. Once I had the slippery thing in my grip, I reversed direction, pulling Noita's spirit from the ankerias—into me.

FORTY-THREE

Sakki retracted his shield.

The ankerias looked at us, its aura a steady purple. I was just as confused, but one thing was certain—the ankerias was free of Noita's spirit.

I was not.

"You're free." I motioned for the creature to swim away.

After several blinks of its dual eyelids, its pupils dilating, it slithered down, disappearing into the murky waters below.

I–I don't know what happened. I swam toward the surface, though I didn't need air. Did I even need to kick? Nay. I thought about rising to the surface, and I did. Because I was buoyant? Or something else?

Sakki was rising, too, without moving. It was like we stood on an invisible lift.

We broke the surface together. Then Rhys appeared. The top half of his merman shape looked like an older, more muscular version of his boy shape. While he had to tread water, Sakki and I didn't. Our bodies remained unnaturally still on the water's surface.

"What is happening?" Rhys's incredulous look flipped back and forth between me and Sakki. "Dragons can tread water?"

What could I say? I didn't understand any of this. I'd somehow siphoned Noita's energy into myself. I could feel it trying to mingle with my own. But it couldn't. It was a foreign entity that didn't belong.

Rhys's gaze moved to my hand, hovering on the water as if it floated.

"Is that... your mother's ring?"

I'd forgotten it was there. "Aye."

He stared, transfixed. "I knew it was powerful, but this..."

"What?" I pulled the ring off to inspect it. The world rippled with a whoosh, and I sank. Holding tight to the ring, I righted myself and treaded water. My heart resumed beating and quickened its pace. I felt my body again. It was tired. So. Very. Tired.

Sakki's long neck extended, his head strained to remain above the water, but it was going under. He retracted back into dolphin form, rose above the surface while his tail kicked, then fell sideways with a splash.

Rhys's värikäsy aura vanished.

"What do you know?" I sputtered, wiping the lake water from my face. He knew something about my ring and never told me? "What just happened?"

"I'm not sure." He waved his arms in the water as he bobbed up and down. "Seems like it stopped the natural laws. Whatever it was, that ring was the cause. To be sure, to be sure."

Or Colleen and Sakki escaped the world and its natural laws.

What do you mean?

Sakki thinks the ring brought Colleen and Sakki into the spiritual realm.

I inhaled water and coughed. *If that's true, why just us? Why not Rhys?*

Colleen and Sakki are bonded.

I relayed the message to Rhys and eyed the ring, expecting it to do... anything. "What should I do with it?"

I didn't want to put it back on. What if this was an unholy ability that would harm me somehow? It had belonged to my mother—a fae. Had it harmed me already? I now had Noita's spirit swirling within me. I felt it. Was this how Rhys felt all the time? Like a foreign invader in his soul made him... irritable? Or was it different for him since he was created to host her spirit?

"Put it away for now. Since it was your mother's, we might learn more about it in Seelie Clós. Until then, try not to use it."

That sounded like good advice. I didn't want to wear it, but I didn't want to lose it either. I tucked it into the pocket of my riding pants, then gripped Sakki's fin, and headed for shore.

WE DIDN'T TELL the others anything until we had changed into dry clothes. Sakki emerged from the lake in dragon form, spewed his catch from his mouth and scorched it, then shifted into his dog form and gobbled the fish with his tail wagging. Hiisi awaited me with leftover kani on a skewer and a wide smile.

I settled by the fire and plucked the skewer from him. "Thank you."

He wrapped his hands behind his back and beamed.

"We cooked it." Liam motioned between himself and Hadwin. "But I'm glad you get the credit, my creepy little friend."

Hiisi didn't seem to grasp the sarcasm or the not-so-thinly-veiled insult. His smile only widened.

Liam had already eaten, so now he was hungry for details. "Out with it. What happened?"

"The ring happened." I took in their confused expressions, then showed them the ring. "My mother's ring came off my chain, and... when I put it on... it *did* something."

"We think it brought them into the spiritual realm," Rhys interjected.

I tried to explain what it had felt like to feel as if I didn't have a body. Not to need air or to swim to move where I wanted.

"That sounds amazing!" Liam's gaze flicked to the ring and flamed with desire.

"Maybe? Maybe not. I mean, the ankerias couldn't kill us and I was able to remove Noita's spirit, keeping the ankerias alive."

"That's great!" Liam stood, waving his arms. "That means we can get it out of Rhys and Ruuta without killing them too."

"It's not so simple. It has to go somewhere. And... when I removed Noita's spirit from the ankerias... it entered me." I huffed out disbelief even as I spoke. "It's in me now."

Everyone sucked in a collective breath, but none louder than Hiisi. Mouth hanging open, he smacked both sides of his face and pulled his cheeks down, dragging his lower eyelids with them.

Liam's face darkened. "But we can get it out of you too?"

I bit the inside of my cheek and shook my head.

Colleen shouldn't be so negative. Sakki is sure there's a way.

I wish I had your faith.

Liam lowered back down to sit, nearly missing the rock. He gripped the back of his neck, ocean eyes flashing. "But if you could take it from the ankerias, there has to be a way to get it out of you."

"I don't know how. Someone might have to pull it out of me as I did with the creature. But I'm the only one I know who can do that."

"Might I suggest"—Rhys's held up one finger, his studious poise returning—"perhaps another elf can."

"Maybe?" Or maybe I'm meant to take it from everyone and die for them. But I couldn't say *that*. Not yet. "I think elves give energy. They help things heal and grow. I don't think they can take it away. I'm afraid..." I didn't want to admit what I was thinking, even to myself. But I had to. "I'm afraid it's the fae part of me." The bad side. More things I couldn't say.

Hiisi stuck by my side, patting my leg.

Liam continued massaging his neck, his face pinched. "We need to find Samu. He can tell us."

"Even if he can, what will happen to him if he takes her spirit?" My question met dire faces. "Are you saying…" I choked on a rising sob. "Nay. I can't let him die in my place."

Liam scrubbed his face and stood. "We'll have to deal with this another day. Right now, we need to get the last piece of Noita's soul and find our friends."

"Agreed." Hadwin's teeth scraped his lower lip hairs, making me want to hold him down and pluck the hairs out. "Since the witch is likely using Ruuta and Samu's disappearance to break us apart and distract us, I say we focus on the last piece. It will be easier to find the others when we no longer have to worry about her."

Although his suggestion made sense, I hated to move on from here without them. It felt like abandonment. But then, maybe it was better for Samu if we never found him again.

Sakki and Rhys will find Ruuta. She has Noita's soul.

I hadn't thought of that. Having a way to find them made me feel slightly better, but I didn't want it to come down to who would be the sacrifice—Samu or me. I didn't know him well, but I guessed he'd fight me on that. But, as Liam had said, that was an issue for another day. I stood and wiped off my pants. "Okay, let's go."

But my heart was no longer in this journey. I was tired and irritable. And I felt squirmy, like something inside didn't belong. Something insidious. Just what would happen to me with that witch's tainted soul skirting mine? I'd probably find out sooner than I'd like.

FORTY-FOUR

Sakki led us through a forest of twittering birds, stopping once in a while to bob his head in multiple directions. He wasn't sniffing. He used some other sense I didn't understand to hunt for Noita's spirit. When he caught the trail, he'd hurry off, struggling to slow himself for us. But I was tired. Body. Soul. Everything within me ached to stop for a long rest.

He stopped, backtracked, sniffed the air, resumed his initial trail, then stopped again and repeated. A bird squawked.

I leaned against a tree. "I'm going to wait here until you figure out where we're going."

Noita's spirit is close, but Sakki can't place it. Maybe if Colleen backed away.

I groaned and relayed the message to the others. As I moved away from Sakki, I called to Rhys. "If it's close, can you sense it?"

"Noita's spirit is near, to be sure, but I can't pinpoint it either. It keeps moving. But Sakki is right." Rhys quirked his lips in a partial frown. "You are interfering."

"Why isn't he interfering?" I motioned toward Rhys and backed further away. "He has Noita's spirit too."

It's different with Rhys.

What about Ruuta? Was it different with her too? We found the ankerias when she was around.

It's the pinpointing that's a problem. Ruuta was on shore. Now let Sakki focus.

I crossed my arms and scowled, then searched the trees where a cluster of birds had gathered. "Could it be one of those birds?"

Hiisi threw me a sheepish look. "Me no like to fly in battle."

Liam groaned. "Of course it's a bird. Whatever the witch can do to make this as difficult as possible. Last time, it was in the water where we might drown, and now... the sky where we might fall. And how in the world are we going to catch a *bird*?"

Sakki can catch a bird.

"I don't think she's going to make her demise *easy* for us, Liam." Hadwin snorted.

"We'll have to use Sakki and Rhys again. I'll go with Sakki." I jabbed a finger between Liam and Hadwin. "Do either of you want to go with Rhys?"

Colleen's not going.

Oh yes, I am, and you can't stop me.

Sakki can stop Colleen. He sat back on his haunches and lifted his front legs. They widened into wings. He flapped a few times for emphasis. Then his wings slimmed to dog legs, and he pitched forward. *Sakki can fly away—without Colleen.*

You wouldn't. My stomach melted to sludge and oozed into a puddle. *What if something happens to you?*

Liam huffed and crossed his arms. "What is going on between you two?"

Something will *happen to Sakki, eventually. But Colleen's presence will make it harder for Sakki to find Noita.*

Creeping crabs, curse this stupid witch! *But what if you need me? I have the ring.*

Sakki swiped the air with his doggy head. *Sakki doesn't need the ring.*

But how will you get Noita's spirit out?

Sakki threw me his half-lidded look that questioned my intelligence. *It's a bird. Dinner. This is no difficult task for Sakki. This is fun.*

I hadn't noticed the squawking overhead until it grew obnoxious. The sky blackened with a cloud of birds—growing larger.

Everyone else's backs were turned until they saw my reaction. Just as they spun to look, I yelled, "Run!"

No! Shield!

Liam lifted Hiisi, tossed him onto his back, and started to run.

"Wait!" I planted my feet and outstretched my hands to still them. "We can't outrun them. Stay by me. Sakki will shield us."

As Sakki ran toward us, he shifted into dragon form. I couldn't see his shield, but I felt the disturbance in the air. He moved behind us as the shield closed, probably to protect his back. The shield hadn't closed yet, and the birds were almost upon us.

The energy within me buzzed to do something, but all I could do was wait for the boundary to seal. I practically vibrated as the birds neared, then slammed into the barrier with such force, I feared they might crack it. Startled, I hopped back.

The birds flapped and squawked, pecking at the shield, slamming into it and one another over and over again. They couldn't get to me. Still, their strikes made me flinch.

Sakki winced. I could feel pain coming from him. They covered his back.

"Sakki! They're all over you!" I waffled, wanting to help, but knowing I couldn't do anything.

The persistent beaks peck, peck, pecked away at him, trying to force him to drop the boundary. I felt it all. He grimaced with every jab, but he held the barrier.

The ring, I had to use the ring. I slipped it on my finger. With a whoosh, the physical pain went away. Not even an echo of Sakki's affliction from mere seconds ago. Only my emotions remained.

In that whoosh, the birds on Sakki's back broke through, filling the boundary and rendering the shield useless. They floundered, clearly surprised by their success. As they regrouped, we stepped back.

It was too late to flee. They attacked, flying straight through me and Sakki, but their hits landed on the others. Liam yanked Hiisi from his shoulders and clutched him to his belly, shielding him from the onslaught.

The others flailed as Sakki and I watched.

Their cries were muffled by the avian cacophony. Rhys dropped to the ground, covering his head, and disappeared under a flapping mound of squawking fowl. Instinctively, I tried batting them off him, but my useless arms cut right through. I could barely see Hadwin and Liam flailing to protect themselves in the winged mass.

The birds were leaving welts and cuts. How could I help them? We had to do *something*.

Maybe...

I grabbed for Liam's hand. It failed to connect.

Please, God. Let this work.

I pushed energy through my hand and reached for the air as I did when I wrapped us in a veil. The air felt different here, but there was something.... If I could just... I strained to connect with whatever it was and felt a rip, like my hand reached through a hole in the atmosphere. A bird's wing graze me. It worked! I snatched Liam's hand and sucked my hand back through the tear.

The birds flew through him and Hiisi. Was that because they were connected?

"Quick! Grab Hadwin!" I pushed my energy through him to his hand as I reached for Rhys.

My hand slid through the swarm attacking his bloodied back. It slipped through the atmosphere, and a sharp beak jabbed me. The moment I connected with him, I closed the breach.

"I've got him!" Liam hollered over the sound of flapping wings.

My energy recoiled back to where it belonged. With each of us linked, the birds could no longer harm us. They realized the futility of their fight and retreated. A few gave last-ditch-effort pecks. But, one by one, they flew away. Once I felt they were a safe distance, I removed the ring, and Sakki's pain from his tortured back inflamed mine once again.

"What was—were we in the spiritual realm?" Liam inspected the cuts on his arms, then his chest.

Holes peppered his shirt like someone had used it for target practice. Hadwin and Rhys too.

"Aye." I moved to inspect Sakki's back. Thankfully, he had scales to protect him. But those nasty fowl still damaged him with their incessant pecking. Blood dripped between scales. His back looked like it had been tarred and feathered.

"Oh, Sakki. That looks bad. Here." I raised a hand, but he backed away.

I waved my rejected hand. *Let me heal you.*

Colleen needs her strength for the others.

It won't take that much. I looked the others over. *Maybe.*

If Sakki gets back to the temple, the temple will heal Sakki.

You'd have to fly with us on your back, you scaly-brained beast! You can't do that with your back like this. But if I heal you, we can get the others to the temple where everyone can be restored.

Colleen shouldn't waste her time going back to the temple. Colleen must find Noita's soul.

But you just said—

Colleen should help the others first. Then see what kind of energy Colleen has left.

I rolled my eyes at his obvious attempts to confuse me... anything to redirect me. It worked. I turned to heal Hiisi instead, held up a hand, and hesitated.

What was making me pause? I'd healed Sakki after he fell into the sea during the airship incident. Sakki was the first being outside of a plant that I'd ever healed, and Hiisi was so small. It would be fine.

I summoned the life force within me. Hiisi's eyes widened as my hand glowed. Then he looked at my face like a kid getting a haircut, staring at the hairdresser while the hairdresser focused on the job.

His ever-changing expression matched the oohs and aahs coming from him as all the little cuts and scrapes sealed before our eyes. As soon as I sensed his injuries had healed, I cut off the flow and retracted my life force. I barely noticed a difference in my energy.

Rhys's injuries were mostly isolated to his back. Like Hiisi's, they were superficial. Both counts would make my work easier. So, I summoned my energy once again and sent it down my arm, through my hand, to Rhys's back. Tendrils of my life force extended for his. I could sense it. So close. Then, like fingers touching a hot stove, my energy recoiled. It slammed back into me with such force, I fell backward. My breath shot out as my back collided with the hard ground, followed by my head. My vision flashed white.

"Ow!"

They rushed to my side, their faces filling my view.

I reached up to feel my head. I didn't feel blood, but I was sure to get a headache.

"Colleen!" Liam's dark hair spilled into his concerned eyes.

"Are you okay?" Hadwin almost bumped heads with Liam.

They parted the way as I peeled myself up onto my elbows, wincing at the pounding in my head.

Liam helped me up, then sat beside me for support. "What was that?"

"I don't know. It's like... his energy rejected mine. Or mine rejected his?" I shook my head, then realized my error and gripped it to stop the pain.

"I have soothing tablets in my satchel." He waved to Rhys. "Go get it, will you? Since you're the one who did this to her."

"You don't have to punish him. He didn't do it on purpose."

"Who's punishing anyone? Someone needs to get it, and I'm not leaving you. It should be him."

Guess I couldn't argue with that. "Still, are the snide remarks necessary?"

"Why are you two arguing like an old married couple?" Hadwin looked like he was hoping for a laugh. He didn't get one.

When Rhys returned, I chewed the bitter pills.

Sakki's lithe cat body wound it's way onto my lap, then went limp. Hating the bits of blood matting his fur, I summoned God's breath within me, into the hand Sakki couldn't see. Then I snatched him in both hands and shoved my energy into his back. The cuts healed as he squirmed. When he escaped my grip, the energy flow slammed shut.

Sakki leaped away, morphing into his dragon form as he went. Then he spun and slammed his front feet on the ground like an angry goat. Head held low, he blasted smoke from his nose.

Jumping to my feet, I coughed and waved the smog away. *Hey! I'm never going to get that smoky smell out of my hair.*

Colleen should have thought of that before forcing Sakki's healing.

But it didn't take much energy at all. I feel no different.

Colleen doesn't know everything. There are more consequences to actions than Colleen knows.

I leaned back as if I might see the truth better from a more distant vantage point. *What don't I know, Sakki?*

He huffed, releasing more puffs of smoke, but much smaller this time. *Every time an elf heals their bonded dragon, it takes away from the elf's lifespan.*

That knowledge knocked me back like a punch to my stomach. *Did you learn that in the temple?*

Sakki shrunk from his dragon to his dog form and nodded.

What else did you learn in the temple?

Too much for Sakki to share without transferring it to Colleen's brain as it was transferred to Sakki's.

"How could you keep something like this from me?"

"Ruuta's right. It's annoying when you two are having a conversation without us." Liam tipped his head so he peered up at me. "How about sharing?"

I obliged, then skewered Sakki with my stare. "I don't know what else he knows that he's not telling me, and I don't care if I lose some of my life if it helps my dragon. They're the years at the end, anyway."

Sakki blew up into his dragon form again, making the earth shake under his temper tantrum. *Colleen doesn't know how much time Colleen has.*

Where's your trust in God, Sakki? You're supposed to be better at this than me.

Sakki pounded the ground with his massive tail.

Liam approached, the color gone from his pinched face. He grasped my hand, and the life force within me reacted. "He's right, Colleen. It could be minutes, hours"—his Adam's apple dipped roughly, and his voice grew throatier—"years. You don't know how much time even a *little* healing may take. Sakki would've healed on his own. Please, don't take these matters into your own hands."

I yanked my hand from his, my eyes blazing. "Fine."

"Colleen, I—"

I took in his slack-jawed expression, then turned away again. "You all don't need me. Just go get the bird."

Fury flamed within me. I did all I could to push it down to a smolder. But I couldn't talk to anyone. I couldn't even look at them. Anything might set the fire to blazing. I stormed off in a huff and slumped by a tree—alone.

FORTY-FIVE

It didn't take long for the fury to simmer down. The flame was still there, ready to ignite at the wrong move, but another, more powerful feeling had set in.

Regret.

I pulled my legs up and wrapped my arms tight around them. How could I be so stupid over something so minor? They were right to be concerned. Sakki had every right to decide if he wanted to be healed or not. It wasn't up to me. I wasn't in control.

But now that I'd fallen into this self-pity pit, I didn't know how to get out. Just go back to the others as if nothing happened?

Nay. I'd look like a fool.

Humph. Look, nothing... I *was* a fool.

This wasn't like me. Was this Noita's spirit within me? Or maybe it was me and I'd just never had the opportunity to respond this way. There was something about the anger... something about the pity... Part of me *liked* it, though it made me feel terrible.

Oh God, what is wrong with me?

This was what we weren't supposed to do. I'd been warned Noita would try to separate us, and I stormed off like a petulant child. But how could I face anyone again?

Crows cawed in the distance. Was Sakki out there now? Trying to fight those birds without me? Without the ring?

I blew out frustration and dropped my head onto my knees.

It was my fault. All my fault.

Something touched my leg, and an image of the hand coming out of the earth jerked me from my pity pit. I scrambled away from the hand before realizing it was Hiisi. He gave me his sad smile, then scooted closer, and resumed patting my leg.

"Where are the others? Are they with you?"

Hiisi looked toward a thick copse of trees, and the others stepped out. Even Sakki. He bounded over, morphed from his dog into his cat form, and crawled into my lap.

I guess this means I'm forgiven?

There is nothing to forgive. Sakki should have told Colleen before. Sakki shouldn't have gotten mad.

I shouldn't have forced you to let me heal you. And I shouldn't have gotten mad either. I braved a meek smile at the others. "I shouldn't have stormed off. Ruuta did that, and now she and Samu are missing. I'm sorry."

Liam crouched by my side. Bits of drying blood mottled his face. He brushed a tuft of curls from my cheek. "I'm sorry too. And what is it they say in Ariboslia? You are loved."

Though I understood the meaning behind those words referring to God's love, somehow, hearing them from him made my face erupt in flames. But I couldn't do anything about the blush without bringing more attention to it. With his gaze so intent on mine, he didn't seem to notice.

I struggled to pull myself out of the foul mood. Noita's spirit must be having some effect on me. I was far from perfect, but this felt... different. Maybe she was working her magic on me to separate me from my friends from the inside.

Liam was still holding my hand. Beyond the initial shock of

reacting to his energy so strongly, I could now sense the damage to his body. I'd never healed him and Hadwin.

"Will you allow me to heal you?" I asked.

He twitched. "If it won't shorten your life. Or take much out of you."

"It won't." Sakki didn't speak up, so I assumed it wouldn't shorten my life. But it might take more energy than I'd let on. "The wounds are superficial."

But what about the strange thing that happened any time I touched him? Was that because he was human? Or because we had some sort of connection? What would happen when I tried to heal him? *Did you learn anything about healing humans in the temple?*

Elves and dragons avoided humans. Sakki isn't aware of any elves healing a human.

Creeping crabs. *I guess we'll find out then.*

He stood up on my lap. Alert. *Sakki will be here if anything goes wrong.*

"Anything you care to share with the class?" Liam's nervous laugh sent a fresh wave of trepidation through me.

"I–I've never healed a human before."

He squeezed my hand and peered into my eyes, captivating all my attention. "You don't have to do this."

I could stare into those ocean eyes all day, but I had to tear myself away. "Nay, I want to. But I don't want to hurt you."

"You won't."

I plucked my hand from his, hesitated, took a deep breath, then reached for his face, trying to ignore his energy surging at my touch. *God, help me heal him.*

I summoned God's breath within me and sent it to my hand, watching for a reaction as my hand lit, warming his face. His eyes widened, but I didn't find hints I caused him pain, so I continued. I sent tendrils of my energy into him and connected with his.

For a moment, I feared his life force would reject mine as Rhys's had. I could feel it so strongly. But it didn't. It *embraced* mine, pulling it until our energy intermingled and almost danced. I sucked in a breath. Never had I experienced anything like this. It sent a thrill through me. Judging by the dreamy look in his eyes, he felt it too.

The cuts closest to my hand sealed. Then the healing spread out until all the visible abrasions had regenerated new skin. But there were more on his arms, back, legs... everywhere the birds could reach. My energy continued to course through him, still entwined in his, until I sensed every cut had healed. Then I began my retreat, hesitating. My energy wanted to stay and continue this dance. But I couldn't. There was Hadwin to heal and a witch to hunt. So, I retracted to where my energy belonged until my hand dimmed and I retreated.

Liam looked like he was in a daze, tranquil. He blinked, the sharpness returning to his eyes with each blink. "Whoa."

"Are you all right?"

"More than all right." He yanked his pant leg up past his calf. "My scar is gone. You've healed my scar."

That was unexpected. I didn't know what to say. But whatever just happened, I felt slightly... embarrassed. But why?

Because, though I'd never kissed anyone in a romantic way, whatever just happened had felt as intimate. Maybe more.

Hadwin stepped forward. "How are you, Princess? Are you able to heal me too?"

Liam jumped up and faced Hadwin as if ready to fight. Then he ran a hand through his hair and held on. With a fistful of hair and a flustered look, he swung his gaze between me and Hadwin. "Uh, I don't know if that's a good idea."

Hadwin's jaw slackened. "Why not?"

"It—I—"

I had to spare Liam with whatever he was thinking. "It will be fine. I think."

Liam released his hair and dropped his hand. "It will?"

I wasn't sure, but I had to try. How could I leave Hadwin with all those injuries if it was within my power to help him? And how could

I explain why Liam was clearly struggling with this? Or that I understood? I just had to hope nothing so... intimate... happened with Hadwin. Somehow, I didn't think it would. "Just... let me try."

God, please don't let whatever happened between me and Liam be the way it is with every human, or I'll never heal another human again... aside from Liam.

Liam's mouth flattened, and his eyes flashed. But he didn't try to stop me. Good enough.

I moved to Hadwin, summoning my energy as I closed the distance. Rather than touch his face, I grasped his bare lower arm. This time, when I sent out tendrils, Hadwin's energy accepted mine, but it didn't embrace it like Liam's had. I let out a relieved breath, then set to work seeking out the injuries. It was faster work, and I had no trouble disconnecting. Nor was I embarrassed.

Thank You, God.

Liam looked from me and Hadwin and back again. "Was that it?"

"Was that it?" Hadwin ran his hands down his legs, then twisted to inspect the skin beneath the holes in his shirt. "She just healed me!" He pulled me into a tight hug, lifting my feet from the ground, then put me back down. "I feel great! Thank you."

At least now I could heal humans, and it wouldn't result in whatever had happened with Liam. Somehow, healing them seemed to have healed me too. I felt more energized, and my headache was gone.

But what had happened with Rhys? It must have had something to do with him being created by Noita. The poor creature looked at us dejected, still suffering with his abrasions. "Liam, do you have that healing balm?"

He moved to his satchel and rooted around until he came up with the tin. "Got it."

I held my hand out for it. "Let's do what we can for Rhys."

Rhys smiled, perking up, and removed his shirt.

I set to work slathering each cut with the balm. Thankfully, he'd curled up in a ball so his injuries were mostly on his back and arms. "What are our plans now? We have a witch to hunt."

We deliberated until Rhys was slippery with the greasy ointment, finally agreeing that we'd stick together, traveling as long as we could on the ground.

As we set off, Liam gripped my wrist, holding me back from the others. "Can we talk about what happened when you healed me?"

Forty-Six

My face grew hot, and I fought to squash the sensations arising within me at the mere memory. "I don't know. I– I'd never healed a human before."

"But now you've healed two, me and Hadwin. Whatever happened with me didn't seem to happen with Hadwin." His jaw twitched. "Did it?"

"Nay, I—"

He rounded on me with a pointed finger. "Then you *did* feel it!"

I took a deep breath and pressed my lips together. What could I say? That I'd never experienced something so intimate? How embarrassing. So, I said nothing and resumed walking.

Hiisi glanced back from Hadwin's shoulders. Rhys and Sakki ventured on, oblivious to Liam and me.

Liam's gaze darted to the others. Then he pulled me to slow. "Look, I don't know what happened, but... I–I care about you. And I don't want what happened between us to happen with anyone else."

"It won't."

"So, whatever happened between us didn't happen with Hadwin?"

He was growing infuriating. "I said it didn't, didn't I?"

We walked side by side in silence. Then Liam caught my gaze askance and grinned. "You felt it too."

I didn't know if I should laugh, reach out and kiss him already, or slap him. But the feelings I'd felt when healing him pinged around within me at his grin—his presence. Liam was a rather pleasantly maddening distraction. He was infuriatingly adorable—infurable. And yet, every time he looked at me, a tingling sensation swept over me.

This was going to be a long road ahead.

I'd never in my life felt so elated. Was this what it felt like to be in love? Or infatuated? I didn't know the difference. If only I could talk to someone about this. My mind drifted to Ruuta, and a pang stabbed my stomach. Here I was basking in Liam's glow and whatever was growing between us. And she was... where? Was she in danger? And we weren't even looking for her. Would I ever see her again? I shouldn't care. She'd fooled me into thinking she was my friend and was there for me when all along she was serving some demon.

But there had to be help for her. Didn't there? I couldn't abandon her.

Nay. I wouldn't. We had to find her and release Noita's spirit, or we'd all be trapped in here forever. It was a matter of time before we found her.

But the guilt wouldn't go away. And even though I tried holding onto my euphoria, it slipped away. Never before had my emotions been so unstable.

Liam had gotten ahead, and he looked back with a goofy grin. As soon as he saw me, his face fell. "Are you all right?" he asked, more attentive than ever.

"Aye. I think." But as I walked, my surroundings wavered. I stopped to steady myself before I fell. The path turned to stone as the trees morphed into small cement homes stacked upon one another.

Bandia?

Nay. Nay, nay, nay. This wasn't happening. I was *not* in Bandia.

But my eyes told me otherwise. Before taking another step between the homes, I called out for Sakki in my mind. Then listened.

But I heard nothing. No response.

Then I smelled it. That telltale electric smell.

Fasgadair.

My heart seized and rammed into my throat.

Nay. Nay, nay, nay. I fled—up the stairs along the path I'd taken all those years ago. But this time, I was alone. I wasn't carrying baby Beagan or urging Corwin and Nialla to stifle their cries and hurry. That should have made my flight easier. It didn't.

I found the first opened door and went inside—alone—with no one else to usher in, then pushed the door closed as quietly as possible. The sound of footsteps approaching and the growing electric stench were like an invisible cattle prod pushing me backward, into the cookstove. The moment my back collided with the stove, I fled into an adjoining room I knew all too well to hide under the table. But... there was no table.

Where was the table?

I crammed myself into the corner and squeezed my eyes shut.

Please hide me. Please hide me. Please hide me.

"Why are you hiding?" A strong, yet gentle voice spoke into my ear.

I jerked awake. Pressing my back into the corner and searched the room for whoever—or *whatever*—had spoken.

"I freed you from this room when you were a child."

"God?" It had to be Him. Never had I heard Him audibly. But no one was with me. I was alone. And who else could make that claim?

"Why are you still here?" he asked so gently, yet firmly.

I studied the room, the prison of my childhood, and fought to control the shaking the mere sight of this place induced. "But I've faced this already. I've overcome...."

Hadn't I?

"You have never let this place go. Not fully. It is your prison still. A prison of your own making."

His voice... His words... They sliced me open and laid me bare. My heart wrenched as tears slipped down my face.

"I didn't create you to have a spirit of fear. My spirit resides in you. With Me, you have overcome. Nothing is impossible with Me. Yet you choose to remain here."

Overcome, I threw myself prostrate before Him and wept. "Forgive me. I didn't know. It didn't feel... like I had a choice."

"Put on your ring."

Choking on sobs, I peeled myself off the floor, rummaged through my pocket for the ring, and slid it onto my finger. The moment it slid into place, I saw Him and averted my gaze. He lifted my chin to face Him. But how could I look upon God? My gaze drifted toward His, shied away, then returned. The depth of emotions there were overwhelming—compassion, grace, truth... love. It made me want to both melt, dissolving into tears, and jump onto my feet and run toward whatever He called me to. But I remained still, staring into the depths of His soul.

"You have done well, my child. You have overcome much, but you hold yourself captive when you should be free, filled with My power."

With the ring, in the spiritual realm, I no longer felt my body, but my emotions were raw. Sorrow and regret threatened to overtake me, but His gaze held me together.

I cast my gaze downward. "Forgive me."

"You are forgiven. Now go forward in My power."

"But what of Noita's soul within me?"

"My child, if I am for you, who can be against you?"

"But I don't understand? How do I free myself from it?"

"Have you learned nothing? What should you do if you want something?"

"Ask?"

He gave me a small smile.

"Can You... I mean, *will* You free me from the witch?"

He reached into my body and pulled out the silvery spirit. It writhed in His hand. "I will put this where it belongs."

With that, the thing disappeared. Did it go back to Noita's body? To Hades? I didn't ask. It seemed to be a private matter between Him and Noita, not me.

"Now, Noita can no longer trick your mind into returning to this place. It wasn't difficult for her to manipulate you once her spirit connected with yours. But you tend to revisit this place on your own without prompting from others."

The look in His eyes made me shrink away.

He held my chin to face Him again. "You must make every effort to stay away. When you feel yourself drifting back, call out to Me. I am your ever-present help in time of need."

"But what am I supposed to do? Am I supposed to kill the witch? Go to Seelie Clós to Queen Rhiannon?"

"Ah." He laughed, and His joy rippled through my spirit. "What do you hope to gain with such questions?"

I shrugged. "Answers?"

"Control." He stroked my cheek with His thumb. "Life is not about gaining control but learning to trust... learning to follow Me. If you know everything that will happen, how will you trust? What will you need with Me?"

I had never thought about it that way before. "But not knowing makes me so unsure. What if I make the wrong choices?"

"Are you so powerful that you can thwart My plans?"

I shrank back. "Nay. Forgive me. I just—" My excuses fell dead in His presence, and I had nothing to say.

"As I told you when you began this journey, seek Me. Trust Me. You can't change my plans. But if you walk with Me, you will find your way. Cast your cares on Me, for I care for you."

I had nothing to say, so I stared into His eyes and soaked up the love within them.

He held my hand and stroked the ring. "As for this ring. When you are ready, remove it. Only use it when I prompt you to do so."

"What happens when I remove it? Will you be gone again?"

He pulled me into His embrace. "My dear, dear child. I have never left you. I will never leave you nor forsake you. Though you can't see me, I am with you to the ends of the age."

I wrapped my arms around Him, never wanting to let go. He didn't say a word, but let me remain in His embrace. Though I wanted to stay this way forever, I couldn't. He had plans for me. And others were counting on me. So, I peeled myself from His grip.

"I love you." I slid the ring from my finger.

My surroundings wavered, and God's smiling face winked. The house in Bandia disappeared with Him. But, unlike the house in Bandia, God was still here. I looked up into my friends' concerned faces.

"She's waking!" Liam, kneeling beside me, squeezed my hand.

"Thank God!" Hadwin said.

Hiisi leaped to his feet and gripped his heart with exaggerated relief.

Rhys just smiled.

"What happened?" I peeled myself away from the tree I'd slumped against and searched the woods.

"You were in some kind of a trance." Liam rubbed the back of his neck. "I wasn't sure you'd ever come out of it."

"It was Noita. Her spirit with mine. She tricked me."

"How'd you escape?" Rhys narrowed his unearthly blue eyes. "And why don't I sense Noita in you?"

"God." A broad smile stretched out my lips, and my spirit lightened at the mere thought of Him. "He freed me. Noita's spirit is gone."

Liam sucked in a breath, his eyes wide with astonished relief. "Oh, thank God."

"We're wasting time." I stood and brushed myself off. "We have a witch to hunt."

FORTY-SEVEN

Rhys kicked a pebble in his path. "I don't know how Sakki senses Noita's soul from so far off." He lifted his chin and squinted at something. "I had a hard time sensing the other pieces with you—or with Ruuta—so close. I don't know how he does it with me around."

I wanted to ask how he handled having her in there with him. Did he have his own soul or only Noita's? Did she make him do things he might not otherwise do? Was he trapped in any prisons? He certainly wasn't free. But what good would come from such conversations? It wouldn't get rid of the spirit plaguing him.

But God said if I want something, I have to ask.

God, please help Rhys get rid of Noita's spirit too. I don't know what Your plans are for a creature like him, but I pray he can be saved. Please save him.

Something in the asking made me feel better. "I wouldn't worry about it. Just be glad we have a way of finding the pieces."

Rhys eyed me askance, his mouth twitching like he wanted to ask me something, but changed his mind.

I was concerned about facing another bird attack and Noita and how to eliminate her soul from my friends. But my worries were nothing like before. God was with me. *Thank You. Thank You. Thank You.*

Colleen is welcome?

I barked out a laugh, earning looks from Rhys and Liam. *I was talking to God.*

Like Sakki has said so many times, Colleen should address God.

He knows I'm talking to Him. You're the only one who's confused.

Sakki's dog form continued trotting ahead, but he looked back at me. *What has happened to Colleen?*

God has.

Liam kept looking at me funny. What must he be thinking after what happened between us and then after what just happened to me?

He bent closer to speak to me alone. But, when he opened his mouth, his gaze tore away, and he spoke to everyone. "Do we have a plan to find this bird and suck Noita's spirit from it? I don't know about the rest of you, but I'd rather not face another murder of crows."

Hadwin agreed, and Rhys grimaced. He couldn't take another attack. If only I could have healed him. Why hadn't I asked God how when I'd had the opportunity? Now that I was no longer in His presence, all the questions I should have asked ran through my mind in an endless loop.

I could ask still. God was still with me.

God, if there's a way to heal Rhys, please show me. And show us how to get Noita's soul from this bird.

I tried to listen for God's reply over the others speaking, but I heard nothing.

"We shouldn't separate again. But we should meet them in the air where we're less likely to get overrun."

"Thanks for your contribution." Liam bowed. "But we already said that."

"Oh." My face reddened. I had to pay attention. "Rhys should fly on his own, if he can, without passengers given his back."

"Said that too." Liam smiled, flashing his gleeful ocean eyes at me.

"Did you already say that the rest of us should be passengers on Sakki's back?"

"Yep. But I'm glad to see you agree." Liam's smile turned to a frown as he looked upon Hiisi on Hadwin's shoulders. "Your little friend isn't too happy about it, though."

With the way Hiisi had jutted his teeth against his lip, he might be trying not to vomit all over Hadwin.

An idea came to me. "He's small. What if we wrap him up so he can't see anything and stuff him in one of our satchels? We can attach the satchel to Hadwin's stomach so he can hold Hiisi and Hiisi can be strapped in."

"I like it." Hadwin searched the skies. "The sooner we're off the ground where we're the prey and in the sky where we're the hunter, the better."

"Why him? Why not you?" Hiisi asked me with enormous eyes glistening.

"I'll need to hide us. Keeping up the veil takes energy. Hadwin will keep a better grip."

Hiisi did not look happy at all as we rearranged our things to empty a satchel for him. And, as he stepped inside and I pulled it up around him, he gave me the most pitiful look.

"Why are you having such a hard time with this? You flew with us before."

"Me no like to fly. Me really no like to fight birds in air."

"I'm sorry, Hiisi. We have to keep you safe and with us."

"What if me fall?" He jabbed a thumb at himself. "Me no fly. Me fall hard."

"I will do everything within my power to keep you safe."

He dropped his head. "Me afraid of that."

"Oh, Hiisi." I hugged him, satchel and all. *Please, God, do not let any harm come to him. Or any of us.*

Once we were ready, we took to the sky. Two grown men, me, and Hiisi were about the maximum Sakki should handle. All of us weighing him down would make for an interesting journey.

THE DIVIDE DIDN'T LOOK so bad from up here. Particularly as I was beginning to see things for how they were, not as Noita wanted me to see them. What if I had seen those birds as she'd wanted me to? What would they look like? Skeleton birds or giant winged beasts? I could only imagine. But the fact that they were just birds didn't make the task any easier. If they should gather and swarm us, being in the air might be worse. Birds were crafty, agile things. While Sakki would be sorely limited.

At least we had Rhys. Though he was injured, he was unencumbered, free to move as his pained body allowed.

So far, I'd seen nothing. Not a bird in the sky.

Noita's spirit is down there. There was no way for Sakki to point. He couldn't move his head without changing our trajectory, and all I saw were treetops.

What should we do?

Can Colleen use the ring?

Nay. Only when God tells me to. He was clear on that.

Then Sakki will land where Noita's spirit is.

I cringed, but what choice did we have? At least we were hidden in my veil. *Okay. But try to land somewhere where we won't be seen. No tall grasses.*

As we descended, storm clouds gathered and swirled, darkening the sky. Thunder clapped, and lightning charged up at us from the ground. Sakki dipped to avoid being hit by the jagged, electrified spear. It smelled like fasgadair. My heart thundered. Rhys tucked into a dive, something Sakki couldn't do.

Use your shield!

Shield doesn't work on Sakki's back! He continued using evasive maneuvers and lowering in altitude as best he could without making us sick.

Creeping crabs! I should have thought of that.

Another thunderclap made me flinch. I almost slipped from my seat. Another lightning bolt cracked the sky, tearing through my heart, electrifying everything within me, and forcing all my hairs on end.

Sakki banked again, rougher this time, nearly spilling us.

"Why is lightning coming from the ground?" Liam yelled.

"It must be the witch!" Hadwin hollered back.

I put a finger to my mouth and strained to ensure they both saw me. But why was I so worried about her hearing us? If she was shooting lightning at us, she must know where we were. But how? Was my veil not working?

Sakki can't wait. He tucked into a dive toward the spot where the lightning seemed to come from, swerving right and left. My heart rammed into my throat while my stomach stayed above. We plummeted, leaving my stomach behind.

Are you insane? You're flying us at the lightning!

It seems to take time to generate power between strikes.

Two! There's only been two!

I nearly slid from my seat as I pressed into Sakki's neck, holding on for dear life. Liam and Hadwin rammed into my back. Poor Hiisi must be squished in between them. I hoped he could breathe.

Thunder sounded. Lightning struck.

Sakki pulled up, yanking us. We almost fell backward from the sudden change. The lightning crashed underneath him, splitting a tree. As it fell, Sakki jerked us away, then landed.

Quick! Dismount! Sakki will use the shield.

I shouted the order to the others. We scrambled from his back. Sakki's shield closed us in. Where was Rhys? I searched, hoping he'd make it inside in time, but he was nowhere to be seen.

"Did you really think you could defeat me?" A familiar voice called.

The witch.

FORTY-EIGHT

I yanked my head toward the voice to find her looking different from when we'd met. She was tall now, angular, with those antlers like dead trees. She pressed her palms together, swirling them in a circular pattern as if she were making a dough ball. Electric tendrils formed, crackling broken buzzing sounds.

Noita opened her palms with a thundering boom, and an electric bolt shot from her, hitting Sakki's shield. The buzzing grew louder. The fasgadair smell triggered me to hide. But there was nowhere to go, and I wouldn't be that scared girl anymore. God had healed me. I couldn't live defeated.

But what *could* I do?

Sakki's shield seemed to amplify the electric bolt. It buzzed and raced around the shield endlessly.

Is it hurting you?

No. Noita's lightning is only affecting Sakki's shield. But Sakki doesn't know how much the shield can withstand.

The charge choked out a few more zaps before petering out.

Noita was swirling her hands again, preparing for another attack. "How dare you threaten me in my *home*."

"Rotko doesn't belong to you!" Hadwin shouted.

Noita ambled toward us. "You think it belongs to you, human? You've no place in this realm."

"The Divide belongs to the dragons. The elves. Even the fae who sought refuge here," he seethed. "Not you!"

The fae?

Noita launched another attack. As the lightning zipped and zapped the shield, I sensed Sakki tiring.

Sakki, we have to do something! You won't make it!

Use the ring.

That wasn't Sakki. That was God.

"Hold on to me." I pulled the ring from my pocket. God knew what He was doing, but I'd do what He commanded *and* protect my friends, if possible. As soon as Liam and Hadwin each gripped an arm, I slipped the ring onto my finger while she prepared her next strike.

Once the ring was on my finger, the shield lowered. Noita's hands stopped swirling. Her feet stopped advancing. "You have the ring."

Sakki leaped over us. Powerful flaps of his wings blasted us with wind. His dangling feet barely missed our heads as he charged for the witch. Her eyes widened when he neared. He opened his mouth, and a blast of fire shot out. A puff of purple smoke engulfed the witch just before the fire reached her. Sakki's fire shot right through the smoke.

The witch was gone.

"What was that?" Liam raked a hand through his hair. "You were sensing Noita, not the bird, this whole time? We can't kill the witch while a piece of her soul is out there. Isn't that right?"

Sakki can't sense the difference between Noita's spirit and Noita.

I relayed his message.

"Facing the witch before we've disposed of her spirits will only get us killed." Hadwin's face was turning red.

"Take it easy. It was an honest mistake." I rubbed the velvety scales on Sakki's shoulder.

Hadwin blew out a breath. "An honest mistake that's going to get us killed."

"Hold on." Liam held out his hands to stop the argument. "Did we think it would be so easy? Noita's protecting the bird. That's what I would do."

Nice of Liam to try to calm Hadwin down. I clapped him on the shoulder and gave him an appreciative smile. "We faced her twice now and lived."

"Third time's a charm?" Liam gave me a sheepish grin.

"Humph." Hadwin crossed his arms.

There was no talking to him right now. I chalked his combativeness up to nerves. He'd been trapped in here for a long time and seen his opportunity to kill the witch. He wanted it done. I understood that. But rather than continue senseless arguments, I hurried to the satchel hiding Hiisi. A figure emerging from the woods stayed my hands.

Rhys.

"Where were you?" The fight had gone from Hadwin's voice, slightly.

"Hiding. I wanted to get to you, but you were in the shield and under attack."

I stopped listening to their conversation and peeled back the flap. Hiisi shivered inside. I dug him out and held him close, crooning. "You're okay, now."

"Me no like Noita. Noita eat Hiisi." His voice shook as badly as his body. "Me no fly."

He wrapped his arms around my neck. "I hate to say it, but we still haven't found the bird. If we're to stick together, we will need to fly again."

"I can stay back with him," Hadwin offered.

"But if we're separated—"

"Hiisi and I have lived in this place a long time. After countless attempts over decades... well... it shouldn't surprise me if it takes longer than I'd hoped." Hadwin motioned toward Hiisi. "Do you want him caught up in all of this?"

Hiisi's wide eyes pooled with tears as his bottom lip quivered. "Me help elf get out," he said in the most pitiful, heart-wrenching voice I've ever heard.

I sat on the ground, pulled him onto my lap, and hugged him. "Hadwin's right. It's too dangerous for you. You helped me get this far. I will make it out of here. And if God wants you to show me the rest of the way, we'll be reunited first. But I want you safe."

"Me want to stay with elf."

"Even if you have to fly again?"

Hiisi shrank back, then closed his eyes, and wailed. I pulled him close and rocked him, filling myself with calm and sharing it with him until he quieted. "You are loved, Hiisi. You are loved."

I continued to comfort him. "If Noita's protecting the bird, how are we going to get it?"

"I'm sure she is." Hadwin scraped his facial hair. "Her spirit remains in Rhys, Ruuta, herself, and that bird. It's the last of her soul's hosts that aren't herself or against her. If I were her, I'd stay close to protect it."

"Then every time we try to go after the bird—"

"You'll have to face Noita."

At Hadwin's interruption, Liam grasped the back of his neck and shook his head. "I don't know how to get past her."

I felt the circular lump in my pocket. "She seemed afraid of the ring. Didn't she?"

Hadwin continued working on his beard with his teeth, then stopped. "I have an idea."

"What?" I leaned closer while trying to avoid disturbing Hiisi.

The others stepped closer, eager for anything to help.

"Her hut." He smoothed the facial hair he'd disturbed. "Her potions, crystals—everything she uses for spells and hexes and to rejuvenate when you harm her—it's all in her hut."

Liam lowered his hand from his neck, clenching it into a fist. "We could set it on fire."

Rhys raised a finger in the air. "And it might provide the distraction we need to get the bird. *And* find Ruuta and Samu."

"Or it could just enrage her." I didn't want a witch on a rampage coming after me.

Quirking his lips, Hadwin shrugged.

"It's a plan." Liam slapped his fist against his thigh. "And it's the only one we've got."

Hadwin gathered his things, then came back for Hiisi. He reached out a hand.

While taking Hadwin's hand, Hiisi kept his gaze on me. "If elf need Hiisi, Hiisi will appear."

I hugged him and kissed his cheek. "Then we will see each other again soon because I will need you."

Hiisi smiled a wide smile, and hope glinted in his teary eyes.

Rhys morphed into a dragon, and I climbed Sakki's back with Liam. Just the four of us. Not too long ago, there were eight.

God, please... if this plan is foolish, stop us. I can't lose anyone else.

After listening to Hadwin's directions to the hut, Sakki took to the sky. Now, I could only hope Noita was with the bird and that, if we were successful in destroying her hut, we'd get out of there before she arrived.

God, please help us.

FORTY-NINE

We flew through the dark sky, following Hadwin's directions. Was it night? Or did Noita still have enough power to make it appear so? Shimmers of wavy lights rippled through the darkness. So perhaps the witch was losing her hold. At any other time, flying in the dark like this, I'd enjoy the light show. I might even find it calming.

Not today.

I kept an eye out for anything witch-shaped to appear in the darkness. For lightning to strike us or something to shoot us down.

God, I hope our plan is working and the witch is far, far, away from here.

Sakki, do you sense Noita's spirit?

Sakki senses something to the left, but also up ahead.

Please, please, please be Ruuta up ahead.

The giant moon I'd seen outside Noita's hut began to take shape. Whatever that was, it was *not* a normal moon. With its unnatural size, we should have seen it from afar. But nay, as we approached, the area lightened until the moon took shape.

We must be near the hut.

I tried to swallow my anxious thoughts. But my stomach squeezed, rejecting them.

Please don't let me throw up all over Sakki.

Yes, Sakki agrees with this prayer.

The hut's silhouette on the cliffside took shape, and my hands shook visibly. This was the last place I wanted to be. If we destroyed Noita's hut, how mad would she be? How much might she do to retaliate? What might she be compelled to do to me, Rhys, Liam—I gulped—or Sakki?

I had to stop with the what-ifs. It was making me feel more and more sick. More and more incapable.

But God was with me.

Must remember that. I wasn't alone. My friends were here, and God was with us.

Light in. Dark out.

Light in. Dark out.

I am not alone.

You are with me.

Great is Your faithfulness...

Sakki circled the hut, flying closer and closer with each cycle like liquid in a funnel.

Rhys shifted into his normal boy shape as he landed. He climbed the steps I couldn't see upon my escape, peered in the window, then waved to us to land.

We alighted by the steps.

Tell Rhys to make sure Noita's home is clear and to be quick. Sakki wants to set Noita's home on fire before Noita returns. Sakki sat back, ready to conjure his fire.

"Rhys!" I yelled in a hushed voice.

He reappeared from the side of the porch and held up his hands. "Stop!"

His volume made me grimace and search for Noita, who must've heard him from any distance. I sensed Sakki's groan through our bond.

"They're in there!" Rhys ran to the door and pulled it open.

"Who's in there?" Liam and I both asked, giving each other a bewildered look.

Could it be Ruuta and Samu? Or Eliina and the other elves. Were they real? Or part of the ruse? We ran for the stairs. Liam took giant leaps, skipping every other one.

Inside the hut, a shocked Ruuta and Samu huddled there with glazed eyes.

"Where? How?" Still blinking, Ruuta raised her head. "How did you walk through the wall?"

"There's a door." I swung it open and closed as proof.

Her expression scrunched even further. "No, there isn't."

I sighed. Even with it open, she couldn't see? Did she think I was just swinging my arm? "There is. You just can't see it. I went through the same thing, only I had to wait until I could see it. We don't have time to wait for you. Come on." I waved her to come.

She didn't move. "Something's wrong with Samu. He's unresponsive. I've been trying for hours. Or days." She squinted up at me. "How long have we been here?"

"He must be under her spell." I shuddered. Is that what I looked like when she had me seeing her visions? But where were the other elves? They'd seemed so real. But were they?

"Is there anyone else in here?" I only saw one other door. Was that to the closet where I first woke up? Where I met Hiisi?

Rhys opened the door, then shrugged. "Nothing but a bunch of junk."

Aye... It was. The supply closet.

"I'll get Samu." Liam crossed the floor, crouched beside his slumped form, and slapped his face. Hard. Red fingerprints were already appearing.

Sharpness returned to Samu's eyes. Then he gasped at his attacker. "Wha—"

"You were under the witch's spell. But we've got to get you out of here." Liam flung Samu's loose arm over his shoulder and hauled him to unstable feet.

Rhys ran to help. While they stumbled away, I reached out to Ruuta.

"You have to come with us. Now."

She took baby steps toward me, looking like a kid caught in a pile of candy wrappers. Both penitent and slightly sick. "I apologize, Princess. Not for helping you become queen to bring down the Divide. But... I should have told you. Everything."

I waved, growing impatient. "We can talk about it later. We don't have time. Sakki needs to burn this place down before the witch returns."

Still, she hesitated. And a full-body groan ran through me. What I would've given for some firecrackers to throw at her feet and incite her to move. I yanked her to the door. "Come on!"

"How will we get out? There's no—"

I pulled her through what must've looked like a wall. "Aye, there is. You just can't see it." I tried picking up speed down the steps.

She tugged her hand free. "Are you trying to kill me?"

Of course. She couldn't see those either and thought I was pulling her off the ledge. "Do you think I've learned to levitate since we last met? There are steps. You just can't see them."

What was that in the sky? Was it? Dread froze my gut, then fanned out, icing my veins.

"Sakki! The witch!" I grabbed Ruuta's hand again, tighter, and would not take no for an answer. With a strength I didn't know I was capable of, I dragged her down the steps.

Once we were clear, Sakki filled his lungs with a deep inhale, then pitched forward, sweeping his spewing fire until it petered out.

Noita landed and began charging her hands. "How dare you sniveling little maggots threaten my home!"

"Sakki! Look out!" I yelled past my heart in my throat.

He shot into the sky and flew to the other side of the house. He rose above the flames and blasted it once more.

Noita shot another lightning bolt at him, hitting her house and adding to the damage.

Sakki's head reared back in a roar.

Then he fell.

FIFTY

"Naaaaaaaaaay!" This couldn't be happening. Sakki hadn't fallen.

"Sakki!" I ran to the ledge, but the flames were spreading. I could only get so close, and the firelight cast nothing but dancing shadows that failed to reach the depths. "Saaaaaaaa-keeeeeeee!"

My heart stopped. Everything stopped except the incessant blinding flames that wouldn't allow me to see anything. Cursed flames!

He'd come flying up from the depths any second. He evaded the hit. It was all a ruse to fake the witch. He wasn't hit. He wasn't.

He couldn't be.

Please, please don't be hit.

"Saaaaaaakeeee!"

"Your dragon is dead." Noita stepped toward me.

"Nay." I'd feel it if he was gone. I'd know. Wouldn't I?

With a burst, he flew up from the depths, rising over the flames, and straight at Noita.

"No." Her eyes bulged out of her cruel face. She rubbed her

hands together, summoning another jolt of lightning. "Would you die already, you wretched beast?"

"Sakki, get back!" *You'll get yourself killed!*

As I feared for my dragon's life, I was only half aware of Samu's glowing hand and the silvery light transferring from Ruuta to him. Was he taking Noita's spirit into himself? But why? Nay, I couldn't be bothered with that whilst Sakki had the witch's attention. I had to do something. But what?

Noita's lightning zapped and buzzed in her hand, begging to be released.

I ran at her, not thinking about anything but stopping her. I'd tackle her to the ground if I had to. I'd fall on that bolt and let it zap me before I let it hit Sakki.

Before I reached her, she sent the bolt zipping through the air, straight at Sakki, hitting him square in the chest.

"Nay!" I screamed as I veered toward my falling dragon.

He landed with a sickening thud. "Nay! Nay, nay, nay. Nay!" I caught up to him and slumped over his fallen body. "Naaaaaaaaaaay!"

"Did you honestly expect to defeat *me*, you miserable twit?" The witch gloated. "I am beyond death."

An anger unlike any I'd ever experienced burned in my heart and scorched every inch of my being. I touched Sakki's face. *Wake up, Sakki. Please, please, please wake up.*

Use the ring.

"Wake up!" I screamed, pushing him so that his head lolled. I still didn't sense that he was dead... yet. And part of me recognized God's voice. But His voice was a small buoy bobbing on the deep sorrow swirling within me.

"I may not be able to kill you, half-breed, but I can make your miserable life more miserable." At the nasty witch's taunting tone, my sorrow further boiled to rage.

My heart and my eyes filled with a sea of hatred as I spun to face —and kill—my enemy.

"Duck!" Liam yelled.

I saw the black cloud in my periphery, but it was too late. Just as I turned, the shapeless mass slammed me, pushing me down beside Sakki onto my back. It poured into my mouth and nose like reverse vomiting, choking me. It went down my throat, and into my lungs, then from my lungs, to my heart, where it settled. It burned like gaseous acid. Once it was done passing through my mouth and throat, I rolled and hacked as if I could cough it up. But it was no use. I could feel the burn in my heart. Whatever Noita threw at me was there to stay.

Use the ring.

I couldn't think about whatever she'd done to me. Not now. Not with my dragon dying by my side. I threw my head onto him to listen for his heartbeats, but it was too difficult to pick up through the scales in his back. Or his heartbeats were too weak to hear. But I still didn't sense his death. Yet.

My heart couldn't handle this. I was losing him.

Use the ring.

I jumped to my feet and shook my fists at the sky. "Now You want to help? It's too late!"

Use the ring.

I wanted to rebel against the command and spend Sakki's last moments with him. Or better yet, die with him. But I couldn't ignore that voice. What happened wasn't His fault—it was Noita's. And I was a fool not to accept His help. I dug into my pocket and slid the ring on my finger. The moment it fell into place, all pain ceased. My touch slipped right through Sakki as I tried to touch him one last time. "I love you."

"I love you too." He coughed and smiled a little. "To be sure."

Wait. What? My heart thumped so hard it pushed me back. Sakki couldn't speak out loud. Nor did he say "to be sure." "Rhys?"

"God has come." He coughed. "For me." He pulled his Sakki duplicate mouth into a weak smile. "Despite... what... I... am."

I looked everywhere, hoping to look upon God's face once more. "I don't see Him. Where—?"

But the light had left his eyes. Noita's silvery spirit slithered from his dead form along with another white spirit. The white one winked in and out, seeming to say goodbye, then rose upward as the silver one charged for Noita.

"No!" The dread in the witch's voice was unmistakable as she stared at her oncoming spirit. It rammed into her, jolting her. Bent in half, she staggered backward. "The dragon. Where's the dragon?"

If this was Rhys, that meant—"Sakki!"

Sakki flew up over the ledge and landed beside me. He burped, and a feather flew from his mouth, followed by a silvery spirit. *Sakki told Colleen catching a bird was easy.*

"You're alive!" I hugged him and, since we were both in the spiritual realm, our bodies connected.

While the witch was still staring, dumbfounded, Samu tackled her. "Now!"

Liam aimed his pistol and shot the witch and Samu. His body fell, pinning her to the ground. As soon as her spirit slinked away from him and struck Noita, Liam shot her again. And again. Until she stilled.

"Samu!" I yelled and ran for his fallen body.

But his dead eyes didn't look back at me. Nor did Noita's. As Samu's white spirit floated from him, blinking like Rhys's had, I waved goodbye.

Tears rolled down my cheeks. "Thank you."

When his spirit was gone from sight, something came from Noita. But it wasn't white like the others. Nor was it the silvery, mercurial substance. Nay, this was a black ooze that seeped from her opened eyes. It pooled beneath her until the ground seemed to suck it away like water around a thirsty flower.

"I guess we know where she's going." Although my rage was gone and I wasn't sad she was dead, I felt a pang for her. No one deserved the eternity that surely awaited her.

Nay, that was wrong. We all deserved it. Thankfully, God made a way to be with Him instead. But it was sad for those who missed out on His grace, choosing to go their own way instead.

Just as I had only moments ago.

As soon as the ground had thoroughly devoured Noita's black soul, the air charged with electricity. Jagged lights zapped and buzzed in every direction. Noita's moon impostor fizzled out as lights of varying colors waved like a flag on a windy day. The sky began to lighten, making the wavy lights more difficult to see. But they were still there.

FIFTY-ONE

Remove the ring.

Forgive me for taking so long to obey. I should have put it on the moment You told me to. I tugged the ring off my finger and past my reluctant knuckle.

The moment the ring was off, the pain in my heart hit me anew. I doubled over and nearly dropped it.

"Colleen!" Liam rushed to my side and grabbed me, keeping me from falling.

"She. The witch. Did something to me." I coughed as if there still might be a chance to purge myself of it, but even now, I could feel it settling into my heart, weakening me. If only I'd listened to God right away, rather than allowing myself to revel in my misery and anger.

"I saw." Grim lines tautened his face.

"I don't know what it is. Or how to get it out." This time, I choked on a sob.

"We'll figure something out. She said she couldn't kill you, so whatever it is, you won't die."

"But how much *damage* did she do?" I tucked the ring back into my pocket before I could lose it.

"Queen Rhiannon will take care of it," Ruuta said as if I trusted her or Queen Rhiannon even a little. "She's the master of potions and spells."

And the last person I wanted to entrust myself with. But God had said to go to her, so go to her I must.

I checked Noita once more, just to be sure she was dead. Perhaps I should have been more broken up about her and her tortured soul, but I wasn't. She was gone. Her threat was gone. All that was left was her cursed parting gift.

Then I looked at Samu. Liam rolled him over so he was no longer lying on the witch. They planned this. "How did you and Samu—?"

Liam crouched to Rhys's fallen dragon form. His mouth quirked, and his eyes shone bright. "Rhys sensed the witch returning and all her spirit pieces converging here. So, while you were busy with Ruuta, he hid over the ledge in Sakki's form, waiting for Sakki to finish lighting her hut on fire. When he was done, he was to disappear over the edge and go after the bird while Rhys took Sakki's place."

"He knew she'd kill him." My words seemed to travel from somewhere far away.

His forlorn gaze moved to Samu. "Samu wasn't caught up on all that was happening, but he knew all the spirits would be here if we were ready to fight the witch. He willingly took Noita's spirit from Ruuta. I have no idea how he knew he could do that."

"They both—" I choked. "Sacrificed themselves?"

It was supposed to be me. It *should* have been me.

Liam grasped my hands and tried to meet my gaze, but I couldn't. "They both wanted to sacrifice themselves for this. Rhys always wanted to be accepted by God despite being one of Noita's creations, and Samu dedicated his life to stopping the witch. That's all he ever wanted since she killed his dragon."

I knew all this, and it helped a little. But not enough. Tears coursed down my cheeks.

Samu was the only other elf I'd ever met besides my father. Now both were dead. Why did Samu have to die? He was good. It should have been Ruuta. My guilty gaze darted toward her, never landing. How could I think such a thing? I wasn't God. It wasn't for me to determine who should live and who should die.

And I shouldn't want Ruuta dead. I didn't. Did I? Nay, I didn't.

"Why didn't you tell me?" Why was Sakki being so silent?

"You were with Ruuta, so there wasn't time." Liam laid a gentle hand on my shoulder. "But also, we needed it to be believable. The witch had to believe she'd killed Sakki."

I shrugged his hand off my shoulder. Why did I do that? I was angry at him for deceiving me, though I understood why he did it. And I felt like a fool for buying into the ruse. Then there were Rhys and Samu. I'd already lost Pirkko, Taneli, and Valtteri. How many more would die?

I could feel whatever Noita had plagued me with. It squeezed my heart, making it more difficult to breathe. But I had to stop focusing on the sadness and be grateful. We were alive, the witch was dead, and the Divide—"Has the Divide fallen?"

Ruuta shook her head. "I can still feel the energy, but it's no longer under the witch's curse."

"Well, that's good, isn't it?" I asked.

"It needs to fall. There's no need for division between the fae and the elv—humans," she said.

"Well, God seemed to think there was a need for it, and I'm inclined to believe Him." Especially now that I knew they were a bunch of demon followers. *Sakki, why aren't you weighing in on this?*

"If the Divide isn't down, will we be able to get out?" Liam scrubbed a hand down his face.

"I don't know, but we have to try. We must get out of this cursed place and go to Queen Rhiannon."

Creeping Crabs! If Ruuta said that one more time, I was going to—

Why wasn't Sakki interjecting with some sarcastic condemning retort? *Sakki? Can you hear me?*

He shifted into his dog form and stared into my eyes, head cocked like he was trying to understand me... or say something.

My heart bled. *I can't hear you. Can you hear me?*

He nodded, but those puppy-dog eyes looked sad.

So, it's me? I can't hear you?

Another sad nod.

"I think... I think whatever Noita did to me damaged my bond with Sakki. I can't hear him." My heart sobbed, and I took a deep breath and held it, keeping my heart in check. "We need to get to Queen Rhiannon. Now."

Sakki shifted back into his dragon form, and Liam, Ruuta, and I climbed aboard and flew to the border. Though we should have been at peace, able to savor this time, knowing our enemy was gone, I couldn't. Not only could I not talk with Sakki but also I couldn't sense him. I was on his back, flying with him, but I didn't know if he was tiring.

And I still wasn't seeing auras. Should I be able to see them now that the land was no longer cursed? Maybe something about this place stifled them. I'd find out when we made it across the barrier to Seelie Clós.

Just what had the witch done to me?

The infinite possibility of answers plagued me, along with the endless parade of what-ifs until we arrived at the glowing barrier.

Sakki landed, and we all slid from his back.

"Here we go." I moved toward the barrier, and the others walked with me, Sakki following. I reached up a tentative hand, looking at the others doing the same, then felt for a barrier. My fingers touched something solid. "Nay." I pressed my fingers against more spots. I smacked against it with my palms. "Nay, nay, nay."

The others were doing the same.

Liam stepped back. "It's no use. We can't get through."

"Nay!" I hammered the thing until my palms smarted. Rubbing my red hands, I joined Liam to look at the barrier from more distance.

"What do we—? Hiisi." I spun to Liam and grabbed his shirt. "We have to find Hiisi."

"Okay, okay." Liam held his hands up, and I unhanded him.

"But where will we find him?" Ruuta asked.

My shoulders slumped. How many regrets could one person take? "We should have planned for this. He said I needed him to guide me to King's Road to get out."

"You need me?" Hiisi came running from out of nowhere with Hadwin loping behind him.

"Hiisi?" Was I seeing things? "Where did you come from?"

"Me appear when you need me." He slammed his solid body into my legs.

"Also, we saw you in the sky and ran." Hadwin pitched forward, bracing himself on his knees, and caught his breath.

I dropped to hug Hiisi. He played with my hair.

"Did you know we'd be here?" Liam asked.

"God show me." Hiisi beamed with his open-mouthed smile. "Me say you need guide." He jabbed his puffed-up chest with his thumb. "Me guide."

Relief buoyed me despite the burning death plaguing my heart. "Well, then"—I motioned for him to take the lead—"show us where to go. We need a way out of here."

With his chest puffed out and with exaggerated steps and arm swings, he marched through the boundary.

I stared after him. "Hiisi, we just tried going through there, and we couldn't."

Hiisi turned and drooped his shoulders, flinging his long arms so his spindly fingers touched the ground. "You need *me*! Try again."

Liam, Ruuta, and Hadwin gave me bewildered expressions and shrugs. Sakki looked sad.

Together, we held up our hands and tried again. This time, we broke through to the other side. As elated as I could be with Noita's curse within me, I picked Hiisi up and kissed his cheek. He closed his eyes and smiled. I put him back down on the ground, leaving him staggering with a goofy grin.

But Sakki had yet to come through.

He stood on his hind legs. His doggy limbs shed their fur and lengthened. His head morphed into my father's, and I gasped. Hadwin ran to him to throw his cloak around him.

"Sakki?" I asked, fearful of what he had to say that he would take on King Auberon's shape.

"Sakki can't go with Colleen to Seelie Clós."

"Is it not safe there?" I eyed the way with newfound suspicion.

Sakki shook my father's head. "Sakki cannot leave. Now that the Divide is restored, a dragon must stay for protection."

His words punched my chest, causing the continual slow burn to flare up. "Nay. You can't stay."

"Sakki must."

"What would happen if you leave?"

"The Divide would be vulnerable to another attack, like Noita's."

"There are no other dragons?"

I knew the answer. Still, I couldn't stand the depth of sadness in his eyes. They must mirror my own. First, I was hit with whatever Noita left in me, damaging my bond with Sakki, and now we had to part? Nay. Nay, nay, nay.

"This isn't forever." I shook a fist. "I will find a way to fix this. I will see Queen Rhiannon—see if she can fix whatever Noita did to me and restore our bond. Then I will not rest until I find another dragon to take your place. Or I'll return and stay with you here."

Ruuta sucked in a sharp breath. She opened her mouth to protest until I shot daggers at her through my gaze. She clamped her mouth shut, probably deciding it best to get me to Queen Rhiannon as if she might change my mind. But the queen was gifted in spells and potions. And she had her motives and desires that didn't include me staying in the Divide with Sakki. I'd have to be vigilant against her schemes.

God, protect us. Help restore me and reunite me and Sakki.

Hadwin walked back into the Divide. "I will stay with him."

I ran through the barrier and hugged Hadwin. "Thank you."

He bowed his head. "It's an honor."

Then I embraced Sakki and didn't want to let go. But I had to. I kissed him on the cheek. "I will be back."

"Sakki will be waiting." Emotion thickened his Auberon voice.

"You are loved, Sakki. I love you." Tears welled in my eyes, making him blurry.

"And Sakki loves Colleen. Go in perfect peace." He wiped the tears that had spilled over.

A sob lodged in my throat, and I returned to where Hiisi, Liam, and Ruuta waited for me. Hadwin blocked Sakki from view and tugged off his cloak. Sakki morphed back into his dragon form. My tears flowed freely, and my breathing hitched. He gave a sad wave, and I waved back.

"Me watch her." Hiisi gave Sakki a solemn nod, then grabbed my hand, and pulled. "You come with me."

I wanted nothing more than to run back to Sakki and stay with him forever. But I had to fix what had broken between us. I was almost grateful for Hiisi's insistence, or I might not have left. But I did. With one last teary look over my shoulder, I watched my dragon as I walked away until I couldn't see him anymore.

I'd return to him... no matter what.

SHAMELESS REQUEST FOR REVIEWS

Authors need reviews! They help books get noticed, and I love to know what my readers think of my stories. So, if you enjoyed this book, please consider leaving a review on Amazon, <u>Goodreads</u>, <u>BookBub</u>... anywhere you think a review might be helpful. I'm forever grateful!

You are loved,
J F Rogers

About the Author

J. F. Rogers lives in Southern Maine with her husband, daughter, pets... and an imaginary friend or two. She has a degree in Behavioral Science and teaches a 5th and 6th grade Sunday School class. When she's not entertaining Tuki the Mega Mutt, her constant companion and greatest distraction, she's likely tap, tap, tapping away at her keyboard, praying the words will miraculously align just so. Above all, she's a believer in the One True God and can say with certainty—you are loved.

amazon.com/J-F-Rogers/e/B01G7N0KSK

bookbub.com/authors/j-f-rogers

facebook.com/jfrogerswrites

goodreads.com/jfrogers

instagram.com/jfrogers925

A jaded elf. A feisty dragon. And a deadly curse that threatens them all.

Samu would do anything to be bonded to a dragon, even serve a king he doesn't trust. But when a strange mist falls over his city and the humans massacre the elves, the last thing he wants is to come to the king's rescue.

Then the dragon eggs are threatened, and the Divide grows dark.

This was no ordinary curse.

Someone... or something... is staging an extinction-level attack against the elves and their dragons.

But Samu won't let that happen. He can't. He'll rescue the dragons or die trying.

The Darkening Divide is the action-packed prequel
to *The Cursed Lands* Christian fantasy adventure. If you
enjoy mixing up genres with elves and dragons in a
steampunk world infested with humans, download *The
Darkening Divide* today! You'll love this intro to J F Rogers's
exciting new series.

http://jfrogers.com/free-book/

Astray

A mysterious amulet leads Fallon to everything she's ever wanted...and possibly her death.

Adrift

Fallon returns to Ariboslia to save lives...but the creatures she wants to save want her dead.

Aloft

Fallon and Morrigan face off for the ultimate battle ... in their minds.

Alight

Three friends. Evil seeks to corrupt them. If they survive... what will it cost?

Pepin's Tale

Can one small peach make an eternal difference?

STANDALONE NOVELETTE

The Smeraldo Flower

Beauty and the Beast meets the Phantom of the Opera in the Secret

Garden in this standalone novelette. A retelling of the Italian folktale, La Citta di Smeraldo, inspired by BTS's song *The Truth Untold*.

STILL LOOKING FOR MORE?

Be among the first to know when new books are released.

Join her clan at jfrogers.com/join/

Join the conversation at discord

Acknowledgments

God always comes first. He is my inspiration and my purpose. If not for Him, I'd have nothing to share. Therefore, I must thank Him first and foremost.

My family is always next. My husband and my daughter inspire and encourage me like no one else.

Special thanks to:

- My Realmie critique partners, Damascus Blades - C W Briar, Gina Detwiler, L G McCary, Katherine Massengill, A K Preston, and Tracy Sassaman. I miss you all terribly!
- Dierdre Lockhart with Brilliant Cut Editing. You are amazing, as always. So glad God sent me to you!
- 100 Covers and the infinitely patient Phyllis Ngo.
- My local writer friends who support me in so many ways —Sharon Gamble, Amanda Ovington, and Marlene McKenna. Thanks for keeping me on track.
- Julie Bernier and Sarah Daniels—thanks for being such amazing friends.
- Claire Gagne—thanks for remembering all the little details I forget. You know my books better than I do! You are such an encouragement to me and I so look forward to our meetings.

- My beta readers - Jenny Cardinal, Angel Cross, Gina Detwiler, Claire Gagne, Carla Greathouse, Vickie Grider, Debbie Harris, Maureen Henn, Birgit Lehmann, and Deb Shaw.
- My street team - Nicole Burns, Dani Coquat, Angel Cross, Sarah Daniels, Claire Gagne, Steph Gagne, Angela Grimes, Debbie Harris, Barbara Harrison, Maureen Henn, Bill Long, Pamela Anne Reinert, Mariel Renaud, Sharon Selig, Deb Shaw, Monique Summers, Jackie Tansky, and Lena Karynn Tesla.
- My ARC readers, clan members, family, and friends.
- And to my readers. I pray my stories encourage you, strengthen your faith, and remind you that you're not alone and you are loved.

So many people showed up to encourage me along the way in God's perfect timing. I am beyond blessed. Thank you! I love you all!

You are loved,
J F Rogers